ONE ~~TWENTY~~ MORE

WITHDRAWN

Books by Mandy Baxter

ONE TOUCH MORE

ONE KISS MORE

ONE NIGHT MORE

Published by Kensington Publishing Corporation

ADULT
PBK
ROMANCE
Baxter

ONE TOUCH
MORE

Mandy Baxter

WITHDRAWN
Beverly Hills Public Library
444 North Rexford Dr.
Beverly Hills, California 90210

ZEBRA BOOKS
KENSINGTON PUBLISHING CORP.
http://www.kensingtonbooks.com

ZEBRA BOOKS are published by

Kensington Publishing Corp.
119 West 40th Street
New York, NY 10018

Copyright © 2015 by Amanda Bonilla

All rights reserved. No part of this book may be reproduced in any form or by any means without the prior written consent of the Publisher, excepting brief quotes used in reviews.

To the extent that the image or images on the cover of this book depict a person or persons, such person or persons are merely models, and are not intended to portray any character or characters featured in the book.

If you purchased this book without a cover you should be aware that this book is stolen property. It was reported as "unsold and destroyed" to the Publisher and neither the Author nor the Publisher has received any payment for this "stripped book."

All Kensington titles, imprints and distributed lines are available at special quantity discounts for bulk purchases for sales promotion, premiums, fund-raising, educational or institutional use.

Special book excerpts or customized printings can also be created to fit specific needs. For details, write or phone the office of the Kensington Sales Manager. Attn.: Sales Department. Kensington Publishing Corp., 119 West 40th Street, New York, NY 10018. Phone: 1-800-221-2647.

Zebra and the Z logo Reg. U.S. Pat. & TM Off.

First Printing: November 2015
ISBN-13: 978-1-4201-3483-4
ISBN-10: 1-4201-3483-3

eISBN-13: 978-1-4201-3484-1
eISBN-10: 1-4201-3484-1

10 9 8 7 6 5 4 3 2 1

Printed in the United States of America

ACKNOWLEDGMENTS

Thanks so much to my amazing agent Natanya Wheeler and everyone at NYLA as well and my editor of awesomeness Esi Sogah and everyone at Kensington who helped to make this book great including the cover designers, copy editors, and proofreaders. Thanks to Angela Carr for your advice on how to properly sew someone up, to Lenny DePaul and Dianne Moates for your expertise, and to Niki Baxter for teaching me the ins and outs of the hotel business. To anyone I might have missed, you know who you are and how I feel about you!

Chapter One

"Parker? Did you hear me? I asked if you've been taking the trazodone like I prescribed. You haven't had a prescription refilled in almost six months."

Parker Evans looked up at the expectant face of Dr. Nancy Meyers, the therapist the Marshals Service forced him to sit down and talk to whenever he completed an assignment. Was there a special course in college that all psychiatry majors were required to take where they practiced their calm, understanding facial expressions on each other? "It's Damien," he replied. "And, no, I haven't been taking the trazodone. It makes me groggy."

"Parker. We've discussed this. You need to learn to separate the fantasy of your undercover work from the reality of your life. Damien is a name that should only be affiliated with your undercover persona. Here, you're Parker."

"Damien is my middle name. Isn't that still me? I mean, I guess I could go ahead and compartmentalize my last name, too. Maybe just use it on Mondays, Wednesdays, and Fridays?" He eyed the ink on his fingers, the symbols permanently etched into his skin that helped to sell the package of his criminal status. Parker Evans was a ghost, a name affixed to a Social Security number so the USMS could cut him a check once a month. No one outside of the Marshals Service had called him Parker since he'd graduated from SOG training four years ago. The name didn't mean anything to him anymore.

Dr. Meyers pursed her lips and pushed her square-rimmed glasses up higher on her nose. Did those frames come standard issue with her crisp navy-blue suit and practical two-inch heels? "I understand that a deputy was shot and seriously injured during your last assignment. Would you like to talk about that?"

"No."

He'd left the dude with nothing more than a single Ruger under the seat of a van, and he'd prayed to God he'd be able to get his hands on it before a trio of Mexican arms dealers managed to put a bullet in the guy's dome. He'd gambled with Landon McCabe's life, not to mention the lives of three innocent civilians. The gamble had paid off, and McCabe had proved he had the stones for the job, but the guilt still ate at Damien's gut and kept him awake at night for a week afterward. It could have just as easily gone the other way . . .

"You know I can't sign off on you going back into the field unless you open up and talk to me."

She made it sound like he was some sort of wild animal, about to be tagged and released. He supposed that wasn't too far from the truth. He spent his days and most of his nights in the company of wild things. Just another mindless beast that should probably be put down before he turned rabid and hurt someone.

"What do you want me to say? That I'm scarred for

life because a guy got shot? Sorry to break it to you, but that shit's another day at the office for me. Or I guess I could tell you that the PTSD is getting to me." Damien cracked his neck from side to side. Jesus, if he didn't get out of here soon, he was going to lose his shit. The walls were closing in on him, squeezing the air from his lungs. "You seem to think that if I come in here every once in a while and spill my guts that I'm good to go for the next job, when really I'm just starting the cycle all over again. So why bother talking about it? This circular logic is nothing but a waste of time."

"Does it bother you that you're not in control here, Parker?" Dr. Meyers settled into the cushions of her chair and regarded him with that infuriating and infinitely patient expression that made his teeth itch. "Perhaps opening up and talking about your experiences is a surrender of power, and that's what makes you the most uncomfortable."

What made him *uncomfortable* was the fact that nearly every sentence out of her mouth was a goddamned question. "Look, I get that it's your job to peel back all of my painful layers until I'm nothing but a raw, exposed nerve. And I know that you guys think that by making me talk about this shit, it keeps me level and more capable of coping with undercover assignments. But I gotta tell ya, all it does is fuck with my head and my ability to effectively do my job."

"Parker, could it be that you use your job as a shield? An excuse to keep your emotions buried?"

Their sessions were becoming more hostile by the month. In the beginning, Damien had been all on board with being psychoanalyzed. He'd had a lot of shit to unload, and the prospect of dishing it all out to an impartial stranger made him feel better about sounding like a pussy when he spilled his guts. But the more he talked, the more he opened himself up, the more vulnerable Damien began to feel. And vulnerability wasn't his friend when he was hanging out with heartless bastards who'd just as soon put a bullet in his spine than play nice. He began to realize that burying his emotional baggage was the only way to survive.

He'd had six years under his belt as a marine before he joined the USMS, and two of those years working in the field as a specialist before applying to the Marshals Service's Special Operations Group. His gruff exterior and lone wolf personality were suited for undercover work, and when he was approached, Damien went all in, more than ready to take down the bad guys from the inside, no matter the cost. If he could go back and do it all over again, he would have told his supervisor with the SOG to stick his undercover assignment straight up his—

"Parker, you're wandering again. What were you thinking about?"

Wandering. It was what Dr. Meyers called it when he zoned the fuck out. "Wondering if I left the coffee-pot on this morning," he responded with a shrug.

Dr. Meyers pursed her lips and fixed him with a stern eye. Definitely not amused. "We can keep doing this dance for as long as you want, Parker." She scribbled something on a yellow legal pad that he assumed outlined his inability to cooperate. "But the fact of the matter is, *you* are the one determining whether you return to the field or sit at a desk for the next six months."

"Well, if it's all up to me, then I say I return to the

field. If you wouldn't mind signing off, I'll be out of your hair and—"

"I said you were the one making the determination, but I'm the one who has final say." Dr. Meyers cut him off and pointed her pen at him to drive the point home. "And right now, you are bound and determined to man a desk for the next half of the year. Wouldn't you agree, Parker?"

Damien focused his gaze at the bridge of her nose. An intimidation technique he employed regularly in the field. Eye contact was easy to break, but by staring right between her eyes, his attention was damned near unbreakable. Too bad the doc was a seasoned pro of the stare-down herself.

"I have all the time in the world, Parker."

She used his name the way that a skilled interrogator might use a torture technique, water-boarding him with his true identity until he couldn't take another second of breathlessness. And he knew that the only way to find relief would be to buckle under her pressure and let her dig around inside his head for the next hour. Let Parker out to play, so to speak. And as a reward for his cooperation, he'd be allowed to walk out of this office as Damien Evans, leaving Parker behind on that goddamned couch where he belonged.

Knowing what he needed to do and actually following through were two different things, though. "You get paid whether I talk or not, so what do you care if I spill my guts? Why not sign me off, collect your fee, and call it a day? I won't tell if you won't."

The indulgent smile that curved her lips was something a mother would give her errant three-year-old. "I'm not here simply to collect a paycheck, Parker." Again with the Parker bullshit. His chest constricted as though fighting for oxygen. "And I don't think you are, either. We both do what we do because we want to make a difference in people's lives."

They could talk for hours about his supposed hero complex, but that would just drag out his session, and it wasn't what Dr. Meyers really wanted to hear. "What if I don't want to be helped?"

He sensed that she was holding in a sigh. He had a tendency to wear on people's nerves. It wasn't his job to be personable or even polite, though. He interacted with criminals almost on a daily basis. Coldhearted bastards who'd just as soon kill him than give him the time of day. Ruthless sons of bitches who only respected him after he proved that he was just as ruthless as they were. And he was expected to turn his emotions on and off like they were a fucking light switch or some shit. Off in the field. On in this office. Damien on the street, Parker on this god-damned couch.

"You're the only one who can decide if you want to be helped or not, Parker," Dr. Meyers said in a calm and practiced tone. "But I'm telling you right now, if you don't talk to me, you are *not* going back into the field. Period."

Damien let out a measured breath. No way was he going to sit on the bench for the next six months or longer. Looked like Parker would be making an appearance today whether he liked it or not. "All right, you win. It freaked me the fuck out when I heard that the deputy from Portland had been shot. Is that what you want to hear?"

"This isn't a win or lose situation, Parker. This is about helping you. I think this is a good place to start. Let's talk about the Sousa case and Deputy McCabe."

Everything was win or lose. What Dr. Meyers didn't realize was that Damien had been losing for so long, he didn't know how to win.

"Thank you for calling the IdaHaven Inn and Suites, this is Tabitha, how can I help you today?"

"I need a suite for the weekend."

Adrenaline dumped into Tabitha Martin's bloodstream at the sound of her ex, Joey's voice on the end of the line. He was *the* mistake. The guy she wished she'd never met and the one she couldn't seem to get out of her life. One of too many regrets. He was also the reason she couldn't leave this job, even though she wanted to. Their relationship had ended a year ago and he still had her right where he wanted her. The urge to hang up the phone overwhelmed her, but Tabitha took a deep breath. No use worrying over what she couldn't change.

"I don't know if I have any suites, Joey." Her fingers flew over the keys as she brought up a list of available rooms. Maybe if they were booked, she could convince him to go somewhere else. "There's a district basketball tournament this weekend and all of the suites are already reserved."

His silence made her stomach twist into an anxious knot. "Move someone," he said after a tense moment. "I need the room."

"It's not that easy."

"You're the assistant manager, Tabs. It *is* that easy. Move someone. I need the room for Friday and Saturday nights. Make it happen."

Liquid nitrogen couldn't have been colder than Joey's tone. He brooked no argument and Tabitha knew the consequences if she failed to deliver. "I'll have a suite ready to go," she assured him.

"Good girl," Joey intoned just before he hung up.

Tabitha released a shuddering breath that she felt all the way to her toes. Her relief would be short-lived since, thanks to Joey's last-minute bullshit, she'd have an angry guest to deal with come this weekend. Not to mention the fact that she'd be seeing him in person in less than two days. She'd hoped that his hotel "stays" would become less and less frequent, but if anything, they'd only picked up in the past few months. Proof that his business was booming.

How could she have ever fallen for that piece of trash?

"Hey, Tabitha. Anything I need to know for tonight?"

She looked up from her computer screen to find Dave, the secondary front-desk clerk, strolling through the lobby. Panic surged as she quickly transferred the Sheldon family's reservation to two adjoining rooms and assigned Joey's company information to the suite. It's not like Dave would be suspicious, but whenever she did one of these "favors" for Joey, she couldn't help the guilt that plagued her.

"Hey, Dave." She exited the property management software and grabbed the logbook from under the counter. "We still have fifteen arrivals and room 321 is going to need a shuttle to the airport at six a.m. Oh, and keep an eye out for the guys in room 245, they got a little rowdy in the hot tub earlier and I had to kick them out."

"Oh yeah?" Dave's interest was piqued at the

mention of hot tub antics. "A little soft-core porn on the security cams tonight?"

Tabitha rolled her eyes. "Not quite. And for the record, unless you want to clean that hot tub yourself, you'd better not let anyone get frisky in there in the name of entertainment. I think they were a little south of tipsy and just being rowdy. I had a couple of complaints so I gave them the boot."

"You're a hot tub dictator, Tabitha. And it's sad."

Tabitha Martin, oppressing the propagation of staph infections in public hot tubs since 2010. "Totally proud to wear that badge of honor, Dave." She grabbed her purse and jacket from underneath the front desk. "Okay, I'm out of here. See you tomorrow?"

"Same bat time, same bat station," Dave replied. "'Night."

"Good night," she shot back as she headed for the door.

She tried not to think of the mess Joey had gotten her into as she walked through the breezeway toward the parking lot. Her shift at the hotel might have been over, but her night was just getting started. Nothing like hours of studying anatomy and physiology to round out the perfect night.

As Tabitha pulled her car out onto Ninth Street, her phone buzzed from the front seat. She reached over to retrieve it, just barely missing a red light in the process. Lucky for her traffic was light at ten o'clock at night, though that didn't excuse her reckless driving. She slid her thumb across the screen and hit the speaker function as she rested the phone on the dash. "What's up, Lila?"

"Hey, sugar-booger. Did you miss me today?" Lila was like the Energizer Bunny. "Get your ass over here and let's go out. I heard there's a new DJ over at Liquid. Let's go get our dance on!"

Her enthusiasm was admirable, but just the thought of going out exhausted Tabitha. "Can't. I've got a ton of homework and I need to study for my medical terminology final."

Lila blew raspberries into the receiver. "Lame. I can't go out without a winglady, Tabs. For once, can you just ditch responsibility and cut loose? You're twenty-three years old. Stop acting like you're an old lady."

"Dude. I'd love to ditch responsibility for a while. As for being an old lady, I'm going to remember you said that when your birthday rolls around." Lila was coming up on twenty-five—closer to ninety than Tabitha was—and still partied like she was sixteen. Of course, when your dad owned a chain of car dealerships, you could afford to be an immature slacker.

"*Ta-habs . . .*" Lila whined. "*Puh-leaze* go out with me. It's two-for-one shots."

Well, at least Lila had her priorities straight. Two-for-one shots? Who could resist? "Sorry, Lila, but I don't want to be hungover for tomorrow's finals."

"You don't have to be," she said in a pouty tone. "You can be the DD and cart my drunk ass around."

"When you put it that way, how can I resist?"

"Come on, you need to let off some steam. You're going to blow if you don't."

True. But running interference while Lila drank her body weight in gin and tonics wasn't the way she wanted to release the valve. "Tomorrow is my last day of classes. I'll blow off steam and whatever else you want on Saturday. And every day for the entire semester break if you want. But tonight, I've got a date with the human body."

"Boo."

Tabitha checked her mirror and switched lanes. "Sorry, dude. Take it or leave it." She steered the car into the turn lane for her apartment complex and put her palm over the phone to keep it from sliding across the dash. "Let me study tonight and I'm all yours on Saturday."

"Fine." Lila would pout over not getting her way, but she'd forget all about it by the weekend. "But your ass better be good and ready to go out after your shift. I'll be picking you up at the hotel."

"Deal." It's not like Tabitha was interested in battling downtown traffic anyway. "See ya Saturday night."

"All right, Florence Farthingale, go be responsible and study," Lila said. "Bye."

"It's Florence *Nightingale*, Lila." She laughed. "Bye."

Tabitha pulled into her covered spot below her unit and stuffed her phone in her purse. She snatched her backpack, containing what felt like a metric ton of books, from the backseat. As she began the arduous climb up the stairs to the second story, a twinge of regret pulled at her chest. She hated that she had to always be the responsible one. What she wouldn't give to be as carefree as Lila, living off of her dad's money and partying her twenties away.

Twenty-three was too young to feel so old.

On the flip side, she had a nice apartment, a job that paid the bills, and she was on her way to a B.S. in nursing. True, it was taking her a little longer than it would most students, but the time frame didn't matter to her as long as she got that degree in the end. She flipped on the light above the kitchen table and spilled her books out on the surface. After she changed into a pair of sweats and brewed a pot of coffee, she settled in for a long night of cramming.

Tabitha was on track to finally getting her life together. The only thing left was to get rid of Joey and his baggage. All she needed to do to make it happen was jeopardize the future of someone she loved.

Chapter Two

As usual, his give-and-take with Dr. Meyers had earned Damien a pat on the head and the privilege of being allowed to resume his undercover work. Unfortunately, if he'd known Bill Crawford—the SOG director for the Pacific Northwest—was going to ship him off to Boise, Idaho, he might have saved himself the trouble and just taken the desk job. As far as assignments went, he reminded himself that it could always be worse.

For the past year the U.S. Marshals Service's Fugitive Task Force had been hunting Gerald Lightfoot, a heavy hitter who'd managed to slip federal custody before they could slap his ass in the nearest super max. A veteran of the drug trade, Lightfoot had a finger in everything from weed to heroin, and word was that he was now operating his syndicate in the States from somewhere in Russia. By using the waterways, he'd been smuggling product down into the port of Seattle and distributing throughout the Pacific Northwest and California. His most recent specialty was a synthetic that went by the street name of Stardust because of its glittery physical properties;

and its ability to give the user a quick high was likened to being shot up into space. It had shown up in Idaho a few months back. Sales were quickly gaining traction and had grabbed the attention of the USMS only after several teens had died. The Boise PD had assigned a special task force to stop the flow of Stardust into the city, but they couldn't keep up with the suppliers and dealers. Bastards got craftier every fucking month.

It was a revolving operation, never staying in the same place for more than a month or two. Seattle, Portland, Spokane, and now Boise. The task force figured that they only had a window of about four weeks to nail Lightfoot's contact here before he pulled his product and moved on to the next city. The distributor in Boise was the key to finding Lightfoot, and had become the Fugitive Task Force's number one priority.

Damien had been brought in to work the chain from the bottom up. First, locate the dealers, then hook up with Lightfoot's distributor. With such a tight time frame, he didn't have long to lay the groundwork.

"Hi! Are you checking in tonight?"

Damien looked up at the sound of the chipper voice and his brain went abso-freaking-lutely blank. The woman behind the counter gave him a wide smile as she tucked a section of her short hair behind her ear. Wide blue eyes the color of a deep mountain lake stared back at him, fringed with dark lashes that made the blue that much brighter. He towered over her, yet he sensed in her a confidence that was far larger than her petite frame. And that smile . . . holy shit. It was the sort of expression that skirted flirtatious and made his chest hitch.

"Yeah," he responded with a smile of his own. "I'm early though, so if you can't check me in yet, it's not a big deal."

"Oh, I don't think it'll be a problem. Can I get your name?"

"Damien Evans."

Her voice rippled over him, smooth and sweet as whipped cream. He checked her name tag—Tabitha—and noted that she was also the assistant manager. She might be helpful later down the line, especially if this place did in fact turn out to be one of the hotels that Lightfoot's man was dealing from. Managers spent more time at the hotel than anyone, plus they made it their business to know the regular guests.

"Okay . . ." Tabitha scanned the computer screen and puckered her lips in concentration. Damien found the act entirely too distracting, his gaze locked on the dark pink flesh that looked as soft as flower petals. "Looks like you requested a room on the top floor. Is that still okay?"

"Yep." A bird's-eye view would help him to notice anything out of the ordinary in the parking lot or street.

"And you also requested a room facing the parking lot?" She cocked a brow and gave him a wry smile. "I have to admit, that's a first."

He smiled back, couldn't help himself. Damien wasn't exactly a playful guy. Gruff described him to a tee. But he found that he wanted to try, for the first time in what felt like forever, to be a little flirtatious back. "Would you believe me if I told you I was a writer for *Parking Lot Monthly* and this place made my top-ten list for spacious parking spaces?"

Her laughter was infectious and it tingled down

Damien's spine in a warm rush. "You know, our guests comment all the time that our parking spaces are extra roomy."

"It's all in the lot design," Damien agreed.

"Totally." Their eyes met and Damien swore the air sizzled between them. "Okay, well, here are your keys." Tabitha tucked two plastic cards into an envelope and slid them across the counter to him. "And I need to swipe your credit card. You won't be charged until you check out."

"No problem." Damien pulled the Visa that he used for undercover operations from his wallet and handed it to her. She swiped the card in the machine and handed it back.

"I have you down for seven days, and if you need to extend or shorten your stay, just let me know."

"Sounds good." Damien tucked the card back into his wallet and retrieved the large duffel with his clothes.

"Then you're all set. By the way, I'm Tabitha." She reached out her hand across the counter. "I'm here most evenings until ten if you need anything."

He took her hand in his and the contact was electric, sending a jolt of excitement through Damien's bloodstream. Of all the shitty timing . . . After months, he meets a woman that he's attracted to and he's on a goddamned job. "Damien," he said in return, his voice only a little strained.

"Have a good one, Damien." Damn, that smile was enough to bring him to his knees. "If you need anything, don't hesitate to ask."

"I won't. Thanks."

Was it his imagination that she seemed interested, too? She was definitely throwing off some sort of vibe, but Damien was clueless when it came to women.

Maybe this was just Tabitha's usual customer service charm. Still, he had at least a week to test the waters, didn't he? Dr. Meyers said he needed to loosen up a little and try to live some sort of life. This week was as good a time as any for a trial run.

"Hey, um, I was wondering. You wouldn't happen to know what's hot downtown? Bars or clubs." He didn't want her to think he was on the prowl or anything, but he wanted a local's take on the city's nightlife.

"Scouting out locations for *Parking Lot Monthly*?"

Damien's lips tugged in a reluctant smile. He'd never been funny, but he racked his brain for something—anything—comical to say, if only to make her laugh. That sound was like the sweetest music. A song he could listen to on repeat. "Even nightclubs deserve a chance at the top-ten lists."

"Totally," Tabitha agreed with a chuckle. "Parking lots downtown can be tricky. But if you're also including parking garages—"

"Garages are just parking lots on steroids. Bigger and beefier."

"Exactly!" Damn the sound of her laughter. It had a calming effect on him that none of the drugs Dr. Meyers had prescribed could manage. "Okay, so if you use the parking garage on Eighth Street, you can hit several downtown clubs from there. Liquid on Eighth and there's Fatty's on West Idaho. I think a new place just opened up near there called Equilibrium that's supposed to be pretty hot, too."

"Thanks." Three locations were more than a decent jumping-off point. From there he could ask around, maybe find out where the bulk of the product was being moved. "I owe you one."

"I won't forget it, either. Have a good one, Damien."

He took a faltering step away from the front desk, wishing he could talk to her for another hour or so. "You too, Tabitha."

"'Night," she called after him with a wave.

Maybe this assignment wouldn't be too bad after all.

"Check you out, getting your flirt on."

Tabitha turned to face Dave and shook her head at the conspiratorial grin affixed to his face. "It's called good customer service. You should try it sometime."

"Uh-huh." He clucked his tongue at her as he approached the desk. "I don't blame you. If I'd gotten to work a few minutes sooner, you can bet I would've flirted my ass off. Did you see those tattoos? And oh my God, his arms." Dave mocked a swoon. "Tall, built, and inked. *Yum.*"

Tall—pushing six-two at least—with the body of an MMA ass-kicker and an expression that screamed *cross me and suffer the consequences*, Damien had *dangerous bad boy* written all over him. Three-quarter sleeve tattoos covered his corded forearms and ran up his wide, sculpted biceps to disappear under the sleeves of his T-shirt. And though he looked like he frequented dive bars and back alleys often, Damien didn't have that nasty, grunge-coated look to him. In fact, when he smiled, the soft openness of the expression had stolen Tabitha's breath. Deep dimples pitted his cheeks, and they'd lent a youthful lightheartedness to him that she never would have known was there if he hadn't smiled at her.

Yep, tall, built, and tattooed hit everything on Tabitha's *yes, please!* list, but those same qualities in a guy often came with their own sets of problems. "Oh, he's yummy," Tabitha agreed. And he seemed like a genuinely nice guy, too. "But yummy can be trouble."

"Yes, it can."

Tabitha laughed at Dave's suggestive tone. Sure, Damien's golden-brown eyes had been hypnotic and his messy thatch of light brown hair practically begged to be touched, but he was a guest at the hotel. "Good thing for us he's off-limits, then." She and Dave had the same taste in men, which was why they were both often in the dating doghouse. Bad boys had their allure, but they only broke your heart in the end.

"I don't know," Dave said on a sigh. "I might be willing to lose my job over a shot at that."

"I would have your head." Tabitha swatted at him and Dave sidestepped her mock assault. "It's too hard to find decent front-desk people. You can't ever quit or get fired, which means no hitting on guests for you, mister."

"Not that it would matter," he replied as though hurt. "Because that tattooed god was obviously hot for your lady bits."

She didn't want to admit that she'd felt a spark of connection between them. Or that in the course of their banter, her stomach had begun to gradually unfurl until it felt as though someone had let a swarm of butterflies loose to fly around. "My lady bits aside, I'm swearing off guys like that."

"You mean drop-dead gorgeous, walking pieces of art?"

"I mean guys who look like trouble." And despite the soft brilliance of his smile, Tabitha had no doubt that Damien was just as dangerous as he looked. "It's tax accountants and guidance counselors for me from here on out."

"Great," Dave replied. "That means more bad boys for me."

"You say that now, but after your next breakup you'll be begging me to help you find a nice guy."

"True. But until then, I'm sowing my oats."

"As long as you don't reap from the company fields, I'm a-okay with that."

"Fine. But I'm telling you now, if Mr. MMA even blinks at me with so much as minimal interest, all bets are off."

Tabitha laughed. "Deal."

"Speaking of gorgeous bad boys, how's your brother?"

Dave had been crushing on Tabitha's brother, Seth, for as long as they'd known each other. He also knew how much trouble Seth caused in her life. Since they were kids, Tabitha had been bailing her younger brother out of one bad situation after another. And it's not like she could have ever counted on her less-than-responsible parents to help him out. He was the king of making bad decisions for the right reasons. Somewhere under his rough, troublemaker exterior was a good guy. He just needed someone to give him a chance to show that good side off.

"He's all right. He's trying to get a job working construction. If I can keep him on track for the next six months, I think he'll be set to start school in the fall. I've got him talked into a junior college to start. I really think he might follow through this time."

"I love a man with a tool belt." Dave flashed her a grin.

Another wave of guests entered the lobby, breaking

up any further conversation, which was totally fine by Tabitha. She let Dave take care of checking them in and returned to her office to complete the food order for next week.

Seth might be trying to get his act together, but the fact of the matter was this was his last chance to make a change. Tabitha had saved his bacon for the last time. Getting him out of his latest bout of trouble had cost her dearly, and now she found herself an unwilling partner to her ex's less-than-legal business dealings. Joey had been Seth's friend first. Tabitha had hooked up with him because wherever Seth was, Joey wasn't too far behind, and he'd been truly charming in the beginning. Well, charming in that dangerous bad-boy way that inevitably curled Tabitha's toes.

If she could go back and do it all over again, she would have taken Seth and left Boise in their wake before either of them could fall prey to that bastard. Hindsight was certainly twenty-twenty, but no amount of coulda, woulda, shouldas would change the fact that she'd found herself in a situation that was becoming more inescapable by the day.

Tabitha settled in at her desk and opened a browser window on her computer. Her fingers hovered over the keyboard, the cursor flashing in the Google search bar. The keys clicked as she typed: FBI, Boise, Idaho. Her pinky paused before clicking Enter. Did the FBI even deal with guys like Joey? She hit the backspace and typed: *Boise Police Department, narcotics* and clicked the first search result: *City of Boise, Bandit Narcotics Vice Unit.*

How many times had she stared at this phone number on her screen? Tabitha's hands began to shake and she twined her fingers together to keep them still. One phone call shouldn't have been so hard to make—after all, she'd done it before in the interest of protecting her brother—but it was Joey's promise to bring Seth down with him that kept her from dialing the phone. Empty threats weren't Joey's style. No, the asshole had tremendous follow-through. Both Seth and Tabitha knew that he had enough evidence gathered against her brother to put him in jail for a good decade at least. Joey was one of those rare sleazeballs who actually had brains enough to keep himself out of trouble.

By getting others to do his dirty work for him, he reaped all of the benefits of being a slimy criminal while keeping his hands marginally clean at the same time. It was Seth's bad luck that he'd trusted Joey, and Tabitha's own stupidity that she'd turned a blind eye to what he was doing until it was too late. Despite kicking him to the curb, Joey was a permanent fixture in her life. He wouldn't let her quit her job, and unless she wanted to see her brother thrown in prison, she had no choice but to let him use the hotel as a front for his dealers to sell their drugs from.

Not exactly the life she'd imagined for herself.

Closing the browser window, Tabitha clicked the icon for the hotel's NiteVision property management software and typed in the name Damien Evans. His reservation popped up and Tabitha scanned the information he'd provided. He'd rented a single. No additional guests, so he was presumably unattached. She hadn't noticed a ring, anyway. He gave a California address, so definitely not local, and he didn't use a company credit card, so he probably wasn't traveling on business.

"Trouble," Tabitha reminded herself as she exited NiteVision to focus on the food order. Damien might be the embodiment of her perfect man, but the trouble Joey had brought into her life was more than enough proof that she needed to lay off of bad boys for good. She let out a derisive snort. At the rate she was going, she wasn't going to be *laying* anyone anytime soon. The past year of celibacy hadn't been too bad. No man? No problem. One less complication in her life. She needed to focus on finishing school, anyway, and getting Seth on the straight and narrow for good. Tabitha didn't have time for a relationship right now.

"Tabs?" Dave poked his head into her office. "Do you have a sec? Night audit accidentally double-booked a room, and neither of the guests is willing to take a double instead of the suite."

She'd take trauma victims and sick kids any day over angry hotel guests. Though if Joey got his way, it wouldn't matter if she was an RN or not, she'd never get the opportunity to put the degree to use. "Yeah, I'll be right there."

Angry guests might not have been her idea of a pleasurable distraction, but at least she wouldn't be worrying about Joey. Or the tattooed bad boy she couldn't seem to get out of her head.

Chapter Three

For the past week Damien had been trolling the local bars, eavesdropping on conversations, keeping his eye out for potential targets. Tonight, he was at Liquid, one of downtown's newest "it" places. The Boise PD's Bandit task force had given him the name and background of a well-known dealer they'd busted a couple of weeks ago. And with the guy currently spending time in the Ada County jail, Damien was free to name-drop a little.

"So, how you know my man Tanner?" The guy shooting pool—Damien was pretty sure his name was Joey—took a swig from his bottle of Budweiser before leaning over to aim his stick.

"We did a stint together up at Sheridan. 'Bout five years ago."

"They throw guys into the federal pen for holding a couple of ounces of weed, huh?"

"Nah," Damien replied, taking the bait. He would have been surprised if Joey hadn't tried to test him. "But they do when you get pinched with fifteen pounds of Salmon River Quiver in your trunk."

Joey made a quick pocket shot and straightened,

leaning against the table while his buddy lined up his stick for a bank shot. "That ain't no shit, man. Fucking Tanner. I told that stupid motherfucker he was gonna get caught hauling all that weed around in his car." He laughed as though reliving a fond memory. "I heard he got picked up again last week. Fool doesn't know how to be discreet."

Damien took a sip from his 7 and 7. "That's the fucking truth. I'm not even gonna try to bail his ass out this time. I'm outta work because of him, and even if he does get out, I'm done with his ass. He'll have way too much heat on him after this."

"You looking to sling?"

This was why Damien always hit up potential connections in bars. Get enough liquor in a guy's system and he did most of the work for you. It took half the time to earn someone's trust when he had a fifth of Jack coursing through his veins. He had a feeling that everybody was Joey's best friend and confidant when he got shitfaced. "Could be. You have product to move?"

Joey flashed him a crooked smile. "Could be."

Damien had broken the ice; now it was time to back off. If he pressed for more information or acted too eager, it might make Joey suspicious. From here on out, all Damien had to do was play the part and wait for Joey to come to him with an offer. Lucky for Damien, Joey had an ego. The cocky ones were always easier to hook. Way too eager to show off and throw their weight around. It worked to his advantage though, so Damien wasn't about to complain.

Damien drained his glass and ordered another, plus a couple of beers for his new friends as they racked up the balls for another game. He was still a little on edge from his last session with Dr. Meyers. It really fucked up his mind-set when he had to get too in touch with his emotions. Especially since he'd confessed to her during their last session that he wanted out of undercover work. He was ready for a real life and some fucking stability for a change. Maybe even a relationship. His mind wandered to the hotel manager and his fingers curled around his glass in a tight grip. He couldn't wait to see her again.

"Hey, Joey, your ex just walked in."

Damien's curiosity got the better of him and he turned to where the gazes of the two men had zeroed in on a couple of women with their backs turned, making their way toward the bar. Beside him, Joey set the pool cue down on the felt table and took a long pull from his beer, his eyes glazing over as he stared. Seedy sons of bitches like Joey were part of the reason why Damien was itching to get out of undercover work. He almost felt sorry for any woman unfortunate enough to get his attention, but then again, considering the type of guy Joey was, Damien assumed his ex couldn't be that much classier.

"Damn, dude. Tabs still has a fine ass. I can't believe you're not hittin' that anymore."

Damien cast a quick glance at Joey's friend. He was a class act.

"Bitch is more trouble than she's worth," Joey replied. "But she does have a fine ass."

The ogling was beginning to make Damien feel more than a little uncomfortable. He liked to admire a beautiful woman as much as the next guy, but Joey and his buddy were simply leering. Nasty.

"So get this." Joey leaned in conspiratorially. God, Damien hoped the dude wasn't about to tell him some kinky sex story. "Tabs works at this hotel a few blocks from here. Before we broke up, I got her to let me use a suite on the weekends to do business out of. I can move twice the product with no nosy-ass neighbors wondering why there's always so many cars parked at my place. Plus, I'm not shitting where I eat. The cops aren't going to ever find anything at my place, so I'm clean. Sweet setup, right?"

Yeah, it was. Which proved that Joey wasn't quite as stupid as Damien had initially given him credit for and that he was definitely the guy he'd been looking for. "If your name is on the registry, the cops can trace you that way, though."

"I got that covered, too. I use the name of a fake roofing company and I only pay cash. Tabs is the assistant manager, so she handles the reservations and she can cover my tracks if I need her to. I'm telling you, man, it's fucking brilliant. I'm bringing in twice as much coin as I used to."

Well, Damien's opinion of Joey's ex just dropped another ten points. "All it takes is a nosy guest or a too-loud customer to bring a hell storm down on you, though."

"Truth," Joey remarked. He turned his attention back to the pool table and picked up his cue stick to break. "I don't dick around with my clientele. You can't keep your shit straight, I don't sell to you. Period. Plus, no one is allowed to use on the property. They've got to take that shit somewhere else. Tabs is trained. If anyone complains, she comps them a free night or some shit to make them happy."

Joey's friend butted in. "Yeah, until she graduates and quits that place."

"She's not allowed to quit and she knows it. Besides, at the rate she's going, she's not gonna graduate for another year or more."

The smart-ass yukked it up from the other side of

the table and Damien made it a point to get the guy's last name. He'd be running a background check on his ass the first chance he got. "You worried that her boss might catch on?"

"Not really. My crew always comes in when she's on shift. When we check out in the morning, my guys are dressed like they're ready to hit a job site. My roofing company"—he waggled his brows—"is a regular customer there. And the IdaHaven treats their regulars really well."

Damien's heart stuttered mid-beat and his breath stalled out. *Damn it.* "Did you say the IdaHaven? Dude, I stayed there last fucking week. Crazy."

"You really ought to see the operation in action, man," the friend—Tony something—piped in again. "It's a thing of beauty."

"I'd like that." The words left his mouth mechanically, but Damien was already scanning the crowd for the woman Joey had identified as his ex.

"I bet you would." Joey smirked before turning to his buddy. "Hey, jackass, it's your turn. What in the hell are you waiting for?"

Damien all but ignored the game as his gaze found a petite blonde with a crooked bobbed haircut. Tabs. Tabitha. Obviously a nickname for the hotel manager he'd met a week ago. Disappointment soured his stomach at the realization that not only had his first impression of her been wrong, but that she was an accessory to a crime. Granted, his only interaction with her had been that one time, but he'd felt a connection. And that didn't happen to Damien often. He tipped back his glass and drained the fresh 7 and 7 in a couple of guzzles. What had he expected? He was on assignment, for fuck's sake. It's not like he had time for dating, and even if he had, no woman in her right mind wanted damaged goods like him. He'd straddled the line between criminal and cop for far too long. And now, there was nowhere he fit in, and no one with whom he truly belonged.

"Is Joey still staring at us?" Tabitha sat with her head bowed, allowing the short strands of her hair to curtain her face. "I swear to God, Lila, if he doesn't leave pretty soon, I'm out of here."

"Relax." Lila grabbed her gin and tonic as well as Tabitha's vodka soda and pulled her friend away from the bar and closer to the dance floor. "If he looks this way again, I will kick that sick bastard square in his nuts. That'll get him out the door."

Tabitha chanced a quick look behind her at Joey and his friend Tony, who'd gone back to playing pool. Her step faltered as her gaze landed on the hulking form of Damien Evans, the star of her dreams and her every waking fantasy for the past week. Her heart took a nosedive into her stomach and a burst of anxious energy dumped into her bloodstream. She'd recognized him in an instant, her body perking up like a flower under the sun at the sight of him. But her reaction withered the moment realization sunk in. If he was hanging out with Joey and Tony, Damien was definitely up to no good. What was wrong with her? She was a total loser magnet. If she was attracted to a man, you could bet he had a criminal record—or was at least on the road to having one. And the worst part of seeing him with Joey wasn't that it proved he was just another slimeball. It was that he didn't look even a little out of place. In fact, with his bulky frame, tattoos, and the deep, serious crease marring his brow, he gave off the vibe that he was an even higher level of criminal than Joey and his idiot friend, which was saying something.

Most of Joey's friends made Tabitha's lip curl when they walked into the room. As though all of the showers in the world could do nothing to wash the layer of slime and nastiness from their bodies. Despite his rough exterior, Damien lacked that oily, clingy dark aura. Tabitha reconsidered her earlier assessment of him. It wasn't that Damien appeared to be the most seasoned criminal of the group. Rather, he was without a doubt the most dangerous-looking man she'd ever laid eyes on.

And why did that make her heart beat a little faster? Heat the blood in her veins? Why in God's name would that turn her on even a little? There was clearly something seriously wrong with her. Tabitha suspected that beneath the tattoos, the shaggy light brown hair that was meant to look unkempt, and the stubble of his jaw—which was more like a ten o'clock shadow than five—was a complicated man who fought with his demons because he wanted more than the life he'd found himself in.

Yeah, right. Tabitha turned her attention from the pool table and focused once again on Lila. That romantic, optimistic outlook was what had gotten her into trouble in the first place. Always giving people the benefit of the doubt, looking for that silver lining on even the darkest of clouds. She'd been convinced that Joey was a good guy beneath his rough exterior and poor choices. How wrong she'd been. And now, after they'd been broken up for almost a year, it was Tabitha who was losing sleep over the fact that he was still a fixture in her life, while Joey reaped the benefits of having her in his.

She guzzled her drink in a few swallows. Boise was small as cities went, but it still pissed her off that she couldn't even go out for the evening without running into her ex. She refused to let him scare her away, though. If Lila could blow reality off in favor of a good time, so could Tabitha.

"Incoming, two o'clock," Lila said close to her ear.

Tabitha's stomach clenched at the prospect of having to make small talk with a guy. She'd sworn off the bar scene as a means to meet men after the nightmare that was her relationship with Joey. "Not interested."

Lila ran her fingers through the length of her straight, auburn hair. "You've got to get back in the saddle sometime, Tabs. You haven't dated in a year. I'm sexually frustrated on your behalf."

"Coming from the woman who hasn't dated in almost as long."

Lila flashed her a lopsided grin. "But that's not to say I haven't been looking. I just have a very strict catch-and-release rule. Unfortunately, the dating pool has been full of minnows lately. I'm baiting for shark."

That was the truth. Lila wasn't shallow by any means and the woman was as shrewd as they came. Sure, she let her dad pay her rent, but Lila had plans for her life, and with a business degree under her belt, she was ready to launch a line of to-die-for handbags in the next year. Likewise, she wasn't about to waste her time on a man-child who aspired to nothing more than working minimum wage jobs and camping out on his buddies' couches. She was looking for a partner. An equal. But just because she'd baited for shark, didn't mean she wasn't doing a little sport fishing for some of those minnows in the meantime.

"What's up, ladies? Can I buy you two a couple of drinks?"

Mister Two O'clock stepped up to them, all charm and smiles. Tabitha had to admit, he was sort of cute: blond, blue eyes, clean-cut and wearing a nice dress shirt and slacks. Her gaze wandered to his feet, because a guy's shoes said a lot about him. Leather loafers. This one might actually be gainfully employed. Huh. Wonders never ceased.

"Well, aren't you a cutie," Lila said with a slow smile. She extended her hand and he took it in a brief shake. "I'm Lila."

"Charlie."

He didn't do anything cheesy like kiss Lila's hand, earning him a couple of points. Tabitha accepted his proffered hand and said, "Tabitha. Nice to meet you."

"Okay, girls. What are we drinking? I had a stellar day at work and I need someone to help me celebrate."

Lila's gaze warmed. It didn't take much for Tabitha to make the decision to back off and let her friend take the lead. Maybe the currents had changed and the bigger fish had finally come to the surface from the deep water. "Ooh, tell us all about it." Lila snatched a tall, circular table that skirted the dance floor and made room for Charlie in-between her and Tabitha.

As Charlie went on about his promotion—she was pretty sure he'd said he was an investment banker—Tabitha's gaze was inextricably drawn to Damien at the far end of the bar. She watched him from behind her hair as he nursed a drink and played a round of pool with Joey and Tony.

Maybe it was a sign of her totally messed-up childhood that she went for guys who lived a life she'd spent years trying to escape. Her parents had been addicts for as long as she could remember, dealing on the side to fund their habits and paying about as much attention to their kids as other people paid to the mice living in their walls. She and Seth were forced to fend for themselves, and whereas her brother had chosen to follow in their parents' footsteps, Tabitha had shunned their lifestyle. Her life's goal was to aspire to something more than poverty and addiction, yet her choice in men didn't help to elevate her from that station.

"So, what do you ladies do?"

Lila nudged her and Tabitha turned her attention back to the conversation. Lila said, "I'm a designer and Tabitha is studying to be a nurse."

"A designer?" Charlie leaned in and Lila scooted her chair closer to him. "That sounds interesting. Tell me more."

Nursing wasn't exactly one of those professions that screamed, *Tell me more!* Nurses were the unsung heroes of the medical profession, and Tabitha was totally okay with flying under the radar. She didn't want to be a nurse for the glory or attention. Rather, she wanted to help people. Make a difference. Do something that changed someone's life for the better.

Lila continued to tell Charlie all about her handbag line, and as a money man, he seemed more than eager to lend a few tips. Tabitha's gaze slid once again to the pool tables and she couldn't help but wonder, what would it take for a woman to make a difference in Damien Evans's life?

Chapter Four

"I made contact with a distributor Friday night. Joey Cavello. Selling out of a downtown hotel, so I'm willing to bet he's Lightfoot's man. He's cautious, but he'll call. He's got the ego and I think he's looking to work his way up in the organization. If Cavello wants to impress his supplier, he'll need trustworthy dealers to do that, and name-dropping Tanner Beckstrom gave me a leg up. With any luck, he'll be in touch by the end of the week."

The conference room at the USMS Boise office wasn't exactly packed, but most of the key players were present. Representatives from the Boise PD's Bandit narcotics task force, U.S. Deputy Marshal Ryan Gates—Damien's official contact at the Idaho district headquarters—and the chief deputy, Dennis Callihan. The only one not present was Jenna McIntyre, the federal prosecutor representing the federal Fugitive Task Force. But since she wouldn't be brought in until they located Lightfoot, Damien wasn't too concerned over her absence.

"We had a feeling that they were using local hotels to deal from." John Rader, the narcotics detective, scribbled down a couple of notes on a legal pad. "Usually, we'll get a heads-up from the hotel staff if something suspicious is going on. Vice took down a prostitution ring a few months back that way. But this guy must be keeping a pretty low profile because we haven't heard a thing."

"That's because Cavello has someone on the inside." Damien scrubbed a hand over his head and leaned back in his chair. It was too damned early to be at work after spending the entire weekend drinking and networking. He was getting too old for this shit. "An ex-girlfriend who's setting up the rooms for him to use and covering his tracks with the staff and guests. Cavello is running a pretty tight ship. He's got a good thing going and he's not about to do anything to jeopardize his operation."

"You want us to run the girlfriend's name?" Gates asked. "See if we can find anything to bring her in for?"

"No," Damien responded. "Flipping the girlfriend is a last resort at this point. Cavello seemed interested in bringing me into the fold, so for now, we're good. Lightfoot is the prize here. We have to look at the big picture."

"Got it," Gates agreed. "Business as usual."

"We'll make sure it's covered on our end as well," Detective Rader added. "My guys will be sure to lay off Cavello. He'll have some smooth sailing for a while. Though I gotta tell you guys, shutting his operation down would be a big feather in my cap."

"If we get our hands on Lightfoot," Chief Deputy Callihan chimed in, "you're welcome to him."

"So what's the plan from here?" Rader asked.

"We just wait," Damien said on a sigh. "Cavello has to come to me. If I press him, it'll look suspicious.

I laid the groundwork Friday night and it's solid. He'll call."

"Hopefully sooner, rather than later."

Damien gave Gates a rueful smile. "No doubt."

"I do want to add that I'm not thrilled about you working solo on this," Chief Deputy Callihan said. "If you don't want backup, I think you should at least wear a wire."

"No," Damien replied. It might have been crazy, but he liked working solo. "Cavello doesn't trust me yet. I don't want to risk the chance of being made because I'm wearing a wire. I don't think he's dangerous and he might be the link to getting close to Lightfoot."

"It's some real cowboy shit," Callihan said. "But it's your call."

Damien nodded. He could handle himself out there. He'd been doing it for a long damned time.

"Okay, I think we've covered everything." The chief deputy pushed his chair out from the conference table. He rapped his knuckles on the surface before heading for the door. "Parker, keep us posted."

Parker. Here he was the upstanding deputy U.S. marshal. One of the good guys. It was the side of his personality he found harder to identify with, the deeper undercover he went. For this particular case, he'd be toeing the line between fantasy and reality, living the criminal life on a part-time basis with lower-level criminals than the type he'd more recently hung out with.

"I'll be in touch." The rest of the men at the table packed up their notebooks and briefcases, and tossed paper cups in the trash. Damien stayed put, though. He needed a few minutes of silence and solitude. A brief meditation to get his shit straight.

Damien slouched down in his chair and let his head fall back on his shoulders. A couple hours' sleep wasn't enough, and he thought about propping his feet up on the table and taking a nice, long nap. He doubted that would go over well though, so he opted for a couple of minutes of rest. Eyes closed, he let the silence sink into his skin. His brain was always too goddamned busy, too full. And this was a rare moment of stillness that he treasured.

During his last session with Dr. Meyers, she'd asked why he wanted out of undercover. His response: "I miss the peace and quiet. I want a little stillness in my life."

A smirk tugged at his lips as he released a deep breath. Check him out, being all introspective and shit. The doc would be so proud.

Damien woke to the sound of his phone playing the tune of Nirvana's "Heart-Shaped Box." He had a soft spot for emotionally damaged nineties grunge rockers. Spoke to his own raging angst. The blackout drapes in his hotel room were drawn—it could have been three in the morning or afternoon for all he knew or cared. He'd crashed hard after this morning's meeting, hitting the mattress like a felled tree. Jesus, he was exhausted.

He swiped his finger across the screen and put the phone to his ear. "Yeah." The one word barely qualified as anything more than a grunt.

"This Damien?"

His eyes opened and he came more fully awake at the sound of Joey's voice. "Yeah. Who's this?" No use acting like he was waiting on the dude's call. He wanted to appear interested, not anxious.

"Joey Cavello. I met you at Liquid a few nights ago. You said you might be interested in slinging a little product for me."

"Yeah," Damien said. "I remember."

"You still want in?"

"Sure." This was good. He'd expected Joey to reach out but not so soon. The guy was eager and it would help to bump up their timetable. "What do you have in mind, man?"

"How 'bout you meet me at Liquid later tonight so we can discuss terms. I don't do business over the phone."

The smart criminals knew how to cover their bases. Joey came across as clueless, but he was much shrewder than Damien had initially given him credit for. "Yeah," Damien said. "I'm down. What time?"

"I've got some shit to do this evening, so around ten."

Damien's gut clenched. It was that nerve-racking moment when the gears began to grind, a plan being set into motion. "I'll be there. See you then."

"Later."

Once the call was disconnected, Damien took a few cleansing breaths. His head was pounding like a motherfucker and his mouth felt like it was coated with a layer of fuzz. Damned dry, forced air. He flexed his arms, loosening the stiff muscles before he pushed himself off the bed. A few stumbling steps got him to the window and he brushed the curtains aside, staring down at the parking lot of the Hilton he'd relocated to after discovering that he'd been camped out at the very hotel Joey was doing business from. He glanced back at the digital display of the alarm clock on the bedside table. Three in the afternoon. He exchanged the burner cell for his work phone, which was tucked away in the nightstand, and searched through his contacts, pulling up Deputy Gates's number.

"Gates," he answered after a few rings.

"Hey, Ryan. It's Da—uh, Parker. Cavello made contact. He wants to meet tonight. How quickly can you get me some cash? I want to be sure I have enough to impress him. In case he needs me to prove that I'm capable of moving a shitload of product." Cavello wanted to work his way up in the syndicate, and Damien wanted him to think that he was equally ambitious. The faster he was accepted into Cavello's inner circle, the closer he'd be to finding Lightfoot.

"You must have made an impression for him to get ahold of you so quickly."

Which was why the SOG loaned Damien out regularly for interdepartmental operations. He was damned efficient. "It's good for our timetable," he agreed. "Definitely a good sign."

"I'll get the paperwork started, and Callihan will need you to sign the request," Gates said. "But I'm sure we can get you what you need by the end of the day."

"Great. I'll swing by the office this afternoon."

"Sounds good. I'll get the ball rolling on our end. See you in a few hours."

"Thanks."

"No problem," he replied. "I'm here to make sure you have everything you need to do your job."

He disconnected the call and Damien tossed his phone onto the bed. He had more than enough time to shower and grab a bite to eat before he headed over to the office. After that, he'd spend the rest of the evening getting into the right mind-set for his meeting with Cavello. Undercover work wasn't the picnic that outsiders thought it was. The necessary compartmentalization of his life was what kept him level as he prepared to dive headfirst into his criminal persona.

See ya later, Parker Evans. Damien was there for the duration.

Tabitha stared at the list of arrivals, her stomach curling up as tight as a fist. Joey's business was certainly picking up. Two weekends in a row was unusual for him, and it was something that Tabitha never wanted to become a common occurrence. She'd been hoping that he'd slowly fade out of her life, not stick around indefinitely. Luckily it wasn't a busy weekend; the hotel was pretty empty. She just hoped that Joey would keep a low profile, conduct his business, and get the hell out of there with as little contact as possible. She'd rather deal with his smarmy "employees" than Joey any day, and that was saying a lot.

The front-desk phone rang, startling her from her thoughts. Jeez. She was a total basket case. "Thank you for calling the IdaHaven Inn and Suites, this is Tabitha, how can I help you this evening?"

"Hey."

Joey. Adrenaline shot through her system in a nervous rush. She hated that he could affect her in such a negative way. "I've got your suite ready, Joey. What else could you possibly want?"

"Oh, I can think of a few things."

Gross. Tabitha's stomach lurched at the thought. How could she have ever dated him? "I'm busy, Joey. Get to the point."

"I've got a new guy coming in tonight. I want you to make sure he's set up."

A little ray of sunshine poked through the dark clouds of her week. At least she wouldn't have to see Joey in person. "I'll set him up like I would any other guest, is that what you mean?" Seriously, what did he expect? That she'd give him turn-down service with a chocolate on his pillow?

"I want you to treat him better than you would a regular guest. We throw a lot of business your way, Tabs."

Business that Tabitha could do without. "It's really nice how you make it sound like I'm not working with you under duress. As if I have a choice—" A woman approached the front desk and Tabitha lowered her voice. "I'll be right with you," she said. And then to Joey, "Don't worry, your new employee will be well taken care of, Mr. Cavello. Is there anything else I can help you with this evening?"

"Good girl." It took all of her willpower not to cringe away from the phone. "We'll talk soon."

Tabitha hung up the phone and released a shuddering breath.

"I was a waitress for ten years." The woman gave her a commiserating smile. "There are some customers who are impossible to please."

If only Joey were nothing more than a difficult guest; Tabitha could have managed him, no problem. Unfortunately, he was a lot more dangerous than just some guy with a beef about his room rate. "Isn't that the truth?" Tabitha fixed her best customer-service grin on her face. "How can I help you this evening?"

* * *

When Joey's new "employee" walked into the lobby rolling a large suitcase behind him, Tabitha wasn't exactly surprised to see Damien Evans. According to Dave, he'd checked out the morning after she'd seen him at Liquid with Joey. Also not a shocker. He'd more than likely heard through the grapevine that people could buy drugs out of the hotel, and had no doubt been casing Joey's operation. Tabitha's assertion that he was more dangerous—and likely smarter—than her ex was obviously correct. He'd totally played Joey. Maneuvered himself into a job. The question was, why?

Tabitha had forgotten how commanding his presence was up close, his frame larger, more muscular and imposing than she remembered. Guys like Damien thrived on intimidation, threw their weight around on a regular basis. She studied him as he walked across the lobby, his rolling gait slow and graceful, like a grizzly bear prowling through the woods. This guy was at the top of the food chain and had been for a while. Which begged the question: How did someone like that wind up working *for* someone like Joey?

"So, I take it *Parking Lot Monthly* decided to cut you loose?" No use trying to be even a little bit personable. Damien wasn't a guest. He wasn't even a nice guy. He was just another asshole drug peddler.

"The economy just hasn't bounced back enough to support the parking-lot aficionados." His voice rippled over Tabitha's skin in a prickle of heat. Deep and gruff, but without the hard edge of sarcasm she'd expected. He placed his hands on the counter, fingers splayed. She tried not to look at the tattoos marking his knuckles, no doubt affiliating him with some gang or another. "Gotta pay the bills, you know?"

"I hear Applebee's is hiring." His brow furrowed and for a moment she was helpless to do anything but stare. Like she'd noticed on the first night she'd met him, Damien lived in the shell of a well-seasoned criminal, but beneath his rough exterior, there was an inner light. An unmistakable aura that made Tabitha think there was more to him than met the eye.

He cocked his head to one side, returning her gaze and looking even more like a wary animal. "Do I look like I could get a job at Applebee's?"

She imagined him towering over a table of elderly ladies, tattoos and all, reciting the night's specials in that deliciously rough voice. A pleasant shiver danced over her skin and Tabitha shook herself from her thoughts and directed her attention to the computer screen. "Okay, so maybe not Applebee's." Why was she even trying to have a conversation with him? If he was associated with Joey in any way, he was trouble. Period. "I've got you all set up in a suite for the weekend. Room 504. You're in a corner room, tucked away from the bulk of the guests. I assume you know the ground rules?"

A crease cut into his forehead, just above the bridge of his nose. In the depths of his golden-brown eyes, something glimmered, as though he fought some inner turmoil and had just flipped a switch of decision. Tabitha knew that feeling all too well. She flipped that same switch every time she was forced to deal with Joey and his business. Did that mean she was becoming too used to this life he'd forced her into, that she could so easily turn off her conscience when she needed to?

"I'm square," Damien said, a little too gruff. "I just need a key and I'm set."

Tabitha coded two key cards for the suite and slid them into an envelope. "I'm on shift until ten o'clock tonight, and after that Kendall, the night auditor, is on shift." She grabbed the cordless phone from the remote unit, and a handheld radio. "Give me a second."

Damien stood stoic, not even a nod of acknowledgment as Tabitha ducked her head into the back office and asked Sam, the sales manager, to keep an eye on the front desk for a few minutes. When she emerged from the office, Damien looked as though he hadn't moved an inch in the sixty seconds or so she'd been gone. Dude was a statue.

"Ready?"

He cocked a brow. "Don't think I can make it down the hallway by myself?"

Tabitha gave him a reluctant smile at the subtle rib. "Just doing my job."

Damien's gaze darkened. "Escorting me to my room is part of your job?"

She didn't know why—hell, she didn't even really know the guy—but she felt like she could level with him. "Look, Damien. I'm just doing what I'm told. I don't know what goes on in the suites that Joey rents and I don't want to know." Okay, so that wasn't entirely true. Maybe she should have said she didn't want to know any *more* than she already knew. "He told me to set you up, and that's what I'm doing."

Tabitha took a left past the lobby and led the way to the elevators. "What's your take in all of this?" Damien asked. "Your cut must be pretty sweet."

Hmmm. Chatty for someone who looked like he'd just as soon throw a punch as exchange small talk.

Tabitha's hackles rose. The fact that Joey's people thought she had any stake in his dealings made her feel like she was covered with a layer of slime. "I don't have a take," she remarked, maybe a little too forcefully. The last thing she needed was for word to get back to Joey that she was running off at the mouth. "Or a cut. See those doors?" She pointed to a set of glass doors leading out to the parking lot. "Your visitors need to exit from there. They shouldn't even be coming through the lobby. I leave that door unlocked for just that reason." Tabitha stopped at the elevators and hit the button for the fifth floor. "Also, tell any guests that you might be entertaining to take the stairs. This late at night, no one wants to be cooped up with some twitchy, shady dude in an enclosed space."

Damien remained silent, his gaze sliding over her in a way that made Tabitha's skin tingle. What she wouldn't give to know what he was thinking right now. The elevator deposited them on the fifth floor and Tabitha took a right down the hallway. "Also, you break it you buy it. If that room is in anything less than pristine condition when you check out, we're going to have a serious problem that has nothing to do with Joey. Understand?"

He paused midstep and Tabitha turned to face him. A grin curved his full lips, revealing deep dimples in both cheeks. "Nothing less than pristine. Got it."

Holy shit, that smile. Tabitha's jaw went slack as something in her brain short-circuited. It transformed his face, intensifying that bright aura until it was almost blinding. It made him look younger. Carefree. Her heart stuttered in her chest at the sight of him, and that was a huge problem. She'd already paid the price once for hooking up with a guy who spent his time south of the law, and she wasn't about to do it again.

"Okay, then." It took an actual effort to put her back to him and keep walking, but she held her course, stopping at the door to the suite marked 504. "Joey made it clear that you pay cash for the room when you check out on Sunday, right?" She didn't want a paper trail any more than Joey did. "I don't work on Sunday, but if you have any issues tell Jackie at the front desk to give me a call."

Damien pulled one of the key cards from the envelope and stuck it in the slot of the door. "Anything else I need to know?"

"Just behave."

He turned to her and quirked a brow as though to say, *Really?*

"You know what I mean." She didn't have the patience to get into any moral discussions with a criminal tonight. "Keep a low profile. I don't really feel like looking for a new job anytime soon." Or more to the point, she couldn't afford Joey's retribution if she got fired.

"There won't be any issues," he assured her as he opened the door. "I doubt Joey is interested in finding a new hotel to stay at, either."

And that was the problem. "Right. Okay, well, I'll leave you to it, Damien." She turned and headed back the way she'd come. God, why was she being so damned polite? She should have told him to fuck off. That she thought they were all a bunch of low-life scumbags. *You're such a coward, Tabitha.*

He called out in a soft voice behind her, "Have a good night, Tabitha."

Her eyes drifted shut for the barest moment. No one had ever said her name with such affection. It left her feeling not a little shaken. The last thing she needed was to be attracted to another bad influence.

Too late, honey. She was already hooked.

Chapter Five

Damien secured the lock and slouched against the closed door. It had been a long damned time since any woman had caught his eye, and he didn't want to acknowledge that the one woman who had was an accessory to a crime. His undercover work made dating pretty much impossible, and likewise, when you hung out with the scum of the earth on a daily basis, the dating pool wasn't exactly overrun with eligible women. Tabitha claimed that she didn't know any details about Joey's operation, but she knew enough. She'd dated the guy, for fuck's sake. No way did she not know what her man had been into.

Still, her expression had been guileless, those big blue eyes of hers showing nothing but honesty. Her short, golden-blond hair looked as soft as corn silk, and in her wake, Damien had inhaled the sweet scent of her perfume. She reminded him of summer. Of the sun, and roses in full bloom. Though she didn't come across as the type of woman who took shit off of anyone, she'd apparently taken it from her ex. Why else would she be helping him by allowing him to set up his distribution operation inside of her hotel? It might've been a good idea to have Gates do a background check on her after all. There was more to Tabitha Martin than met the eye, and Damien wanted to know what it was.

Fuck. It was tough to get into character and compartmentalize when his brain was buzzing with questions. His interest in Tabitha had nothing to do with the job. He had to stop thinking of her in those terms and see her through Damien's eyes. She was a go-between and nothing more. A means to an end. Period. It was time to focus and get his head in the game.

He hoisted the heavy suitcase up onto the bed and unzipped it. Lifting the flap, he took a moment to examine the contents. Joey had gotten himself in deep, for sure. Filled to the brim with Stardust, the cache of narcotics was large enough to put Joey Cavello away for the rest of his life. Jesus. A twinge of guilt pulled at Damien's chest; the knowledge that this shit would soon be out on the streets unsettled him. But the prize was Lightfoot. He had to see the bigger picture. Boise PD would get their chance at Cavello. Just not quite yet.

Damien had refused to wear a wire and he hadn't thought it wise to bug the room, either. At least not yet. That's not to say he was completely alone. Gates had men staged close to the hotel who were responsible for monitoring the comings and goings of Cavello's clientele and to act as backup if shit went sideways. A small consolation, he supposed. Then again, if shit did go sideways, he'd probably be dead before his backup arrived. Callihan was right about it being some cowboy shit. Maybe his recklessness was an indicator that he just didn't give a shit anymore.

He replaced the SIM card in his burner phone and cataloged the contents of the suitcase, snapping pictures of the drugs, the room, anything and everything that could be used as evidence. He might be using Cavello's operation to get to Lightfoot, but that didn't mean he couldn't help build a case against the asshole in the meantime. After he finished, he tucked the tiny memory card into his boot. Even if Joey's crew showed up to further vet him, they weren't going to bother digging around in his shoes.

The next hour was spent dividing Joey's cache into distributable portions. Fifteen different dealers would be stopping by, as well as a few preferred customers who didn't deal but bought enough product to get "platinum level" treatment. Those platinum customers got a discount on their purchases because they didn't have to go through a dealer to buy. They'd earned their status by keeping quiet, respecting Joey's rules about not using on hotel property, and by always paying up front in cash. He might seem like an idiot, but in truth, he was running a top-notch business. The smart criminals were always the hardest to catch.

Which was why they'd had a hell of a time getting their hands on Lightfoot. Obviously he surrounded himself with equally crafty associates.

Damien spent the next hour handing out product to Joey's dealers and clients, all the while making mental notes about each and every one of them. The dude ran a tight ship and the people who bought from him behaved like professionals. A few of them were dirty and already high enough to raise a brow, but for the most part, they handed over their money, took their backpacks full of product, and left. By ten o'clock, Damien had handed out over half of Joey's weekend supply, and he wouldn't be seeing the other half of his customers until tomorrow night.

Silence permeated the air and settled over Damien's skin like shrink-wrap, squeezing all of the oxygen from his lungs. He let out a gust of breath and cracked his neck as he stretched it from side to side. It was too goddamned hot in the room. Too stifling. The walls were slowly closing in on him. If he didn't get some fresh air, he was going to snap.

He snatched the key card from the table and hung a Do Not Disturb tag on the door as he closed it behind him, as an indicator to any of Joey's clients that they should wait in the hallway. Unwilling to be cooped up in another small space, he took the stairs down to the ground floor and left through the side exit that Tabitha had left unlocked. As the cool night air met his lungs, Damien inhaled deeply, holding his breath as he stretched his arms high above him. A cloud of steam billowed in front of him on the exhale. Early winter wasn't exactly balmy in Idaho, but the cold had never bothered him.

"What part of *no* do you not understand?"

The words echoed across the parking lot, spoken with a mixture of anger and anxiety. Damien recognized the speaker in an instant and walked toward the sound of Tabitha's voice. He found her standing next to an older model Toyota 4Runner, both hands on the door handle. Beside her, Joey's friend Tony held the door closed, one meaty arm caging her in while his free hand fiddled with the short strands of her hair.

"Quit being such a frigid snatch. I know you like to party. Joey said you're the best piece of ass he ever had. I don't see a problem here. It's not like you're with him anymore."

Damien's temper surfaced in a wave of heat that seared through his veins with every beat of his heart. What sort of low-life son of a bitch talked that way about his girlfriend? Ex or not. And had Joey indicated that Tabitha was one of the perks offered to his customers? A free sample that you got when you spent over a thousand dollars? She obviously wasn't down with that, and she shoved against the asshole who'd just picked a backpack up from Damien not five minutes ago.

"Not if you were the last man on the planet, Tony. Get away from me and take your hands off of my car door before I call the cops. I doubt Joey would want them taking a look inside your backpack."

Damien picked up his pace to a slow jog. Tony let out a loud bark of laughter. "As if you'd call the cops. As long as Joey has Seth by the balls, you aren't going to do shit."

He leaned in and Tabitha abandoned her struggle to open the car door, to push against Tony's unwelcome advance. Damien swooped in and grabbed the asshole by the collar of his jacket, spinning him away. He slammed him up against the 4Runner with enough force to rattle the bastard's teeth and braced his forearm against Tony's throat.

"I know you aren't tryin' to start shit in this parking lot when you know the rules, right?" He forced the words through clenched teeth and increased the pressure on Tony's throat until his breath wheezed in and out of his lungs. "Because if that was the case, you wouldn't be doing business here anymore. And you know better than to fuck up a good thing. Right?"

Tony's eyes bugged out of his head as he struggled to free himself from Damien's grasp. He choked up tighter and the bastard's face grew red under the fluorescent lights that illuminated the parking lot.

"Answer me, or I swear to God, I won't think twice about snapping your skinny-ass neck."

He let up on the pressure and Tony squeaked out, "Right. Right. I was just playing. Giving Tabs a hard time." His words were spoken with all the desperation of a coward. Tony was obviously only as tough as he perceived his opponent weak. Damien towered over him and had a good fifty pounds on the smaller man. Tony knew he was outgunned.

"Apologize," Damien ground out.

"I-I'm sorry, Tabs. I was just giving you a hard time."

Damien leaned in close, his words for Tony's ears alone. "If you so much as look at her again, I swear to Christ I will *end* you. Do you understand me?"

"Yeah. Of course, man. Loud and clear."

Damien released him with a shove. "Get the fuck outta here and go move some merchandise. Or I'll make sure you don't get another ounce."

Tony nodded in response and hiked the backpack up on his shoulder as he turned to leave. He massaged his throat, muttering something under his breath. Empty threats, no doubt. Tonight wasn't the first time some low-life SOB had cursed Damien, and it sure as hell wouldn't be the last. No matter what Tabitha's role in Joey's operation was, she didn't deserve to be treated like community property.

Residual anger and adrenaline still burned through

Damien's veins and for a moment, he wished that Tony had put up more of a fight. The sight of his hands on Tabitha, his fingers teasing the strands of her hair, had sent Damien into a rage that he didn't understand. Further proof that his head wasn't right even after a few months' worth of therapy sessions. He had no business being back out in the field.

None.

Tabitha leaned against the hood of her 4Runner, her breath stalled somewhere between her sternum and her mouth. Fear turned quickly to awe as she watched Damien throw that slimeball Tony up against her car, his forearm like a log lodged against the smaller man's throat. No one had ever stood up for her like that before. Not even Joey, who used to sit back and snicker when guys hassled her, as if he found her distress entertaining.

She had no idea what Damien had whispered in Tony's ear, but Tony looked like he was about to pee his pants. And honestly, Tabitha wouldn't have blamed him. Damien's display only served to solidify her opinion that he was, in fact, far more dangerous than Joey or any of the wannabe thugs he hung out with.

"Are you okay? He didn't hurt you, did he?"

The natural growl of his voice vibrated through every inch of Tabitha's body and she suddenly felt too flushed despite the chill in the air. "I'm okay." She pushed herself away from her car and hugged the two halves of her coat closer together. "Tony's bark is worse than his bite. I've fielded worse from him before."

His gaze darkened at the admission and Tabitha almost felt sorry for anyone his anger might be directed toward. "You shouldn't be keeping company with guys like that."

"What about you? Should you be keeping company with guys like that?"

He hid any reaction to her words behind an impassive mask. Why? Most gangster types wore their associations like a badge of honor. Tabitha got the impression that those relationships embarrassed Damien.

"Buy a can of pepper spray," Damien said. "If you're leaving work this late all the time, you should have the canister in your hand before you even walk out the door."

Tabitha wondered at his concern. "You're probably right. Especially with Joey's asshole low-life friends hanging around."

Damien looked like he wanted to say something, but he kept his mouth shut. A car pulled into the far end of the parking lot and cut the engine. No doubt another of Joey's customers after their score. His gaze followed hers and a scowl marred his expression. "Does that asshole know where you live?"

"Tony? No. No one knows where I live." Not even Joey. After they'd broken up, she moved from her apartment so he wouldn't be able to drop by unannounced, and it made her feel a little safer.

His brow arched with curiosity "Not even Joey?"

What did he care? She barely knew Damien. "I think you have a customer." She indicated the car that was sitting in the parking lot with the engine running. "Thanks for handling Tony for me. I appreciate it."

Damien took two steps toward her, the bulk of his large frame towering over her. She didn't feel crowded or intimidated in his presence, though God knows she should have. Instead, a jolt of excitement shot through her bloodstream as her heart beat wildly in her chest. He reached up, the motion abrupt, and brushed her hair away from her face as though he couldn't resist. A riot of butterflies took flight in Tabitha's stomach, swirling and soaring at the simple contact.

And just as abruptly, he turned away. Stalking across the parking lot with an angry stride that prompted the pleasant butterflies in her stomach to duck for cover. Was he angry? With her? What in the hell just happened?

"Who's Seth?" He turned to face her, not ten feet from her car.

Suspicion crept up her spine like an early morning frost. "My brother," she said. "Why?"

"Go straight home, Tabitha. And if Tony gives you any more trouble, I want to know about it."

Without waiting for her response, he turned and took off toward the hotel, his body rolling with the cautious gait of a skilled predator. In the distance, a door slammed as whatever nasty drug dealer Joey sent over there got out of his car to follow Damien inside the hotel. Tabitha let out the breath she'd been holding in an attempt to calm her trembling limbs.

Her skull tingled from the brief contact of Damien's fingers in her hair. The warmth of his body still occupied the space where he'd stood, close enough for her to touch. She reached for the door handle and pulled against the weight of the door. Tony had scared the shit out of her. She'd played it off for Damien's benefit, unwilling for him to see any weakness in her. But the truth was that he'd always scared her, and despite Joey's warnings, she knew he'd sampled some of whatever was in his backpack before making his way to her car.

If Damien hadn't stepped in . . . God, she didn't even want to think about what might have happened. Tabitha was still shaking when she fastened her seat belt. It took two tries to get the key in the ignition and she didn't know what had her more rattled: her encounter with Tony or the effect of Damien's close proximity.

By the time she pulled out of the parking lot, Tabitha was fairly sure she could drive home without getting in a wreck. If Damien could shake a woman up by touching her hair, she could only imagine what skin-on-skin contact would do. A quick ten minutes—thanks to the streetlight gods—saw her home, parked, and ready to call it a night.

"Hey, I saved you some pizza." Seth was sitting on her couch, flipping through channels with a can of soda balanced on his knee. "What took you so long? Didn't you get off work like an hour ago?"

It wasn't that she minded having her younger brother as a roommate. In fact, with Seth's penchant for getting into trouble, she could keep an eye on him better if he was under her roof. But tonight was one of those nights that Tabitha would have appreciated a little solitude to decompress. Her mind was racing with too many thoughts for casual conversation.

"How'd you pay for the pizza?" It sucked that it was the first thing she was prompted to ask. But she knew that Seth didn't have three dollars, let alone thirty bucks.

He gave her a bright smile. "As of today, I'm officially and gainfully employed. The guy who owns Les Bois Construction, Jack, gave me a hundred-dollar draw to buy work boots."

"And you ran straight over to Flying Pie and bought a pizza?"

"No." Seth rolled his eyes and hiked up a pant leg. "I bought these first. On sale. Then I bought the pizza. Because I'm a boss at money management."

The boots were nice, but he should have used the thirty bucks he'd saved for pizza for a higher-quality shoe. She wasn't going to lecture him about it, though. Seth hadn't worn many bright smiles in the past couple of years. And if she was going to keep him on the right track, he needed Tabitha's encouragement, not her disdain.

"Pretty fancy for work boots." She grinned. "When do you start?"

"Tomorrow," he said through a mouthful of pizza. "I also went over to BSU today and talked with an admissions counselor."

"Really?" She hadn't meant to sound so shocked, but she would have simply been happy to see Seth enroll in a nine-month tech course.

"Yeah. I mean, I still don't know what I want to do, but I thought I could apply for spring semester and figure it out in the meantime."

"That's awesome, Seth." They were only two years apart in age, but most of the time Tabitha felt more like a mother than a big sister. "I can help you with the financial aid stuff if you want. I bet you'd qualify for a few grants, too."

"All under control, sister." Seth tossed a sliver of crust into the pizza box, his gaze focused on the pepperoni, bacon, and mushroom pie. "I know I've been a major fuck-up. And you got my ass out of trouble when you probably shouldn't have. I just want you to know that I'm ready to put all of that behind me. And I don't want you to feel like you have to take care of me anymore."

Tabitha plopped down on the couch beside him and ruffled his blond hair that was just a little shorter than hers. "You're not a fuck-up, Seth. You've just made some bad choices. And I don't feel like I have to take care of you."

"Did you notice I didn't get any peppers on the pizza?"

She smiled. "I did. You're so considerate."

Seth nodded solemnly. "Considerate is my middle name. And I *really* wanted peppers, too."

Tabitha selected a narrow slice from the half of the round that was still left. She leaned back on the couch and propped her feet up on the coffee table. Seth settled in beside her and resumed his channel surfing.

"So, how was work? Anything interesting happen in the land of guest services today?"

A flush crept over Tabitha's skin as she recalled the heat in Damien's golden eyes as he'd swept the hair from her face. The sheer maleness of him as he'd jerked Tony away from her and slammed him against her car and the roll of his muscles as he'd walked away from her. "Same old, same old," Tabitha replied after a moment. "Just another glamorous day of reservations at the IdaHaven Inn."

Seth laughed. "One more semester and it won't

matter, right? You can kiss that place good-bye and go work at a hospital and torture people with your cold stethoscope."

Tabitha let out a chuff of breath. She'd never let Seth know the truth. That if Joey had anything to say about it, she'd never leave that hotel. "That's the plan."

For once, she wished that life could be that simple.

Chapter Six

Damien collapsed on the bed, ready to put this miserable night behind him. For the past three hours, he'd been reliving his time in the parking lot with Tabitha. His fingertips still tingled where they touched her hair. *You stupid, impulsive bastard.*

He hadn't intended to touch her. Fuck, he barely knew her. And she'd just barely fended off that asshole Tony's unwanted attention when he'd reached for her. His gut clenched at the thought of how her gaze had warmed. And whereas she'd cringed away from Tony, he could have sworn that she'd leaned into his touch.

And goddamn it, her hair had been just as soft as he'd imagined. Like corn silk. His eyes drifted shut, and Damien didn't even bother to turn off the lights as sleep weighed down his limbs. All he felt like doing lately was sleep. Probably a sign of depression. Oh fucking well . . .

A knock at the door squashed any hope of oblivion and Damien dragged his ass out of bed. He'd crossed the last guy off his list of "appointments" about a half hour ago. From the dresser, he retrieved his Beretta and held it at the ready as he checked through the peephole in the door. On the other side, Joey Cavello stared at the screen of his phone, his expression pinched and impatient. Checking up on him, huh?

"'Sup?" Damien swung the door open wide and tucked his piece into the waistband of his jeans at the small of his back.

Joey strode through the door and took a quick look around as though trying to catch Damien doing something he shouldn't. As tonight was his first night on the job, Damien didn't blame him for being suspicious. "A buddy of mine did some checking up on you tonight, Evans. Found some pretty interesting shit."

Adrenaline shot through Damien's bloodstream and his muscles bunched in anticipation of a fight. The Marshals Service had done a pretty good job of burying his real identity, but hackers could be crafty. If Joey knew a good one, there was no telling what he might have found. "Oh yeah? And what's that?"

"Said you were arrested a few months back with a bunch of Mexican arms dealers. That right?"

To protect his undercover persona, Damien had been arrested along with Teyo Sousa and his crew as they were getting ready to take possession of a dirty bomb near the Port of Seattle. He had a fake criminal record a mile long, and his colleagues never seemed to tire of throwing the cuffs on him. Their entertainment was a hard-core pain in the ass for Damien. "Yeah, that's right," he replied with a shrug of one shoulder.

"You must know some heavy hitters to get out of that shit. 'Cuz I bet none of those other guys are out walking around like you are."

True. Sousa and his associates wouldn't be seeing the light of day anytime soon. "I do." Again, said as though it was no big deal.

Joey looked him over, a smirk pulling at his thin lips. "I knew taking you on would be a good move. C'mon, I need some help tonight and Tony flaked out on me."

Bastard was probably in a flophouse somewhere coming down from his high. Things were progressing quicker than he'd expected, which in some cases could be considered a bad thing. Since he didn't consider Joey stupid by any stretch of the imagination, he had to be suspicious of his motives for trusting him so easily. He'd thrown him into the deep end of his business without batting a lash, and now he was taking him out as backup for God knew what. Not that Damien wasn't pleased. But he wasn't interested in taking a bullet to the skull anytime soon, either. "Sure. What do you need?"

"I'm picking up a delivery. Some assholes from a syndicate out of Nampa tried to jump us last time, and I'm not putting up with that bullshit tonight."

And no doubt Lightfoot would find someone else to work with if Joey couldn't keep his house in order. "You think there's going to be trouble? If that's the case, you might want to take more than me along." It showed the low level of criminal Joey Cavello was that he wasn't taking an armed entourage along to pick up tonight's shipment. Which made Damien more than a little twitchy. You'd think they were going to the grocery store to pick up a gallon of milk or some shit, not a half million dollars in narcotics. The kid was clueless.

Joey snorted. "I take a big motherfucker like you along, ain't *no one* gonna fuck with me."

Jesus. Damien was big, but he wasn't Superman. It was his reputation that backed up his size, though, and Cavello knew that. Damien wondered how much Joey's competition from the neighboring city would care.

"Don't be so sure." He tucked the suitcase with the rest of the product under the bed and grabbed the Do Not Disturb sign to hang on the door. He led the way out and Joey followed him. "I'm down, though. Am I good to leave my luggage in the room? I don't want anything happening to it."

"You're good," Joey remarked. "As long as that door hanger's up, no one will go in. Tabs runs a tight ship and everyone knows that when my crew is staying the weekend, they don't like to be disturbed. And it's in her best interest to keep me happy."

The threat inherent in Joey's tone made Damien want to beat the fucker to the ground. His statement was yet another indicator that Tabitha might be helping him under duress, and though it didn't pertain to his assignment in the least, he was bound and determined to get to the bottom of it.

They hopped in Joey's tricked-out Ford F-150 pickup and headed from the downtown area to the outskirts of the city, toward Gowen Field. Several shipping companies had their headquarters on the lots that skirted the freeway, and Joey followed Federal Way out to a fenced-in lot with a large warehouse. A sign that read LTC Inc. was hung on a chain-link fence and Joey stopped to enter a code on the automated gate that slid open with several jerks and squeaks of metal.

Questions raised suspicion, and Damien had learned over the course of his undercover assignments that if he kept his eyes open and his mouth shut, he'd learn all he needed to without uttering a single word. Joey flicked his cigarette out the window before rolling it up and drove through the gate toward a large lot full of semitrailers. "The shit's coming down from up north. So far, the state police don't have a clue about what these trucks are really transporting. We're talking high-tech shit. Hidden compartments that the dogs can't even sniff through. It's fucking genius, dude."

Ingenious, dude. For every undercover op Damien worked, he felt his IQ drop another notch. "Sweet." Just to be safe, he'd have to fill Deputy Gates and the chief deputy in, make sure that the Idaho State Police gave the shipping company a wide berth, as well.

"When I started distributing for this guy, I was setting up at the hotel one weekend a month. Now, I'm up to twice a month, and with this shipment, I'll probably have you there every weekend from here on out. This guy is a fucking gold mine. I'm making bank, and if you stick around, I can guarantee you that you'll be pulling in some serious cash."

What Joey didn't know was that Lightfoot would be pulling his operation out of Idaho soon. And when that happened, he'd leave him high and dry. "You thinking of setting up shop somewhere else? Gotta spread the love, you know what I mean?"

"Nah. Why? I've got a sweet deal at Tabitha's hotel. I'm not gonna catch any heat as long as she's working there, and she's working there until I tell her she's not."

Damien resisted the urge to pop the asshole in the face as Joey pulled the truck to a stop just inside the yard and flashed his headlights three times. "She used to be your girl, right?" He'd violated his own rule by asking a question, but curiosity burned him from the inside out.

"Yeah," Joey said in a conspiratorial tone that caused Damien's hackles to rise. "And believe me, I *defiled* her fine ass."

Damien swallowed down the growl that rose in his throat and traded it for an appreciative snort. "But you're not hittin' that anymore?"

"Tabs likes bad boys, but she wants hers to have more of a conscience. Ain't nobody got time for that shit."

Joey's statement, coupled with Tony's not-so-gentle reminder to Tabitha that Joey had her brother by the balls, only helped to confirm that there was more to Tabitha's involvement than Damien had first surmised. It was becoming more obvious that she was being coerced, which made him wonder exactly what Joey had on her brother that would convince Tabitha to help him out.

In the distance, a flashlight blinked in the darkness once, twice, and again. Joey opened his car door. "We're on. Let's get the cargo and get the fuck outta here."

Damien put Tabitha to the back of his mind as he got out of the car and followed Joey. His skin prickled as his senses engaged, fine-tuned to his surroundings and every minute sound that shifted in the distance. It was too damned dark out here. The opportunity for an ambush too perfect. As they approached the three men waiting for them, Damien banished that last bit of concern for Tabitha to the compartment that he stored Parker's sensibilities in.

The exchange was made easily enough. Product was transferred from one of the semitrailers and loaded up into the backseat of Joey's truck. He pulled out of the yard and stopped just outside of the gate to the shipping yard, waiting for it to close behind them, when a disembodied arm reached in through his open window and pointed a gun at Joey's head.

The would-be carjacker leaned in the rest of the way, his face undistinguishable in the darkness. "Both of you fuckers, get out of the truck. Now."

Obviously Joey's rival dealer wasn't done trying to get his hands on Lightfoot's product. From out of the shadows, the guy's backup approached from behind a souped-up Nissan. The car was running, but the lights were off. Damien couldn't see much past the headlights of Joey's truck, but as the dude sidled up to his partner, the light glinted off the chrome of a 9mm clutched in his grip.

Joey eased open his door and climbed down from his seat and Damien tucked his forty close to his hip as he followed suit. They had darkness on their side and with what appeared to be two-against-two odds, Damien had the height and muscle—not to mention the training—that would ensure they got the upper hand.

He kept his stance relaxed as he came around the high front end of Joey's Ford, using the truck's jacked-up height to hide the weapon at his side.

Thug number one jerked his gun in Damien's direction. "Get your ass over here before my patience runs out, asshole."

The fence to the shipping yard rattled closed and Damien used the momentary distraction to strike. He used the butt of the gun and brought it down on the head of the guy closest to him, knocking him out cold.

Before thug number two could react, he brought

his gun up and aimed it at the bastard's head. "You really wanna do this?" he asked. "Just gather up your buddy, back the fuck off, and let us go."

"Yeah, right." Thug number two let out a disbelieving bark of laughter. Dude was either incredibly brave or goddamned stupid. "I'm not going anywhere until you hand over the shit you got in the backseat. I didn't come all the way out here to go home empty-handed again."

Damien lunged in with an elbow and caught the guy under the chin. The gangbanger spun away, his 9mm dropping from his grasp as he slumped to the ground beside his buddy. Small-time gangster bullshit. Damien hated dealing with this petty crap, but at least a clueless thug was easier to take down than a seasoned dealer. Tonight could have easily gone south. Joey was damned lucky.

"Fuck yeah!" Joey shouted as he hopped up into the truck. "You're a certifiable badass, Evans!" Damien hustled back to his side of the truck and hopped in. Joey threw the truck into gear and peeled out onto Federal Way, the tires squealing in his haste. "Damn, am I glad I brought you with me tonight."

Damien stowed his gun and rolled down the window to let the chill wind cool his heated face. Funny, none of what he'd just done made him feel like a badass.

Why had she agreed to a blind date? Or even a double date, for that matter? Lila was chatting up a storm with Charlie, the guy she'd met at Liquid a couple of weeks ago. They'd been going strong since that night, and now Tabitha was being forced to endure small talk with Charlie's friend—what in the *hell* was his name again? Josh?—while Lila seductively fed her date calamari from across the table. Ugh.

"So you're a nurse?"

"I'm sorry, what?" Tabitha dragged her eyes from the spectacle of Lila feeding Charlie and turned her attention back to her date.

He flashed her a knowing smile, as though watching her friend behave like a horny vixen was turning her on or something. Gross. "I said that Lila mentioned you were a nurse."

"I'm still in school." She reached for her wineglass and drained it in a couple of swallows. *Where in the hell is the waiter when you need him?* "I just finished up the current semester and I'm about to start my clinical rotations in a month."

"Cool. So, if I passed out, could you do mouth-to-mouth on me?"

It took all of the self-control she could muster not to roll her eyes. "Only if you stopped breathing," she said, refusing to take his bait.

Josh deflated a little but continued in his valiant attempt to make small talk. "Do you want to take care of babies or work in a swanky downtown clinic?"

She opted to ignore his veiled misogyny. "My specialty is going to be trauma. I want to work in the ER."

"Triage." Ooh, Josh was throwing down the twenty-five-cent words now. "Right?"

"You've got it."

Conversation dwindled and Tabitha caught their waiter's eye. She raised her glass and he gave her a curt nod. It was going to take an entire bottle of wine to get her through tonight. Since yesterday, all she'd been able to think about was Damien. The intense and instant attraction she felt for him had thrown her for a loop. Her body came alive just at the sight of him, and last night's episode in the parking lot had only served to solidify her infatuation. Every solid inch of him was masculine perfection, and Tabitha found herself wanting to reach out and test each and every hard edge.

"Helllllloooo? Earth to Tabitha. Did you hear me?"

Jeez, she must've been coming across like a total flake tonight. "Sorry, I was zoned out there for a second. What did you say?"

Lila cut her a look and let out a slow breath. "I asked if you wanted to order another appetizer."

Not if she had to endure watching Lila hand-feed her date like he was a baby bird. "No, I'm good, but if you guys want something, go ahead and order."

Lila rolled her eyes and Tabitha knew she was treading on thin ice. She needed to kick it into gear and at least pretend like she was having a good time. But how could she when her mind was somewhere else? With someone else. Ugh. She was so stupid. Getting involved with Damien was not a good idea. He was in business with Joey, and that was enough to tell her that he was bad news. Still . . .

Her phone rang from inside her purse and she dug it out and checked the caller ID. "It's work, I need to take this," she said to the table at large. Lila frowned and Tabitha gave a shrug before swiping a finger across the screen. "Hello?"

"Hey," Dave said. "I know you're double-dating it tonight, but I've got a minor problem. The key coder isn't working. Can you come over and reset it real quick?"

Part of her assistant manager duties included acting as a troubleshooter for the night shift. She couldn't help but wonder if Sandy, the general manager, had these kinds of problems during the day, because it seemed like all of their equipment chose to malfunction at night. "I'm just a couple of blocks down the street. I'll be there in a few minutes."

"You're the best, Tabs."

"Yeah, yeah. See you in a sec."

"No." Lila looked horrified. Probably because she wasn't interested in entertaining Josh. So sad. "You took the day off. That means you *don't* go to work."

"It'll only take a minute. I'm the only one who knows how to reboot our key coder. We're dead in the water until I fix it."

"I can order for you," Josh piped in.

"Um, yeah, okay. Thanks." She gathered up her purse and turned to leave. Knowing her luck, he'd order her veal or something that she absolutely refused to eat.

"Don't drag your feet," Lila called from behind her. "Get that stupid thing fixed and get back here!"

Tabitha raised her hand in acknowledgment and beelined it for the exit, more relieved for the distraction than she wanted to admit.

"There. All fixed."

"You're a lifesaver," Dave said. "I swear to God, every single one of our check-ins decided to show up at the same time tonight. I've been swamped."

"No worries." Tabitha logged out of the system and logged Dave back in.

"So . . . how's the date going?"

"Don't ask," Tabitha answered on a groan. "I'm starting to think that nice guys just aren't my thing."

"I could have told you that," Dave said with a

laugh. "If he's not tattooed, he might as well not even bother."

Heh. Probably. Another wave of guests walked through the entrance and Tabitha motioned to a stack of blankets and pillows on the front desk. "What are those for?"

"Oh, I need to take them up to room 502, but I haven't had a free second to run them up."

"I can do it." Tabitha scooped up the linens and rounded the corner. It's not like she was anxious to get back to Josh and his small talk.

"I owe you a dinner," Dave said. "Thanks."

"No worries," she said as she headed for the elevator. "'Night, Dave!"

"See ya!"

It wasn't lost on her that she was delivering the linens to the room next door to the one she'd put Damien up in. Nor was she simply being nice by offering to come up here for Dave. She was sick. Sick for hoping to get even a glimpse of him. God, what was *wrong* with her?

She knocked on the door and as she waited for someone in room 502 to answer, the creak of hinges from the next room drew her attention. Her breath caught in her chest as her gaze locked with Damien's feral gold eyes.

"Are those for us?"

Their moment was interrupted by 502's occupants. Tabitha gave the woman an apologetic smile, all the while aware that Damien was still standing there watching her. "They are," she replied with a small laugh. "Thanks for being so patient. Is there anything else I can get for you tonight?"

"No, uh . . ." The woman looked pointedly at her shirt, as though searching for a name tag.

"Tabitha Martin," she said. "I'm the assistant manager."

"Ah." She smiled as though the confirmation that Tabitha was indeed an employee reassured her. "We're good for now. Thank you."

"Have a good night," Tabitha said as the door swung closed.

For a moment she simply stood there, staring at nothing. From the corner of her eye she noticed Damien lean against the doorjamb, his large frame taking up the bulk of the open space. He crossed his arms at his chest as he studied her, and a thrill went through Tabitha's body. *Well, you came up here hoping to see him. What are you going to do about it?*

She turned slowly to face him. He watched her with the intensity of a hawk about to snatch up a mouse in its talons. "Hi." She hadn't meant to sound so breathy, but she couldn't manage even a shallow intake of air when he looked at her like that.

"I bought something for you."

His gruffness didn't do anything to cool the flush that crept over her skin. He disappeared into the room and Tabitha followed, as though a length of string connected her to him and she had no choice but to go where he led. The door closed behind her with a finality that gave her a start. She knew she shouldn't be in this room. With him. With that horrible shit Joey had tasked him with peddling. But her curiosity about this man who had such a visceral effect on her won out over good sense.

Josh was waiting for her back at the Piper Grill with Lila and Charlie. He seemed like a good guy. A smart choice. Her eyes traveled the length of Damien's muscled back, to the straight line of his hips and lower to where his jeans hugged his thighs. *Holy hell.*

"Here." He turned and tossed her a slender black canister. She reached out and caught it, bemused.

"Pepper spray?"

"Don't think twice about using it." His brows drew sharply over his eyes, lending a severity to his expression. "Trust your first instinct, always. Sometimes it's just a tickle. Like something scratching at the back of your brain. But if you feel that way about someone—anyone—who's approached you, you're right to assume that you could be in danger. Spray the bastard in the eye and then kick him in the nuts. You understand?"

Tabitha nodded.

"Good."

He grabbed her by the hand and hauled her against him before putting his mouth to hers in a crushing kiss.

Chapter Seven

What in the actual fuck are you doing?

The voice of reason shouting in his head was way more Parker, responsible deputy U.S. marshal, than Damien, hardened criminal who did whatever the fuck he wanted. He ignored that niggling voice of his conscience because right now, he wanted Tabitha.

Holy Christ, she was so goddamned soft. So willing in his arms. The sound of the canister of pepper spray dropping to the floor was the only sound in the room save their racing breaths. His mouth slanted across hers, hungry and eager to deepen the kiss, and she responded, opening up to him. A hint of wine sweetened her lips and he thrust his tongue into her mouth, desperate for more of her taste. Tabitha wound her fists into the fabric of his T-shirt, pulling him even tighter against her. Through the thin fabric of her shirt, her nipples hardened against his chest and he swallowed down a tortured moan. He'd never in his life wanted a woman as badly as he wanted her right now.

She nipped at his bottom lip and the light sting only served to rev him up. His cock grew hard in his jeans, throbbing in time with each thrust of his tongue in her mouth. Mindless with the need to have her, Damien pulled her deeper into the room, his mouth greedily devouring hers as he backed through the small sitting area and into the bedroom. He spun her around until her back was flush with his chest. He worked the button loose on her jeans with shaking hands and pushed them and her underwear down over her ass in a hurried sweep. A soft moan answered his actions, all the permission he needed, and he leaned her over the mattress until her ass rubbed against his cock in a way that damn near made him come right then and there.

"Spread your legs." He growled the command in her ear and she obeyed, thrusting her ass out and grinding it against him. She was as wound up as he was, and her scent hit Damien's nostrils, that fragrant perfume of her arousal, and his heart pounded in his chest with all the force of a jackhammer.

"Touch me."

The words were a plea, roughened with passion. Any shred of reason that lingered in Damien's brain evaporated under Tabitha's plea. He let his palm cup the curve of her ass, a slow caress as he savored the softness of her skin. His fingers curved, skirting the crease of sensitive skin, which elicited a low whimper from Tabitha and sent a jolt of desire shooting through Damien's body. He continued his path, so slow that it tested his patience, until his fingertips found the silken flesh of her sex, already swollen and slick with want.

A satisfied growl rumbled in Damien's chest. She wanted him. Was wet and ready for him. He savored every inch of her, delving into her slippery heat as he spread her slick arousal over the stiff bundle of nerves

that jutted out from her lips as though in invitation
of his attention. When he circled her clit with the
pad of his finger, Tabitha let out a desperate moan.
She all but melted onto the mattress, thrusting her
hips up to meet his touch. Her responsiveness drove
him wild and Damien leaned over her. He thrust his
free hand under her shirt and jerked the cup of her
bra down as he took one full breast in his palm.

"Yes." Her voice vibrated through Damien's body
as a low, sensual thrum. He rolled her nipple between his fingers and it pearled from his touch, hard-
ening to a proud little peak that tightened his balls.
"That feels good," she whimpered as he continued to
work his fingers over her slippery flesh. "Don't stop."
No way was he going to stop. It would take an act of
God to pry him away from her now.

He continued to stroke her clit, slow circles and
quick, gentle flicks of his fingers. Tabitha buried her
face in the coverlet, releasing her pleasure in sweet,
drawn-out sobs muffled by the bedding, which drove
him crazy. Damien needed to be inside of her, to feel
the tight heat of her cling to him. He teased her
opening with one finger and her hips jerked toward
him. With a groan, he entered her channel, all the
while working the sensitive bud that continued to
swell and stiffen under his touch. She gripped him
tight, her pussy drawing his finger deeper, and he
thrust gently in time with each flick of his finger,
each pluck of her nipple.

Damien put his mouth to Tabitha's ear, took her
delicate lobe between his teeth before he growled in
her ear, "Come for me."

Tabitha shuddered in his embrace. The orgasm
came on the heels of his command, and she cried

out, the sound so passionate that it tightened the head of Damien's cock to the point that he felt on the verge of coming himself. Her body held on to him, pulsing contractions that squeezed the entire length of his finger as he brought her down from the orgasm. Gentle thrusts and featherlight caresses until her body went limp and she collapsed fully on the mattress.

As far as Damien was concerned, they were just getting started. He needed to see her body, naked and spread out on the bed for him. He wanted to suckle the heavy weight of her breasts, bury his face between her thighs and taste her. God, he wanted to fuck her so badly he didn't even know if he could wait long enough to do any of those other things first.

He took Tabitha up in his arms and positioned her fully on the bed, turning her over on her back so he could get her good and naked. Her eyes were hooded, her face flushed with passion, and the heat in her gaze told him that she was more than ready to resume where they'd just left off. She kicked at her pants to free her legs of the restricting fabric while Damien fumbled with the button of his jeans, his hands shaking so fucking much he could barely unfasten it.

His gaze wandered to her naked, glistening sex and the air stalled in Damien's lungs. Jesus fucking Christ, she was beautiful . . .

A loud knock on the door broke the spell in an instant. Tabitha's blue eyes grew wide as shock and then panic overtook her delicate features. "Oh my God." The words left her mouth in a frantic rush. She jumped up from the bed, tripping on her pant legs as she worked them up her thighs. "Ohmygodohmygodohmygod."

Nothing like a horrified expression on a woman's face to bolster a man's ego. Damien let loose a string of curses under his breath as he stalked toward the door. He was going to murder the stupid bastard on the other side. Another round of obnoxious knocks came on the heels of the first, this time a pounding that sparked Damien's ire to a near unmanageable degree. He yanked open the door, prepared to lay into the son of a bitch with his fist.

"Okay, well, looks like the heating unit is working okay now. Be sure to let the front desk know if you're having any more problems and I'll let maintenance know. Have a good night." Tabitha flashed him a too-bright smile as she ducked under his arm and out the door.

Every muscle in Damien's body tensed as he watched her rush down the hallway, disappearing inside of the elevator. The pent-up energy he'd been unable to release exploded as he grabbed the scrawny asshole in the hallway by his collar and dragged him inside the room. The door slammed behind them and he put the bastard up against it, knocking his head with the force.

"You pound on my door like that again and I'll rip your arms out of the sockets, understand?"

"Y-yeah. I understand. It won't happen again."

Tension vibrated through Damien's body and it took all of the self-control he could muster not to lay his fist into the stupid SOB's face. "You're damn right it won't." He let go of his grip and stalked deeper into the room. "You pull that shit and I'll make sure you're off Joey's buy list for good."

"I hear you, man. My bad."

"All right, let's get this done. I want you out of my face two minutes ago."

As the elevator doors slid shut, Tabitha let out the gust of breath she'd been holding in her lungs for at least the past minute. Free divers had nothing on her as she shut off the intake of air, too afraid that she'd give something away if she looked too winded or even too relaxed. Hell, she might as well have the words *I just had the best orgasm of my life* tattooed on her forehead, because whether she'd kept her cool or not, Damien had just rocked her to her very foundation.

Oh my God, Tabitha. What were you thinking?

She'd never done anything so impulsive in her entire life. Or so blatantly wanton. It didn't matter that she barely knew Damien, she'd spread her legs at his command as though she had no choice but to obey. The memory of that moment sent a thrill through her body, rekindling the desire that had been quenched by their interruption.

His rough exterior and gruff words were such a contradiction to the way he'd handled her. His touch so gentle, the way he cradled her against his body, tender. It had taken nothing more than a kiss to drive her to that point of mindless need that she hadn't even balked when he'd spun her around and yanked her pants down.

The doors of the elevator slid open and Tabitha only now realized that she'd slumped against the bar inside of the car, as though unable to support her own weight. The flush resurfaced on her cheeks as she straightened, glad no one was waiting on the other side of the doors. She exited the elevator, surprised that she could walk on her own steam. No man had ever made her feel so good. And *never* had a man attended to her pleasure while disregarding his own like Damien had.

Such a paradox to the man she thought he was.

Tabitha stopped dead in her tracks. Crap. She'd left the canister of pepper spray he'd bought for her in his room. And—she checked her pockets—*oh no.* Her cell phone. No way was she going back for them. She could get another phone, and the pepper spray was the least of her worries. After rushing out on him like that, it would be too embarrassing to knock on his door and confess that her cell must have fallen out of her back pocket when he'd stripped her pants off. Besides, the moment was over, that state of mind-addling lust, gone. The awkwardness would be too much for her to deal with.

"Oh God." The words left her mouth in a drawn-out moan of regret.

"Hey!" Dave called from behind the front desk. "Everything okay?"

Ugh. Nothing like being caught in a moment of self-reflective angst. "Yeah. I uh . . ." What? *Just thinking about the hot porno moment I just had in room 504.* Oh shit! Her blind date! "I sort of got sidetracked and I might have stood up my date." Might? Oh, she definitely stood him up. There was a pretty good chance she was going to have to find a new best friend after tonight, too. "I'm heading back over to the restaurant. Call me if anything comes up."

She rushed through the automatic doors without giving Dave a chance to respond. Lila was going to *kill* her. At least forty minutes had passed and there was a pretty good chance there was a plate full of food cooling in front of her empty chair right now. And without a phone to text or call, Tabitha had to hope that they'd at least started eating without her. If not, Lila was going to be a force to be reckoned with.

The late-night dinner and drinks crowd was in full swing when she walked into the restaurant. The table they'd been sitting at was still occupied by Lila, Charlie, and Josh. It looked like their meals had barely shown up. Charlie and Josh were eating with gusto while Lila picked at her salad. Tabitha reached up to smooth her hair, and fluffed out her shirt as though worried that the evidence of her sexual encounter was still flashing like a neon sign over every inch of her body. What was she even doing here? Her mind was still back in that room, with him. A wave of desire rippled through her and Tabitha clenched her legs together as though that would stem her body's reaction to her thoughts. But all it served to do was remind her of the delicious pressure of his fingertips, the way Damien had coaxed every cry from her lips. She wanted him. Right this second. And yet, she knew that she could never get up the courage to return to that room.

Because if she did, Tabitha knew she'd gladly beg for another kiss. One more touch. "Sorry I took so long," she said as she slid into her chair. "The hotel is crazy tonight."

"Where in the hell have you *been*?" Lila seethed as she leaned in close. "Did you get lost between here and the hotel? Fall into a black hole? Step into a parallel dimension?"

"I'm sorry." Was she sorry? "It took a bit more to reboot the system than I'd expected and Dave was

swamped with arrivals so I helped him with a couple
of—"

"Yeah, yeah, whatever," Lila said, her attention to
Tabitha's explanation nonexistent. "Josh hasn't been
the best third wheel, and I need you to run interference."

"You mean he doesn't enjoy watching you and
Charlie feed each other with your fingers?" Lila's
brows drew sharply over her eyes, her lips puckered
in a pout, and Tabitha cringed. "You've got to admit.
You guys are sort of self-absorbed."

Lila paused and she leaned in even closer. Her
eyes narrowed with suspicion and she pursed her
lips. "What have you been up to? Your cheeks are
flushed and you're all glassy-eyed." She leaned in and
sniffed. "Did you smoke a bowl with Dave in the back
room or something?"

"Nice." Lila knew that she wasn't into that sort of
thing, and no way would she do it at work even if she
was. "I ran two blocks in ballet flats with no support.
You'd be flushed and glassy-eyed, too."

"Uh-huh." Lila didn't sound too convinced. "I'll
get it out of you eventually. You're definitely up to
something. But right now, put it on the back burner
and entertain Josh."

"Sorry I took so long." She bent her head toward
Josh before her attention settled on the plate in front
of her.

"No worries," he said with a grin. "We only got our
food a few minutes ago. I ordered you the veal."

Tabitha bared her teeth in what she hoped was a
smile. What she really wanted to do was lay into him
for thinking she'd even consider eating veal. Awful.
"Thanks."

She pushed the meat aside and picked at her

steamed vegetables instead. No way was she eating a
baby cow. When their server finally came around, she
ordered a vodka soda. Wine wasn't going to cut it
anymore. Her limbs were deliciously limp, her hands
still a little shaky from her tight grip on the comforter. She glanced over at Josh and noticed that his
lips were moving, but once again, her brain wasn't
registering. Her mind was full of Damien; there
wasn't room for anything else.

". . . and I told her that if she thought we were
going to refund her money, she was crazy. I mean,
we're an investment firm, for Christ's sake. Not
Macy's. It wasn't my fault if she chose to invest in a
stock that I suggested. It's not like I twisted her
arm . . ."

On and on he went, proving with every ridiculous,
arrogant, self-centered word out of his mouth that
Josh would never get to date number two. For the
past year she'd convinced herself that she needed to
follow in Lila's footsteps, look for a guy in a nice suit
with a respectable day job and the paycheck to back
up his reputation. But the more time she spent listening to Charlie and Josh go on, and on, and *on*,
tooting their own horns, the more she realized that
guys like that were never, ever going to do it for her.

None of them compared to the man she'd left
behind in that hotel room.

None of them were Damien.

"Let's go across the street to Fatty's after dinner,"
Lila suggested. "The music is better over there and I
want to dance."

"Sounds great," Josh said as he sliced off a hunk of
his steak. "I bet you're a great dancer, aren't you,
Tabitha?"

She couldn't even bring herself to smile this time.

"Not really. But that's not to say I don't give it my best effort. You could say my style is a cross between a wacky flailing-inflatable-arm tube man and Sweet Dee from *It's Always Sunny.*"

Josh's brow puckered. Her humor was lost on him. Just another indicator that he wasn't the guy for her. Their dinner conversation dwindled and Tabitha focused on finishing as much of her meal as she could stomach. Later, as they filtered out of the Piper Grill, Josh put his hand on the small of her back and she bristled at the contact. After one encounter, her body had been fine-tuned to Damien's touch.

She was officially ruined.

Chapter Eight

Damien shoved open the window and the heavy curtains billowed with the influx of cool air. The wind had picked up and the room filled with the crisp scent of early snow. Clean and sweet. Just like Tabitha.

The weekend had officially come to a close. The last of Cavello's drugs were sold and that left Damien with nothing but his tortured thoughts to keep him company. Oh, and the raging hard-on that had yet to go the fuck away. A chill brought goose bumps to the surface of his skin, but aside from the mild discomfort, the drop in temperature did nothing to cool his lust. He grumbled a curse under his breath and toed off his boots. Stripped off his shirt. Shucked his jeans and underwear. He glared down at his erection and stalked toward the bathroom. Instead of swiveling the shower knob to hot, he left the water cold and stepped directly under the spray. A sharp intake of air lodged in his chest, but he refused to turn up the heat or step away from the cold stream of water.

And still, the stiff bastard between his legs stuck around to taunt him.

Icy rivulets of water sluiced down his body and Damien's muscles tensed. His nipples tightened and he found the sensation pleasurable rather than uncomfortable. What would it feel like to have Tabitha's teeth graze his nipples? Maybe even the head of his cock? Nothing short of a bullet through the heart was going to calm him down at this point. His senses were still awash with her: her scent, the softness of her skin, the sound of her impassioned cries in his ears.

Damien reached down and took the heavy length of his erection in his hand. His thumb brushed the engorged and sensitive head and he shuddered, sending droplets of water rolling down his abs and thighs. He stroked down to the base and back up, imagining that he was pumping into her and not his own goddamned hand. A haze of want clouded his thoughts and Damien thrust again, his pace increasing as he worked his fist over his erection. He braced his arm against the shower wall, a low moan vibrating through him as he came in violent spasms that brought him to one knee.

Christ. A couple of pumps and he'd come all over the fucking shower. Pathetic.

Pushing himself to stand, Damien reached back and turned the knob to the left. The water began to warm and some of the tension left his body, though his legs were still weak and felt like cooked noodles. Steam billowed around him, matching the fog that clouded his thoughts. Tabitha had blindsided him. An unexpected complication that he could never have planned for. He'd never wanted any woman with the sort of desperate, primal need that had driven him to behave so rashly with her. With a groan, Damien knocked his forehead against the wall. He'd treated her with so little respect, bending her over the bed without so much as an attempt at seduction.

But she'd come so easily for him. Shattered under his touch like myriad shards of glass. She'd wanted him, too. He hadn't imagined her eager response.

Damien finished up his shower and dried off, wrapping the towel around his waist as he left the bathroom. The in-room phone rang, a loud digital trill that set him instantly on edge. No one should be calling the room. Cavello had his burner number and Gates knew to keep his distance when Damien was undercover. He lifted the receiver from the cradle and took a deep breath before bringing it up to his ear. "Yeah?"

"Did you order a wakeup call for the morning?"

Damien let out a slow breath as he recognized Bill Crawford's voice on the other end of the line. His SOG supervisor rarely called when he was undercover, but if he needed to reach out, they had ways of getting around suspicious eavesdroppers. "No, thanks, I've got an alarm set," he replied, letting the other man know it was safe to talk.

"Good to know I haven't caught you at a bad time, Evans."

Aside from being alone in the room, Damien had swept the entire space for bugs and was confident that Joey wasn't eavesdropping. Thank God. Otherwise what had happened between him and Tabitha earlier would have made for an awkward working relationship. "What's up?"

"Dennis Callihan says you're making good progress up there." Crawford had a reputation as a hard-ass, but Damien liked him. Ball-busters got the job done, and his success rate was damned near perfect. He wanted Lightfoot as badly as Damien did. An arrest would be a huge win for the Marshals Service.

"I think so. Nothing on Lightfoot yet, but I'm in with his distributor."

"That's good, Evans. You're definitely moving ahead of our timetable. The DOJ has intel that Lightfoot is readying a market in Northern California. The demand for Stardust is snowballing and the deaths are piling up. With all of the interagency effort going into this case, everyone agrees that we want this crap off the streets as soon as possible."

"Agreed." Synthetic shit could be damned dangerous. But the worst part of the synthetic trade was that it was dirt cheap and easy for kids to get their hands on. It was imperative to get Stardust off the streets before it became an epidemic. "Boise PD is working with me to give the distributor a wide berth for the time being. But as soon as I get a bead on Lightfoot, we'll be shutting his operation down."

"Good. The federal prosecutor wants the takedown on this to have a long reach. That means as many arrests as you can manage. I want anyone with a connection to the distributor arrested. This is going to be a zero-tolerance situation. The government is bringing the hammer down on this one. Not only to send a message to all of the other Lightfoots out there, but to the small-time dealers who think they'll make money on his heels in the synthetic trade."

"Understood." Damien's heart rocketed up into this throat before taking a nosedive straight to his gut. "I'll brief Callihan and Ryan Gates Monday morning on what I've got so far. Is there anything you'd like me to include when I talk to them?"

"No, I'll be talking to Callihan next week. Just keep doing what you're doing. And be careful out there, Parker."

Damien ended the call without responding. There was more to Crawford's words than a simple concern for his safety. He'd worked most of his undercover assignments under Crawford's supervision, and the SOG supervisory director knew better than anyone—except for maybe Dr. Meyers—about the blurred lines between Damien's life and Parker's.

The backs of his legs met the mattress and Damien collapsed on the bed as a rush of breath vacated his lungs. He'd told Gates, Callihan, and the Boise PD about Tabitha's involvement in Cavello's operation. By providing him with a place to do business, she was more than just an accessory. The federal prosecutor could bring a list of charges against her: conspiracy, racketeering, trafficking, aiding and abetting . . . *Jesus.*

He flung himself back on the bed and his foot knocked something across the carpeting. He pushed himself up, his brow furrowed at the sight of the cell phone he'd catapulted across the room, resting not far from the discarded canister of pepper spray. *What the hell?* Leaning over the edge of the bed, he scooped the cell into his grasp. He propped himself up on the pillows, and unlocked the screen.

Two faces stared back at him in a wallpaper selfie. One was Tabitha, and she had her arms around a guy with the same golden hair and deep blue eyes. They could have been twins, their features were so similar. The phone must have fallen from her pocket earlier. Damien's lungs seized up as he thought back to their encounter, but he forbade himself from revisiting it.

It was either that or another cold shower, and he wasn't interested in freezing his dick off to keep it from getting hard.

For a moment he stared at the picture. It didn't take an investigative mastermind to know that she didn't belong in the world she'd found herself in. Damien's instincts were razor sharp. He could read people with ease, and Tabitha was an open book. But until he got to the bottom of how she'd wound up an accomplice to Joey's distribution operation, there was nothing he could do but continue to investigate her like she was any other suspect.

Sitting in the palm of his hand was a virtual trove of information. Text messages, call logs, pictures, and the history of any websites she might have visited in the past week or longer; the apps she used most, the apps she'd used most recently, and any GPS information that might have been logged in the maps app.

A peek into the life of Tabitha Martin. Rather than feeling like a cop doing investigative work, delving into the contents of her cell phone made Damien feel more like a voyeur. She'd reached level 349 of *Candy Crush* and amassed a small fortune in coins playing *Bejeweled Blitz.* She used Snapchat, and her Instagram account showcased pictures of downtown Boise, various meals, and a photo of her wearing scrubs and inserting a large needle into someone's arm with the caption, "First stick was a success!"

Was she training to be an EMT? Or maybe a nurse? And if so, what was she still doing working at this hotel, helping Joey Cavello to peddle his nasty shit all over the city? There was more to her than met the eye. He stood by the assertion that she had no choice but to do as Joey asked. And he was positive it had to do with her brother, Seth. Could he be the guy in the picture with her?

Or was he simply making excuses for her? Grasping at straws because of this inexplicable want he felt for her? Was his career worth taking a risk on someone who might burn him in the long run? And if so, would he even care?

"Shut the front door! You did *not*!" Dave's scandalized tone had nothing on the excitement that lit his green eyes. He loved gossip as much as he loved muscle-laden, tattooed bad boys. Tabitha had effectively gifted him with the gossip equivalent of Tom Hardy.

"I'm weak, Dave. So, *so* weak. And apparently a little slutty, too." She hadn't gone into detail about her encounter with Damien, but gave Dave just enough information to give him a well-rounded idea of what had happened. Lila would judge her. Dave on the other hand . . . he shared her weakness for guys that were no-good. She could find solidarity with him. "I couldn't help myself. It was like I was a starving woman and he was a bacon cheeseburger."

"Oh, I can think of several juicy bits on his body to bite. Tabs, you are the most unslutty woman I know. But seriously, can I just interject here and say that I'm totally disappointed that my dream man is hetero? Though I'm not surprised. He was giving you a hardcore vibe the first time he laid eyes on you, and I bet he was sporting a chub the size of a VW bus."

"Dave!"

"Tell me. He's impressive, right? I'm dying to know."

"I don't know . . ." Tabitha cast her gaze down toward her desk. "We didn't exactly get to him."

"Shut. Up!" Dave all but shoved her in his excitement. "Are you telling me he's a giver?"

"He was *very* generous."

Dave made a show of collapsing on the front desk's counter. "Forget my earlier disappointment. I'm officially devastated."

"Hi, Tabitha. Come on in."

Tabitha exchanged a look with Dave as the general manager, Sandy Webber, opened the door to her office. "Good luck," he said under his breath and knocked his knuckles against hers.

Nervous energy pooled in Tabitha's stomach, sending a burst of adrenaline through her body. She felt a little light-headed and wasn't even sure if she'd be able to form a coherent thought. When she got the call that Sandy wanted to see her this morning, she could think of only one reason why: someone had ratted her out and Sandy knew about Joey's weekend escapades. In which case, she was officially screwed.

"Have a seat."

Tabitha closed the door behind her and took a chair in front of Sandy's desk. They usually had a pretty casual work relationship, so her formal tone wasn't doing much to assuage Tabitha's fears. *Crap.* "What's up?" She tried to keep the quaver from her voice, but she couldn't help it. At this point, she was doing her damnedest not to throw up all over Sandy's desk.

"First of all, thanks for coming in on a Sunday. But since I'm leaving for vacation tomorrow, I wanted to get all of my ducks in a row beforehand. You're the acting GM next week, so I want to double check that your school schedule won't be disrupted."

A trickle of tension drained from Tabitha's muscles. If this was a pre-vacation check-off, she could breathe easy. "I'm good. I finished up my finals last week, and aside from a CPR and first responder refresher that I signed up for over the break, I'm available. I've already got it worked out with Dave, and he's agreed to field any issues that might crop up while I'm doing the refreshers."

"Great." Sandy gave her a reassuring smile and she relaxed another degree. "I'm sure Dave can handle anything that comes up, too."

There was a pregnant pause and Tabitha shifted in her seat. The nerves that had abated jacked back up and she was pretty sure she could taste bile at the back of her throat. "Did you need anything else?"

"I did." Sandy's expression was much too grave. Heat rose to Tabitha's cheeks and she tried to control the speed of her shallow breaths and racing heart. "We had a noise complaint last night from the guests in room 502. Lots of coming and going late into the night, some pounding on the walls and door. I checked the system and the room next to that is the one we put the HiTop Roofing guys in. I know that they're your account and that they do a lot of business here, but we don't have anything to worry about with them, do we?"

Tabitha was willing to bet that some of that door and wall banging was going on right about the time she and Damien had been interrupted. Was it possible for someone's face to catch fire from embarrassment? Because she was pretty sure hers was beginning to smoke from the heat. "As far as I know, this is the first complaint, and they stay with us consistently."

"I was hoping that since they're your account, you'd talk to them before they check out this morning. I don't want to lose their business, but I also don't want a bunch of rowdy guys partying and trashing our rooms, either."

"I'll take care of it." Relief flooded her. Speaking to Damien after what happened between them would be marginally less humiliating than giving a speech in her underwear, but it was better than having Sandy investigate for herself and contact Joey personally. If Joey thought that the sweet setup he had there was in jeopardy, there was no telling what he would do.

"Thanks. I'll have my cell on while I'm on vacation and I'll be checking e-mails. If something major comes up, don't worry about giving me a call."

Tabitha took the cue to beat a hasty retreat and she shot up from her chair, earning a questioning look from Sandy. "I'll talk to HiTop's noisemakers before I leave. Have a good trip."

Sandy gave her a pleasant smile and waved as Tabitha left the office.

"What happened?" Dave was as bouncy and eager as a puppy when she closed the door behind her. "Did she fire you? Find out about your *room service*? Did someone complain?"

"Slow your roll, Dave." His mile-a-minute questions weren't doing anything for her nerves. "First of all, if you call what happened last night *room service* again, I'm going to slap you. Second, Sandy was just touching base with me before she leaves for her vacation tomorrow. No scandals for you to sink your teeth into."

"Then why do you look like you got caught with your hand in the cookie jar?"

His arch tone made her wonder if he'd had his ear up to the door. "There was a noise complaint last night from the room next to Damien's. Sandy asked me to go talk to him about keeping it down while he stays here."

"Can I go?"

"No, you can't go." Dave needed to find a hobby. Or a boyfriend. "But you can watch the front desk since, you know, it's sort of your job."

"You're a buzzkill."

She smiled at his feigned pout. "I do what I can."

Chapter Nine

Damien finished packing up the last of his shit into the duffel bag. Checking out of one hotel only to return to another, the glamorous life of an undercover marshal. He tucked Tabitha's cell and the canister of pepper spray into his back pocket and slung his duffel over one shoulder while he grabbed the now-empty suitcase in his other hand. He took one last look around before opening the door—

"Hey."

Tabitha stood on the other side, her fist held up as though she'd been about to knock. His body sparked with excitement at her nearness. Hell, he was worse than some teenage girl, all fluttering nerves and bullshit unease. "Hey." *Way to articulate, dipshit.*

"Can I talk to you for a second?"

Awkward had nothing on this moment. At once, Damien was ashamed of the way things went down last night. How he'd all but climbed over her like a rutting bull, driven by some primal urge. She walked through the doorway, past him, and Damien caught the faint scent of her perfume. The sweet floral bouquet went straight to his head and made him want to seduce her into agreeing to whatever wicked sexual act he could think of. His free hand twitched at his side. She was close enough to touch, and he wanted nothing more than to reach out.

"What's up?" His voice was strained; her nearness affected him right down to his vocal cords. Her lips parted slightly, ready to be kissed, and Damien could think of nothing better than to oblige her. He followed her into the room and set the suitcase down on the bed—trying not to think of the things he'd done to her there last night—and tossed his duffel bag down next to it.

"My manager got a noise complaint about your room."

Goddamn it. He wondered just what had spurred the complaint. The asshole banging on the door after ten o'clock at night, Damien slamming said asshole against the door, or his own fool head banging against the shower wall after Tabitha had left. Probably all of the above. "Sorry about that. It won't happen again." If he could, he'd hit his cranium against the wall right now. If only to jog some marginally less Cro-Magnon conversation from his lips.

"Thanks. She asked me to handle it personally because I'm responsible for Joey's account with the hotel and Sandy doesn't want to lose his business. But if it happens again there's a chance she'll try to contact him directly, and I can't afford for that to happen."

There was a twinge of fear behind her words that spurred every protective instinct in Damien's body. "Why are you afraid of him?" He hadn't meant to blurt the question out, point blank. But the thought of her living in fear made him want to break something. Namely, Joey Cavello's face.

"I-I'm not." The lie was obvious, her body language conveying her deceit in little tells that Damien was trained to identify.

"Then why are you helping him? Why not let him get his ass kicked out of here?"

Tabitha's eyes narrowed with suspicion. "Why do you care? You're selling that crap for him. What difference does it make to you who helps him or where he moves it from? You're getting paid, right? Isn't that all that matters?"

Damien's façade slipped. The barest peeling back of layers that made him feel too damned exposed for his peace of mind. He tucked that very *Parker* part of him away and hiked a disinterested shoulder. "Yup. Who doesn't like money? I'm sure you don't mind the kickbacks you're getting, either."

Damien felt the anger rippling off of her like heat rising off a summer sidewalk when she said, "I told you, I don't take a dime of Joey's money. I don't want *anything* from him."

He quirked a sarcastic brow. "Not a single thing?"

"You're an asshole."

Jealousy had prompted Damien's harsh words. The knowledge that she'd been with that slimy son of a bitch was like a coal burning hot in the pit of his gut. Tabitha's anger lent her beauty a fierceness that took Damien's breath away and he abandoned logical thought. He was tired of living this double fucking life. So tired of upholding the moral right by condoning so many wrongs. And sick of putting everyone else's needs before his own wants.

Fuck that shit. He wanted Tabitha. And goddamn it, he was going after what he wanted.

Her eyes widened as he stalked toward her, but

there wasn't an ounce of fear in her gaze. Rather a defiance that only served to heat his blood. An unspoken challenge, as if she dared him to take another step. To touch her. Put his mouth and hands on her. Damien had never been one to walk away from a challenge.

He took her face in his hands and held her still. Tabitha's breath raced, her chest rising and falling in a quick rhythm. Her lips parted, soft and inviting despite the fire in her eyes. "I'm not afraid of you either, Damien." The words floated to his ears on a whisper.

He kissed her with every ounce of frustration pent up in his body. Though he wanted to be gentle with her, caress her mouth with his, treat her as though she were some fragile thing, he couldn't. Couldn't tame the desire that burned within him, the need that overtook him. His attraction for her was too visceral, too desperate for anything other than fierce abandon.

Tabitha shoved at him and he took a stumbling step back. "Damn you," she seethed before rushing at him, her hand clasping the back of his neck as she pulled his mouth down to hers.

She'd come here to make sure that Damien knew the ground rules. That he'd play the game and lie low. And maybe return her damned cell phone. Kissing him, throwing herself at him, had *not* been part of Tabitha's plan. Damien's effect on her was instantaneous. A rush that went straight to her head and erased all logical thought from her brain. Common sense, decision-making skills of any kind became nonexistent the moment his lips met hers. But, oh God, was he ever worth the consequences.

Damien's hand came around the back of her neck, his fist gripping the short strands of hair that brushed her nape. He tilted her head the way he wanted it, allowing him access to her throat. The control he exercised over her was something she craved. In fact, it wasn't enough. So much weighed on every single decision she'd made over the past couple of years, and for once, she wanted the burden of choice to be taken from her, giving her no option but to obey.

"Damien." His name hovered on her lips, an unfinished thought. The blunt edge of his teeth grazed the sensitive flesh of her throat, the slight sting a delicious precursor to the wet warmth of his mouth. Tabitha's eyes drifted shut. His touch was bliss.

"Housekeeping!"

The warning preceded the click of a key card in the lock and Tabitha shoved at Damien once again, sending him back a few paces. His eyes glinted with a wild light, a feral animal with the night's prey in its sights.

"Don't. Leave." The command was firm and a rush of liquid heat chased through Tabitha's veins, settling low in her abdomen.

When the housekeeper walked through the door, Tabitha was certain that the shocked expression on Lisa's face mirrored her own. "Oh my gosh, Tabitha, I'm so sorry." Lisa's face flushed a deep crimson and Tabitha fought the urge to roll her eyes. What in the hell did Lisa have to be embarrassed about? She wasn't the one almost caught with her pants down.

"No worries. The heating unit was acting up yesterday and I was just checking to make sure it's still working all right."

"I can come back." Lisa's eyes slid to Damien and warmed as a smile spread across her face.

"No need." Damien's eyes never left Tabitha. "I'm checking out."

Damien grabbed his suitcase and hauled his duffel over his shoulder. He cast a warning glance Tabitha's way and headed for the door. She waited for it to shut behind him and took a deep breath. His presence was so overwhelming that she found it hard to breathe when he was near.

After a few pleasantries—and a couple more rushed excuses—were exchanged with Lisa, Tabitha figured she'd given Damien more than enough time to check out and pay his bill. She strolled down the hallway, counting out her steps with measured breaths in an effort to calm her still-racing heart.

"Did you think you could get rid of me that easily?"

His sardonic tone broke her from her reverie and she looked up to find Damien waiting for her near the elevators, one massive shoulder bracing him against the wall. A confident smirk graced his features and Tabitha's heart stuttered in her chest. If he was gorgeous when he wore that imposing, angry expression, then he was absolutely breathtaking when his face showed a spark of humor.

"I wasn't trying to get rid of you." She fixed a stern expression on her face. "I was talking to one of my housekeepers."

"Uh-huh. I know when I'm getting the brush-off."

Heat crept up Tabitha's cheeks. She tilted her head to the side and regarded him. "For some reason, I find it hard to believe that anyone has ever given you the brush-off."

He grinned, showcasing the deep grooves of his

dimples, and her stomach did a backflip. The casual hike of his shoulder did nothing to diminish her attraction to him. Good Lord, she lusted after him like a cat in heat. It was all she could do not to rub herself up and down his body. "I thought you had Sundays off," he said, disregarding her earlier observation.

"I do, but I had to come in to take care of a few things."

"Like a rowdy guest or two?"

She smiled. "Something like that."

"What are you doing now?"

She quirked a brow. "Talking to you."

Damien rolled his eyes, but those dimples stayed put in his cheeks. "You know what I mean."

Tabitha stepped up next to him, so close that her senses were awash with his spicy, masculine scent. Her arm brushed his as she hit the button to call the elevator. She didn't miss the way his gaze drifted to where their bodies touched. A simple shift of his eyes ignited her desire. Could she be any more pathetic?

"Don't you have to meet Joey? Square up for the weekend?"

The look he gave her told Tabitha that Damien Evans didn't answer to a fucking soul. The world waited to do his bidding. And once again she couldn't help but wonder, *what* was he doing working for a low-level criminal like Joey?

A bell chimed as the elevator doors slid open. Tabitha stepped inside and Damien followed with his luggage in tow. He reached across her, as though pushing the button for the first floor was an action devised to give him an excuse to brush his arm against hers. "Leave your car here, and let's get some lunch." Again, Damien didn't ask Tabitha to do anything. He *told* her. "We're downtown, there's got to be plenty of places to eat within walking distance."

The man was a mystery. In all of the months she'd dated Joey, he'd never once taken her out on anything that even resembled a date. If they weren't hanging out at a bar, they were at her apartment. Dinners and lunches consisted of takeout—that she usually paid for—and never anything fancier than a Flying Pie pizza. Joey wouldn't be caught dead in any of the fancier downtown eateries.

"All right." The words left her mouth before she could think her decision through. "I need to check in with my manager before she leaves on vacation, and you still need to check out. I'll meet you out in the parking lot?"

The elevator doors slid open and they stepped out into the hallway. He flashed a quick smile that caused her insides to melt into a puddle of liquid heat. "I'll meet you outside."

Without another word, he walked out in front of her, down the hallway toward the lobby. Tabitha wasn't going to complain as she took in the view of his ass, hugged by the denim slung low on his hips and revealing the waistband of his underwear. *Damn.*

Tabitha scanned the parking lot. She found Damien leaning against a cherry Shelby Cobra with California plates. Stolen? Or did that gorgeous hunk of machinery belong to him?

"The '65 is nice, but if you ask me, the '67 Shelby convertible is the best. The roadster body gives the 1950 Ferrari a run for its money and the V-8 is killer," she said.

His lips spread into a wry grin that caused a wobble

in Tabitha's step as her knees felt like they might have disconnected from her shins. She'd never met a man who made her legs weak until now. Had she become a walking cliché, or what?

"The '67 roadster is okay, but the body of the '65 *is* the American muscle car. Plus, the '65's got a little more torque, and the growl of the engine can't be beat." He pushed himself away from the car and Tabitha couldn't help but notice how his muscles flexed and bunched with the simple action. Damien's body was a living, breathing work of art. "You're the local. So you choose where we're eating."

Again, his words didn't invite discussion. He'd given her a gentle command and it was clear he expected no resistance or argument on her part. It was tough for her to admit, but Tabitha didn't exactly frequent downtown Boise. She worked downtown and that was about it. Besides her epic failure of a double date with Lila the night before, she didn't eat anywhere that wasn't dirt cheap. The downtown restaurants catered to people on a champagne budget, and Tabitha was definitely living on a beer income.

Well . . . he asked for it. "I've heard that Fork is pretty good. I haven't eaten there, but my friend Lila said they have the best burgers she's ever eaten."

"Sounds good to me. Lead the way."

Tabitha took a quick look around as nervous energy skittered up her spine. It's not like she expected Joey to be hanging out in the hotel's parking lot, but she had a feeling that if he saw her with Damien, it would cause all sorts of problems that she wasn't ready to deal with.

"How long have you lived in Boise?" Damien kept his eyes facing front, but Tabitha felt his undivided attention on her nonetheless.

"My entire life," she responded with chagrin. "I know, not very exciting."

He gave her a sidelong glance and a corner of his mouth hitched in a lopsided grin. Holy crap, she wanted to kiss the dimple in his cheek, dip her tongue into it . . . "I move around a lot. There's nothing wrong with having deep roots. I'd kill to settle down for a change."

There was a depth of emotion to his words that caused Tabitha's chest to tighten. Regret, longing, and sadness spoken with an openness and honesty that tugged at her heartstrings and squeezed the air from her lungs. "It's not always so great to be firmly rooted in place." They paused at the crosswalk and started across Main when the little man flashed from red to a walking white. "There are days that I really wish I could just pack up and leave. Start over where no one knows me. It would be awesome to have a clean slate for a change."

"What's keeping you here?"

Tabitha had a feeling that she was being managed. Damien knew how to steer the conversation in the way he wanted, and asked leading questions so that it seemed as though Tabitha was volunteering the information he was coaxing out of her. Still, the realization did nothing to stem the flow of words. There was something refreshing about spilling her guts to him. He was the clean slate she couldn't get anywhere else.

"School. My brother. Work." She could make a list of reasons a mile long, but those were the big ones. "Seth is a . . ." What? Royal screwup? ". . . handful. He's had a rough few years and he needs me."

"Younger?"

"By two years." Though sometimes it felt like twenty.

"He's finally got his life on track and I don't want to do anything to screw it up for him. Besides, it's a total pain in the ass to find a school that will transfer credits, and I'm so close to finishing that it just doesn't make any sense to pack up and leave at this point."

"What are you studying?"

"I'm working toward my RN." Tabitha paused and steered them down Eighth Street. "I want to be a trauma nurse and work in the ER."

"How much longer do you have?"

She gave him a wry smile. "Are you interrogating me, Damien?"

"Yes." His tone wasn't the least bit playful and it sparked every nerve in her body with electric energy.

"I finished up my labs and lectures for this semester last week, and next semester I'll be doing clinicals at St. Luke's." Tabitha paused at the entrance to Fork and held out her arm in invitation. "We're here."

Damien pulled open the heavy glass door and waited for Tabitha to walk in ahead of him. Joey had never once held a door open for her. Hell, Joey had never taken her out to eat. She could hardly call what this was between her and Damien a relationship, but already it surpassed anything she'd ever had with her asshole of an ex. Damien was indeed a mystery. A criminal and a gentleman? Did such a thing even exist?

Chapter Ten

"Two for lunch today?"

Damien smiled at the hostess, and at his nod she retrieved two menus from the tall podium she stood behind, handing them off to a young girl decked out in a long black skirt and crisp white dress shirt. "Right this way." Her tone was pleasant and customer service perfect as she led them past the rustic-style bar, wine rack constructed from rebar and old barn wood, and into the restaurant proper, through a maze of tables.

As their waitress rambled on—something about the weather and the possibility of a snowstorm—he couldn't be bothered to listen as he took a moment to appreciate the sway of Tabitha's hips as she walked, and the luscious curve of her ass that he itched to reach out and take in his hands. He towered over her by at least a foot, and his bulk almost tripled her petite frame. Without a doubt, she'd weigh almost nothing, and he imagined himself lifting her in his arms to settle her on his cock while he took her up against the wall. *Whoa. Put on the fucking brakes, man.* If he didn't curb the erotic trail of his thoughts, he'd be sporting wood before the waitress managed to seat them.

She led them to a booth on the street side of the building, and placed a menu on either side of the table as she waited for them to sit down. Tabitha's attention was centered on the server as she recited Fork's specials, but Damien didn't give a single shit about the soup of the day. He lost focus of everything but Tabitha. God, she was fucking beautiful.

She cast a curious glance at Damien, her full, petal-pink lips quirked in a half grin. "I think we're going to need a few minutes," she said.

"No problem," the waitress responded. "I'll check back in a few."

"What?" From the way Tabitha was looking at him, Damien had a feeling that he'd missed something in the women's exchange.

"I think I must have lost you sometime after the lunch specials. She asked if we wanted to start off with any drinks or appetizers, but it looked like you weren't tracking."

Not even close. Who needed food or water when she was sitting across from him? Sunlight filtered in through the large picture windows, setting her hair on fire with a golden light. Her eyes seemed even bluer, crystal clear like the waters of the Indian Ocean. "Nope. I was too busy looking at you."

She blushed at his comment and Damien's chest swelled. That he could affect her with just a few words stroked his ego and it made him want to test the waters, see what more heated sentiments would do to her. "Why? Do I have something on my face?"

The way she deflected the compliment made him think that she was uncomfortable with any form of praise. He could press on, tell her she was beautiful, that he couldn't quit thinking about her mouth, or her gorgeous pussy, but that wasn't exactly proper lunch conversation. Which just proved that Damien was about as housebroken as a timber wolf. Jesus, he was so out of touch, he had no business sitting down to eat a civilized meal with her. "How long have you been working at the hotel?" Conversation served a triple purpose: he could investigate her on the sly while learning more about her, and maybe if he kept the topics light he'd quit thinking about how he wanted to sink his teeth into the soft flesh of her ass . . .

"A little over four years." A busboy stopped at their table and filled two sawed-off wine bottles that had been repurposed as glasses, with water. Tabitha waited for him to move on to the next table, and continued. "I started working there the summer before my freshman year of college. They worked with my schedule and I could do homework at the front desk when it got slow."

"After you graduate, you'll be quitting?"

Tabitha averted her gaze, triggering Damien's protective instinct yet again. Fear flickered across her features for the briefest moment before she answered. "That's the plan. BSU has a great program, and since I'm finishing up my clinicals at St. Luke's, it's likely they'll hire me right out of school."

He noted the quaver in her voice, the lie inherent in her tone. She might want to quit the hotel, but Damien sensed that if Joey had anything to say about it, she'd be staying put. Why? "Not enough blood and guts working the front desk, huh?" If he pressed too hard, she'd shut down. Damien needed her to trust him, and that was something he couldn't force.

"You've obviously never had to manage a swimming

pool full of ten-year-old boys in town for a soccer tournament," she joked. "I actually liked working at the hotel. I get along with my boss and everyone who works there. The money is decent considering how hard it is to find a good job around here. It could be worse."

"Liked?" He didn't miss the slip. She'd enjoyed her job at one time, but not anymore.

"Huh?"

Her perplexed expression coaxed a reluctant smile. "You said you *liked* working at the hotel. As in, you don't like it anymore."

A hint of crimson tinted her cheeks. Not embarrassment. Rather, guilt that she'd been caught in an admission she hadn't meant to make. "It's not that." Tabitha averted her gaze and traced the lip of her water glass with the pad of her index finger. "I just—"

"Have you guys had a chance to look over the menu?"

Damien's lip curled at the interruption, though it's not like his annoyance was justified. "I'll take the Urban Burger and a Square Mile Cider."

"Great. You're going to be happy with the burger. It's fantastic." The waitress turned her attention to Tabitha. "And for you?"

"I'll have the same." She gave Damien a sheepish grin as she handed her menu over to the waitress.

"I'll get these burgers started for you."

When the waitress was clear of earshot, Damien turned his full attention back on Tabitha. "If you weren't ready to order, you should have said something. I could have waited."

It didn't take much to embarrass her, it seemed. The expression that crossed her features suggested that the people in her life didn't make her feel as though her opinion mattered. An offense that prompted fantasies of breaking the skulls of anyone who'd managed to belittle her.

"It's fine. I've wanted to try the burgers here for a while. A lot of the guests who stay at the hotel eat here, and they rave about the food."

"Why haven't you eaten here before? It's just a couple of blocks down the road. I'd be mowing down everything on the menu if I were you."

"It's sort of out of my price range. This is more of a special occasion place, you know?"

Was there nothing in Tabitha Martin's life that she'd ever felt was worth celebration? "I'm glad your first time here was with me, then."

Her answering smile squeezed his heart. "I'm glad, too."

As they waited for their lunch, Damien tried to keep the conversation light without being too heavy-handed in his questions. It violated his don't-show-your-curiosity protocol, but Tabitha was a tough nut to crack. She didn't have the ego most of the criminals he dealt with sported, which kept her from bragging or divulging too much. And she seemed reluctant to offer up anything about herself unless he specifically asked.

"So, let's say you breeze through clinicals and walk away with a spiffy degree. What then? Will you bounce and take the job at the hospital?"

This was the question Damien was burning to know the answer to. Was she staying at the hotel to help Cavello? Or was she working under duress like he assumed—too afraid to cut him loose and walk away.

"I want to leave. But sometimes what a person

wants and what they get are two completely different things."

Damien leaned forward in his seat, ready to pressure her for an in-depth answer, when their food arrived. He swore the damned waitress was plotting against him. Her interruptions couldn't be more perfectly timed to fuck up his day.

She set two large, square wooden planks on the table, each decked out with a fat, juicy burger and all the fixings. Beside the planks she doled out two conical metal baskets overflowing with Parmesan fries. Damien's mouth watered as he realized that he hadn't eaten in almost twenty-four hours. Hell, he could easily inhale two burgers and three times the amount of fries. Maybe if he turned his attention to his lunch, it would give Tabitha a moment or two of introspection. Reluctant witnesses often opened up after they had a few minutes to process what an investigator asked them.

At the very least, he could enjoy the view while he ate. Goddamn, there wasn't a more beautiful woman in existence.

Tabitha dug into her burger with gusto she didn't feel a damned bit embarrassed about. She hadn't eaten in almost twelve hours and she needed something in her stomach so it would quit churning with the nervous acid that kicked up every time she laid eyes on Damien's tattooed and muscled body. It should've been illegal for a man to look so perfectly made for sin.

Her conscience tickled at the back of her brain, a germ of thought that infected what was sizing up to be a nice afternoon. Damien Evans might be gorgeous. He definitely had the body of an MMA superstar and charm in excess. But he was still a criminal, a hard, unflinching, unconscionable drug dealer who probably had a history of violence that would make Joey's petty squabbles seem like a child's temper tantrum in comparison.

Was it strange that, given all of that, she felt safer with Damien than with any other man in her entire life?

"Can I ask you a question?" So far, they'd talked only about her. Tabitha appreciated that Damien was curious and a good listener, but it was time to turn the tables.

He washed down the gargantuan bite of his burger with a long pull from the bottle of hard cider. "Shoot."

"That first week you stayed at the hotel, were you working for Joey then? Did you come to Boise to work for him?"

"That's two questions," he said without humor.

Tabitha's stomach twisted. She might feel safe with him, but that didn't mean he wasn't a dangerous man. "True. But I'd like you to answer."

He studied her for a moment, his eyes narrowed. "No," he finally replied. "I wasn't working for him the first week and I didn't come here to work for him."

"So . . . you just stumbled into it?"

Tabitha wondered if he'd noticed the note of hope that leaked into her voice. Was it too much to wish that he—like her—had ended up an unwitting accomplice to Joey's less than legal activities? Would that somehow absolve her of the guilt she felt for lusting after him?

"I met him in a bar. Liquid. I needed money, he needed a guy. That's all."

Tabitha wasn't unaccustomed to the need for extra cash. She lived every day of her life needing only a little more than what she had to make ends meet. Surely selling drugs was easy money for some. Her parents had found the money easy enough to make. It was obvious by the way he carried himself that Damien could handle most any situation that came his way. Maybe for someone as fearless and strong as he was, the consequences of his illegal acts meant very little at the end of the day.

"There are safer ways to make money, you know." Her voice dropped with her gaze and she fiddled with a fry, twirling it between her fingers before she popped it into her mouth.

"There are," he agreed. Tabitha dragged her gaze up to his and her breath caught at the intensity of his golden-brown eyes. "But I'll endure the danger factor—and that idiot Joey Cavello—if it means I get to see more of you."

"You want to see more of me?" God, she sounded like a fool, all shaky voice and fluttering nerves.

His gaze heated, warming Tabitha from the inside out. "I do. And wearing a hell of a lot less than you have on right now."

Tabitha was pretty sure that the entire restaurant could hear the sound of her brain sizzling as it short-circuited. Maybe the cider had gone to her head and she was drunker than she thought, imagining the words spoken in a husky rasp that made her skin tingle. One hard cider on an empty stomach was surely enough to give her a buzz. And enough of a buzz to make her feel brazen at that.

"Shouldn't that be my line? You've definitely seen more of me than I have of you."

A wicked smile curved his lips and it was all Tabitha could do not to jump across the table and tackle him. "I'll show you whatever you want to see. All you have to do is ask."

Sin. Incarnate.

Tabitha couldn't remember a time in her entire life that she'd shared a bit of dirty talk over a cheeseburger. She tingled with excitement from head to toe, even though the cautious part of her lust-addled brain reminded her to tread lightly. "Let's say a girl wanted to do just that. Where would she find you on any given weeknight to pose such questions?"

After a week at the hotel, Damien had checked out, and aside from his weekend there working for Joey, Tabitha had no idea where he was staying. He'd asked her plenty of leading questions over the course of their lunch. It was time for him to answer a few of hers.

"Does it matter where, as long as it's private? Maybe you could ask me a few questions over at your place."

"No." Damien might be the sexiest man she'd ever laid eyes on, but Tabitha had worked hard to make sure that Joey didn't know where she lived. No matter what depraved acts she wanted to commit on Damien's body, there was no way she'd risk her or Seth's tenuous sense of safety by inviting one of Joey's associates to her apartment.

Her stern response was answered by a dubious brow. "No?"

Tabitha had a feeling that very few people told Damien Evans no. There was a first time for everything, she supposed. "Sorry, but—" How far should she trust him? "—at the end of the day, you still work for Joey. And there are some things, my address being one, that he doesn't need to know."

Damien studied her as though he wanted to climb inside her brain and rummage through her thoughts. His bright eyes clouded over and Tabitha sensed that his temper simmered close to the surface. "Did he hurt you?"

Emotionally? Yeah. Mentally? You bet. He'd thrown her self-esteem to the floor, stomped on it, torn her emotional stability to shreds, and that was before he'd used her brother as a tool to blackmail her. "He never hit me." Though she hadn't really given Damien the answer she was sure he was hunting for, that was all he was going to get. "But he's bad news and I don't need him in my life any more than he is already."

The cloud didn't lift from Damien's mood. In fact, at her words, it seemed to darken even more. "I'm just like him, aren't I? Bad news is bad news. What are you doing sitting here with me?"

Her voice dropped to almost a whisper. "You're not like him."

Damien braced one massive forearm on the table as he stood and leaned toward her. He reached out and cupped her face in his palm, his grip firm as he forced her gaze to meet his. Tabitha suppressed a shudder that had nothing to do with fear or anxiety. When he took control this way, he didn't realize that he was giving her exactly what she wanted. "You sure about that?"

He'd meant to intimidate her. To put a little healthy fear into her. *Sorry, buddy. It's not gonna happen.* "I'm not afraid of you, you know." She met him look for look, her tone no longer meek but full of fire.

"Oh no?" His grip tightened. Not enough to hurt her, but just enough to let her know that he could if he wanted to. As if.

"No."

His large frame loomed above her as he leaned down for a kiss. Tabitha felt multiple sets of eyes watching them, but Damien seemed not to care. His mouth moved over hers, not roughly as it had earlier in the hotel room, but with a slow, possessive precision that made Tabitha's toes curl in her shoes.

When he pulled away, she was breathless and eager for more. His brow furrowed as he sat back down. "I'm afraid of me. You should be, too."

For the first time since they'd met, Tabitha experienced a tiny trickle of what Damien wanted her to feel. "Maybe we're both a little scary." Or more to the point, scared. Scared of who they were, what they'd done, and how perfect they were together despite the fact that they barely knew each other. "Life is a little scary, don't you think?"

His dark gaze swept over her and every nerve ending in Tabitha's body seemed to respond. He could get to her with a look, enslave her with those golden eyes until she was little more than a mindless minion. "Scary." The word hung in the air, flat. "You shouldn't have to be scared, Tabitha. Of anything or anyone. Ever."

The fierceness of his tone made her think that he'd do anything to reassure her, keep her safe. She believed his earnest expression, the concern etched into every line that marred his forehead. But did protecting her mean that he would also protect her from him? She didn't think she wanted that. Not anymore. "No one should have to be scared, Damien." And that included him, whether he believed it or not.

Silence settled over them like an early winter snow. Peaceful and calm. Each of them lost in their own thoughts. Tabitha picked at her lunch, dipping one of the Parmesan-coated fries into a little silver bowl of fry sauce. Damien wasn't the sort of guy you pushed into anything, but Tabitha was going to do her best to urge him to leave the path that Joey had set out for him. He was a good guy. Too good to live his life peddling drugs and whatever else Joey wanted him to do.

"Here." Tabitha looked up as Damien slid her cell and the canister of pepper spray across the table to her. "You left these in the room last night."

"Thanks." She tucked both of them into her purse and gave him a sheepish grin. "I wasn't too worried about the cell, but replacing a lost canister of pepper spray is *such* a hassle."

He flashed her a grin, the sight of his dimples enough to make her heart race. A breeze of fresh air seemed to blow the clouds of melancholy away and just like that, they were back on track.

"How's it going over here?" their waitress asked as she approached the table. "Is anyone interested in dessert today?"

Their eyes met and Tabitha's stomach flipped at the brilliance of his smile. God, he was amazing. He didn't break eye contact with her as he said to the waitress, "We're definitely interested in dessert."

Damien Evans scared the crap out of her, but not for the reason he thought. The way she felt with him, as though she might actually be falling for him, was scarier than anything he could throw at her.

Chapter Eleven

"Seth Martin. Twenty-one years old, has a record that goes back to juvie."

Damien sat back in the swivel chair, his arms planted on the armrests, fingers steepled at his lips. "Can we get our hands on the sealed records?"

"Already done."

Gates had spent most of the morning digging up everything he could on Tabitha and her brother. Damien's stomach soured as the deputy marshal listed Seth's laundry list of offenses, ranging from petty theft to possession with intent to deliver, and a B and E, all before he'd turned fourteen. "Boise PD picked him up at seventeen for delivery of a controlled substance. Let's face it, the kid isn't exactly a criminal mastermind. I'd be willing to bet he gets caught doing more than he's ever gotten away with."

"What about the sister?" Damien was willing to bet that Tabitha spent most of her time bailing her brother out of jam after jam. It fit her protective personality to a tee.

"A couple of speeding tickets several years back and one parking ticket last June, but nothing major. If she's a player, she's smarter than her brother."

"What was the brother's most recent arrest?" There was more to Tabitha's story than her brother's arrest records and her involvement with Joey.

"Possession with intent to deliver, about eighteen months ago. He did six months and got thirty-six months of probation. I read the transcript and the judge told him if he stepped a toe out of line again, he'd be going away for the duration."

"Six months isn't a long sentence for that type of charge."

"No," Ryan agreed. "But when Boise PD picked him up, he only had a few baggies on him, not more than an ounce of weed apiece. They'd been following him for a while, I guess, but according to the arrest record, the narc guys figured he'd unloaded most of the product by the time they got their hands on him."

If Seth was on probation with a stern warning from the Ada County magistrate hanging over his head, there was a good chance that Tabitha could easily be coerced into giving Joey a hand if he had something on her brother that could get the kid arrested. "I take it Boise PD and Seth Martin are well acquainted?" Then again, Damien could be grasping at straws. Anything to excuse Tabitha's involvement.

"Oh yeah." Gates sat back in his chair and nibbled on the cap of his pen. "I talked to John Rader this morning and he said that they'd been investigating Martin for a couple of years. As clueless as the kid is, they were sure someone was using him as an expendable mule."

"But they never made an arrest?"

Ryan shook his head. "Whoever was supplying Martin with product kept a low profile, and Seth wouldn't give him up even when they offered him a plea bargain."

Maybe Seth didn't give up the supplier because the asshole was dating his sister at the time? "My money's on Cavello for the supplier."

"Yeah, mine too." Damien swore, the way Gates was going to town on that pen cap, he was going to be picking bits of plastic from his teeth for weeks. "He was more than likely dating Martin's sister at the time, and her continued involvement with Cavello indicates that they've had a working relationship with him for a while now. But the last time Martin was picked up, he was still just peddling weed. The Bandit task force said that the synthetic only showed up on the streets a few months ago."

"About the time Lightfoot's organization pulled out of Oregon."

Gates examined his pen and threw it in the trash. Thank God. That Bic ballpoint was no doubt loaded with germs. "Yep. But here's where I'm lost. How did Cavello get hooked up with Lightfoot in the first place? We know now that he's distributing Stardust, and we know how he's getting it—good work, by the way—but there has to be something or someone to connect the two. Cavello was small-time before this. I don't think he would've had the sort of rep to garner Lightfoot's attention."

"True." Damien had been racking his brain for a couple of weeks, searching for that very connection. "But maybe that's the point. Lightfoot knows we're looking for him. High rollers and well-known dealers would bring too much heat. Someone like Cavello—small-time, expendable, who asks very few questions and does what he's told—would be the perfect distributor. What does Cavello care where Lightfoot is and what he does, as long as he's getting a fat paycheck?"

Ryan dragged a hand through his hair. "If that's the case, our chances of getting our hands on Lightfoot through Cavello are slim."

Damien swiveled in his chair. "I disagree."

"Evans, come take a look at this." Chief Deputy Callihan stepped up to the cubicle Damien was working from, his expression pinched.

He exchanged a look with Gates, who was equally nonplussed. "Sure," he remarked as he pushed himself up from the chair. "What's up?"

Ryan joined them and they followed Callihan to the hallway lined with windows that looked out over the parking lot of the federal courthouse building. Sitting in the parking lot was an older model gold Toyota 4Runner. "She's been sitting down there in her car for the past half hour. Security called up because it seemed suspicious. How would you like to handle this?"

Damien swallowed down the groan that rose in his throat. Confronting Tabitha here could potentially blow his cover, and likewise, how would she react to finding out that the guy she'd been fooling around with wasn't what he seemed? He had a feeling that she wouldn't appreciate being lied to. *Fuck.*

"What's she been doing down there?" Not that he thought she was dangerous or even erratic. But why in the *hell* was she here?

"According to security, just sitting in her car. She told the guard at the security gate that she had an appointment, but I asked around and she hasn't contacted anyone here."

Damien continued to stare down at the parking lot, his brain working a mile a minute as one scenario after another played out in his mind. The door of the Toyota opened and Damien watched from the fourth-story window as Tabitha got out of the car and paced from the hood to the back bumper, back and forth, back and forth.

"Is she talking to herself?"

Damien glanced over at Gates before turning his attention back to Tabitha. It did appear as though she was coaching herself, her palms open, forearms stretched in front of her and gesturing as she paced.

"Looks like it," Callihan chimed in. "Is she unstable, Evans? Should we have someone go down there and get her?"

Whatever internal debate she had going on, Damien knew that instability wasn't an issue. "Send Gates to talk to her." No way was he about to blow his cover now. "But don't shake her down."

"So you're saying you want me to pour on the charm?"

Damien's eyes narrowed as he took in the shit-eating grin on Ryan's face. The last thing he wanted was to watch from the fourth-floor window as the suave deputy flirted with Tabitha. "I'm saying that you should go down there and feel her out." *Dude, wrong choice of words.* "See if you can get her to tell you what she's doing here. We'll decide what to do from there."

Ryan looked to his superior and Callihan replied, "It's his show, Gates. Go ahead."

Damien waited with his face plastered to the window, glad that the mirrored exterior surface wouldn't rat him out to Tabitha. The only thing that would make him look more pathetic at this point was if his palms were splayed on the glass, the surface fogging from his breath. A façade of calm indifference was tough to maintain when all he could think about was Tabitha's reaction if she knew he'd lied to her about who he really was. Their lunch on Sunday was the best date Damien had been on in years, and for the past few days he'd been counting down the hours until he returned to the IdaHaven, just so he'd have an excuse to see her again. When had selling drugs become an acceptable excuse to see a woman? Jesus.

"You don't think your cover is compromised? If it is, we might have to take her into custody," Callihan remarked. "Are you ready for that?"

Of course the chief deputy was speaking in regards to Damien's investigation, but all he could think of was the hurt that she'd suffer if they arrested her. "An arrest might be a little overboard. But if I'm compromised—which I don't think is possible—it might be a good idea to take her into custody."

"You want to try and flip her?"

Honestly, Damien doubted it would be too hard, considering her opinion of Joey and what he did. "Maybe. We'll wait to see what Ryan finds out first."

From the corner of his eye, Damien caught sight of the deputy as he emerged from the building and crossed the parking lot. Tabitha continued to pace until Gates got within earshot. She froze midstep and turned to face him.

Damien's breath stalled in his chest as Ryan approached Tabitha. Goddamn it, he wished he knew what was going on down there.

* * *

This is a mistake. A huge, enormous, gigantic mistake.

Tabitha still didn't know what she was doing standing in the middle of the parking lot of the courthouse building. Why she thought the U.S. Marshals would be less intimidating than the FBI was a mystery. She was already terrified, and she hadn't even made it through the front door yet. It's not like she'd never been in this position before. But her past decisions had been made in an effort to protect Seth. And Joey's threats had made it clear that any attempt to protect her brother now would only land Seth in jail. These guys were feds. If this didn't go the way she hoped it would, her brother wouldn't end up in a county jail or state pen. He'd be looking at federal prison time. It was a risk she didn't think she could take.

"Hi. I'm Deputy U.S. Marshal Ryan Gates. Can I help you with something?"

She practically jumped out of her skin when the marshal approached her. She wasn't ready to talk. Had no idea what to say. There was still too much to consider and it wasn't just her own hide she was eager to protect; she had to think about Seth as well.

Cute, clean-cut, with short dark hair, moss-green eyes, and a friendly, open smile, Deputy Ryan Gates was the sort of guy that Lila would sell her soul to climb into bed with. Too bad all Tabitha could think about was a bulky, muscled body, tousled hair, tattoos, and the most intriguing golden eyes she could imagine. What would happen to Damien if she came clean to the marshals? She couldn't ruin his life just to protect Seth. Could she?

"Miss . . . ?"

"Oh, um . . . Lila. Lila Simmons." *Oops. Way to panic, you idiot!* She'd already given her license to the guy at the security checkpoint. If Deputy Gates decided to follow up, she'd be caught in the lie and she might be down a best friend by tomorrow. Too late to worry about it now, she supposed. If she fessed up she'd only come across as crazy. Or guilty. Neither prospect was all that appealing.

Deputy Gates quirked a brow as though he knew she wasn't telling the truth. *Crap!* Maybe he'd already checked with the guy manning the check-in. In which case, she was screwed. "With as much security as we have around here, it can make everyone a little nervous when anyone hangs out in the parking lot for a half hour. Would you like to come up to my office, maybe talk about what brought you here today?"

Tabitha looked down at her feet and wished that the parking lot would split open and swallow her. She thought she could do this when she'd pulled up to the building. Thought she was brave enough to risk the consequences. But now that she'd had time to mull over her decision, she just couldn't do it. "Oh no, that's not necessary," she said with a nervous laugh. "I, um—I wanted to . . ." What? What could she say that would be a passable excuse for being there? "I've been thinking about a career in law enforcement." If there was a desk nearby, this would definitely be a moment to introduce her forehead to it. "Maybe something federal. But just thinking about the training made me break out into a sweat." Another nervous laugh. "I'm obviously not ready."

Deputy Gates's green eyes darkened with disappointment. Had he been expecting a different response? Maybe people showed up in their parking lot to confess to criminal activity on a daily basis. "Why don't you come up anyway?" His soft, charming smile must have made the girls—and probably some of the boys—in the office giddy. "I can give you the tour, show you our offices, and maybe give you a little background on what we do. We might not be so scary if you see for yourself that the U.S. Marshals Service is staffed with some pretty damned good people."

She sensed that he was speaking past the cover story she'd given him, to Tabitha Martin, woman on the edge. It unnerved her to think that he could see through the pretense to the fear and trepidation she was working so hard to disguise. If she didn't get the hell out of there soon, she'd crack for sure. "I can't today. I spent too much time trying to work up the courage to go inside." At least that little bit wasn't a lie. "I'll be late for work if I stick around now. But maybe I could schedule an appointment to come back some other time?"

"Sure." Deputy Gates gave her a sad smile as he fished a business card from his pocket. He held it out to her and she took it between shaking fingers. "Here's my card. The number for my personal extension is listed at the bottom. Call me anytime. I'd love to talk to you—about *anything*."

Panic surged as adrenaline pooled in Tabitha's limbs. Either Gates was a mind reader or he knew she was nothing more than a cowardly liar. She swore he had her number and was just waiting for her to give it up. "Thanks. I'll think about it."

Without another word, she climbed into her car and forced the key into the ignition. It took a couple of tries, but the engine finally turned over and she fought the urge to put the pedal to the metal and tear out of there, squealing tires and all. Instead, she gave him a bright smile and waved as she backed out of the parking space and pulled out of the parking lot. It was only after she was past the security gate that she allowed a tear to trickle down her cheek.

God, Tabitha. You are such a coward.

"Hey, Tabs. How was your day?"

When she woke up this morning, Tabitha never thought that her day would take a downward spiral that crashed and burned and left no survivors. But damn, had it ever. "What are you drinking?"

Seth held up the bottle of Blue Moon IPA and she took it from his grasp. "Hey! I just opened that."

Today had definitely been a three-beer day, but she'd settle for this one. Tabitha brought the bottle to her lips despite her brother's protest and drained half of it in a couple of swallows. "I swear, if I have to fish one more turd out of the swimming pool, I'm going to go postal. Toddlers and swimming pools *don't* mix."

Seth laughed with all of the amusement of a twelve-year-old. "That's gross."

"It's beyond gross." Tabitha plopped down on the couch beside her brother and propped her feet up on the coffee table. "I'm so sick of bitchy, demanding guests, of smiling and nodding when I want to throttle someone. I'm tired of fishing disgusting things out of the pool and dealing with trashed rooms that I don't blame the housekeeping staff for not wanting to clean."

Seth let out a deep sigh and averted his gaze. "You should quit. I'm working full-time. I'll cover rent, groceries, and utilities. You can focus on school and take a break."

She cut him a look that said, *Yeah. Right.* "That's not possible, Seth, and you know it."

"How do we even know that Joey will do anything? I mean, at this point, it's just as risky for him as it is for me. If he turns me in to Boise PD, they could arrest him, too. I don't think he'll talk. He's bluffing and holding it over your head to keep his cushy gig at the hotel going."

"What?" She'd never told Seth about the threats Joey had made. "Seth, I—"

"Come on, Tabs. I'm not an idiot. Give me a little credit here. I know that he's making you set him up with rooms at the hotel. No way would you help him if he wasn't holding me over your head."

She hadn't wanted him to find out. Didn't want to put that guilt on him. But one thing her brother wasn't was stupid, and Seth did have a point. Tabitha didn't want to push her luck or take unnecessary chances at this point. "I know you're not an idiot, Seth. I was just trying to protect you. But Joey isn't stupid, either. I'm sure he's covered his bases. And if Boise PD ever does arrest him, he'll turn State's evidence like he said and put it all on you. I'm not quitting my job on a hunch that he's bluffing. I can suck it up. This can't go on forever."

"But I didn't do anything," Seth remarked. "Not really."

"No. You only hooked him up with the guy who's supplying that shit he's selling." Tabitha couldn't help the accusing tone of her voice. She'd done everything in her power—things that weighed her down with guilt—to make sure that she and Seth could make a clean break from their past. Instead, Seth had kept in contact with the one man Tabitha couldn't seem to get him away from. The man who'd enabled her parents' bad habits and effectively ruined her and Seth's lives. While Tabitha thought she'd made the right decisions, done what she had to do to get Seth out of the life, he'd been going behind her back, working for the most dangerous man they'd ever known. While she and Joey were dating, Seth had introduced him to their parents' longtime friend. Joey promised Seth big-time rewards for the connection, but the only reward he'd given was a warning to Tabitha that if she didn't play ball, he'd give the cops something incriminating on Seth. He was on his second strike and still on probation. Any mark against him at this point would be bad. Worse than bad.

"Maybe you should let me take my chances." Seth had done a lot of growing up over the past six months. A year ago, he wouldn't have cared what Tabitha had to do to get him out of a bind.

"And let you go to prison? Seth, if they find anything to charge you with, you won't be spending a few months in the Ada County Jail. There will be federal charges."

"Hey, at least I'd get three squares a day." She glared at his joking tone. "Seriously, this is something you should think about. I don't want you to have to deal with Joey and his bullshit. You need a clean break, Tabs."

She'd been thinking about it. For weeks. How many times had she looked at the FBI's phone number, her fingers hovering over the keypad of her phone? Searched the Boise PD's Bandit anti-narcotics web page? Sat in the freaking parking lot of the U.S. Marshals Service's home base? She'd thought about it and thought about it until her freaking brain throbbed from all of the thinking. And now, she didn't just have Seth to worry about, but Damien as well.

For shit's sake, Tabitha. What more can you do to screw up your life?

Chapter Twelve

After talking to Gates and getting the lowdown on Tabitha's visit to the courthouse, Damien decided it would be best to give her a little space. But now that Friday night had rolled around once again, he found himself bouncing back and forth between excitement and worry. A combination he rarely felt and didn't like at all.

He'd never been so anxious to see someone, and at the same time worried over what would happen when he did. As he unloaded the heavy suitcase full of Stardust and his duffel from the trunk of his Shelby, he thought about putting a phone call in to Dr. Meyers. Because if ever he needed his head shrunk, it was right fucking now.

As he hauled his stuff through the lobby, a scowl curled his lips as he recognized the guy who worked nights—and not Tabitha—at the front desk.

"She's off tonight."

Damien checked the guy's name tag—Dave—as he typed something on the keyboard. "Who?"

Dave gave him a wry smile. "Tabitha. I got the

feeling that I wasn't who you were expecting to see behind the desk."

Jesus, was it that obvious? Damien spent his life fooling hardened criminals into believing that he was one of them and he couldn't even hide his infatuation from an innocent desk clerk? He might as well turn in his badge now.

"But don't worry. She told me you'd be in tonight and I've got your room all ready to go. Is your crew working on the roof over at the new Village complex in Meridian?"

Damien wasn't at all familiar with the local landmarks or neighboring cities, though he'd heard some talk in passing about this place or that. It didn't matter where he said he worked as long as he kept up the pretense that he worked for a roofing company and left it at that. "Uh, yeah. We'll be on and off the project for at least another month or so."

Dave continued to make small talk, but Damien couldn't manage more than a grunt or two in response. His brain was buzzing, too full of Tabitha. Where was she? What was she doing? Had she discovered what he was really doing by working for Joey?

"Here's your key," Dave said, sliding the little paper envelope closer to Damien's hand. How long had he been zoned out? *Real smooth.* "Can I help you with anything else this evening?"

Dave's flirty smile didn't go unnoticed. Maybe he could coax some information about Tabitha out of the über-friendly front-desk clerk.

Good God. He might as well be some middle school kid passing notes in class. *Did Tabitha talk about me at lunch today? What did she say? Also if she likes me, check this box.* Can you say loser? "No, thanks. I'm good."

"Okay, well, don't hesitate to call if you need anything!"

He held up a hand in acknowledgment as he walked away from the front desk. What he needed was a fucking lobotomy to get Tabitha out of his head. Maybe Dave could grab a butter knife from the breakfast room and give him a hand with that.

The night dragged by on broken legs, painfully slow and debilitating. Damien played the part of amateur drug peddler, doling out the packages to customers based on weight, cost, and the individual dealer's ability to move product. He made small talk when he could, manipulated each and every person through the door into offering up some piece of information, no matter how small. It didn't get him any closer to Lightfoot, unfortunately, but Boise PD and the Idaho State Police would have a heyday when he wrapped up his investigation.

At the back of his mind, though, he fixated on a singular thought: Tabitha and what he could do to get her to the hotel ASAP. A week apart had been torture. True, their current circumstances were less than conventional, and didn't he just feel like a king-size dick for it, too. Their lunch date hardly made up for the fact that he'd thrown himself at her not once, but twice. And truth be told, he could think of nothing more than doing it again. He'd order her to get naked before he laid her out on the bed and enjoyed her in the way he'd been dying to, coaxing those sweet sounds from her once again.

Christ. If he'd thought his head was fucked up before this gig, it was nothing compared to the tangled state it was in now.

Damien's last customer had left fifteen minutes ago and he wasn't expecting anyone else until tomorrow night. A muffled curse escaped his lips as he snatched up his cell and dialed the number he'd retrieved from Tabitha's phone the previous week.

"'Lo?" Tabitha's sleepy voice answered, and the husky timbre raced across Damien's skin in a shiver.

"I want to see you." No use exchanging pleasantries—or giving his name, apparently—at this point. He wanted her here. Now. Ten minutes ago. "Get in your car and get over here."

Silence answered him and Damien's heart pounded in his chest. Why couldn't he just quit being a demanding dickhead for long enough to ask her nicely? *Way to fuck up the only thing in your life you* don't *want to ruin. Idiot.*

Tabitha's voice was like a caress when she answered, "Give me ten minutes."

"Hurry."

He disconnected the call and tossed his phone onto the bed.

The next ten minutes might as well have been ten years as he waited for Tabitha to show up. He'd considered running down to the lobby and buying a package of condoms from the hotel store. He needed to fuck like he needed food to live. But the front-desk guy already seemed to know that something was going on between him and Tabitha. It wouldn't be a good idea to flaunt his need of a booty call in front of her coworker. He wasn't interested in disrespecting her in any way. And really, it was a little presumptuous on his part to assume that's where the night would lead. Sure, they'd fooled around, but that didn't guarantee a repeat, no matter how badly Damien wanted that to happen. He needed to calm the fuck down and let things unfold. Naturally. It was just a sign of how badly he wanted her that he felt

like he needed to rush out and buy a case of Trojans.
Overeager much?

The minutes continued to tick by at a slog. What
if she'd fallen back to sleep after his call? For all he
knew, she'd been talking in her sleep, agreeing to
his ridiculous command. Wound tight as a fucking
spring, it wouldn't take much to send Damien rock-
eting into the stratosphere. His skin clung to his
frame, too goddamned tight, and his breath sawed in
and out of his chest as though he'd been running
circles around the hotel parking lot.

A derisive snort sliced through the quiet. He was
keeping his cool like a boss.

When a soft knock came at the door moments
later, his heart seized up in his rib cage before beating out a furious rhythm that sent the blood zinging
through his veins. He stalked across the room with all
of the collected calm of a disaster movie victim fleeing from a comet hurtling toward Earth, and threw
open the door.

Jesus Christ, every time he laid eyes on her, she
seemed more beautiful.

Her blue eyes glistened, still a little sleepy, and
her short, blond hair was tousled in a way that made
her look as though she'd just been fucked. Which,
strangely enough, turned him on while simultane-
ously causing a pang of jealousy to flare in his chest.
On the right side of her nose, a tiny jewel twinkled.
He'd never noticed the piercing before; she obviously didn't wear it to work. Tight, black leggings
hugged her legs, leaving nothing to the imagination,
and a worn, too-small Soundgarden-concert tee
barely skimmed her waist along with a short, black
leather jacket. A pair of fawn-colored sheepskin boots

rounded out her outfit, and she'd never looked hotter. Just the sight of her made him hard.

"Hi."

His eyes dipped to where the cropped top of her shirt revealed her belly button, and Damien couldn't form a coherent response to save his life. He'd never wanted a woman the way he wanted Tabitha, and that mindless need was slowly ripping his composure to shreds.

With a mechanical step to the right he opened a path for her to come in. She placed a hand on her hip, cocking it to one side and said, "Should I be expecting anyone else to stop by tonight?"

"No." The word worked its way up his throat, grating on his vocal cords like gravel. "Worried I might misbehave?"

A sweet smile curved her lips. "Maybe a little."

He couldn't help his own answering grin. "Get in this room. Now."

When Damien gave her a command, Tabitha found herself helpless to deny him. A man she'd once sworn she'd keep her distance from, now her body responded to the gruff timbre of his voice, drawn to his side like lapping ocean waves are drawn to the shore. She'd been a wreck all week. Thinking about Damien. Worrying. Wondering where he was. What he was doing. Who he was with . . . A week of sleepless nights had her collapsing into her bed, exhausted, only to be woken by his call. The gruffness of his voice sparked her to life with the first word he'd spoken, and the decision to throw on a pair of boots and get in her car was one of the easiest of her entire life.

His gaze devoured her as she stepped into the room, the heat in those golden-brown eyes enough to make her sweat. Any words she might have wanted to say lodged themselves in her throat, but really, was it necessary to say anything? She knew why he'd called her and why she agreed to come.

As she walked to within touching distance of him, Damien reached out and wrapped his large hand around her waist. A low thrum of desire settled in her abdomen and Tabitha knew that if he were to slide his fingers between her thighs, he'd find her wet and more than ready for him. She was completely shameless in wanting him like she did. The tension of his arm stopped Tabitha dead in her tracks, and a low groan rumbled in Damien's chest. His palm curved a path over her hip and settled on her ass. "What are you wearing under these pants?" he asked low in her ear.

She looked up at him from beneath lowered lashes and murmured, "Nothing."

His free hand settled on her opposite hip and he took a step to his right so that he stood fully in front of her. Lord have mercy, he towered over her, his heavily muscled frame overwhelming and magnificent. Tabitha shivered as he traced a path up her torso, his fingers skimming the curve of her breast. "And under this shirt?"

Shameless. "Nothing."

"Were you naked under the covers when I called?"

Tabitha shuddered at his words, loving the game he played. No man had ever talked to her this way before, and it gave her permission to be as brazen as she dared. "Yes." Up and down, up and down, his fingers brushed her torso beneath her jacket, teasing the swell of her breast until her nipples hardened and she ached for him to touch her there.

Damien's body went rigid with each question asked, a slight tremor transferring through his touch into her skin. His barely veiled restraint caused Tabitha's breath to race in her chest, and with every intake of breath, her breasts rubbed torturously against the rippled muscle of his torso. If he didn't do something—*anything*—soon, she'd go out of her mind!

As if he sensed the maddening desire building up inside of her like carbonation under pressure, Damien took a step back and regarded her, his gaze raking over her with a hunger that sent her heart beating madly. With an arm's length between them now, Tabitha's body chilled in the absence of his touch. She moved to close the distance and he said, firm, "Stay where you are."

Under his spell, she had no choice but to do as he told her.

For a moment he just looked at her. Her skin tingled with his appraisal, flushed with heat as though his hands were still on her. With a slow breath, Damien reached out, took the strands of her hair between his fingers. "Your hair is like silk."

The wonder in his tone caused Tabitha's chest to swell with emotion. Such a contrast to his hard, commanding presence. He let the strands fall through his fingers and cupped her face in his palm before tracing the shell of her ear. A featherlight caress brought chills to the surface of Tabitha's skin as he trailed his fingers past her earlobe and down the column of her throat, skirting the neckline of her T-shirt.

Anticipation coiled in her stomach as every nerve

ending in her body grew hypersensitive. The quiet in the room was deafening, the only sound that of their quickened breaths. "Look at me."

She brought her eyes to his and fought the urge to drop her gaze. Was this how prey felt in the clutches of a powerful predator? Or perhaps a lowly wolf in the presence of its alpha? He reached beneath her jacket and with the pad of his thumb circled one nipple. Tabitha's lips parted on a sharp intake of breath, the sensation so intense despite the thin layer of cotton fabric that separated her skin from his.

With his left hand, he cupped the back of her neck, as if concerned she might suddenly look away. Or bolt. He held her fast, slowly circling her nipple as he studied her reaction with an intensity that caused Tabitha's breath to come in desperate little pants that ended on a quiet whimper. She could come like this. With nothing more than his eyes on her and his thumb teasing her nipple to a diamond-hard peak.

"Does that feel good?"

He had to have known that he was driving her crazy. But it was part of his game, wasn't it? The control he needed to exercise and the commands that Tabitha needed desperately to obey. "Yes." The word burst from her lips in a low moan and Damien's nostrils flared as his grip on her neck tightened and his thumb brushed along her jawline.

"Tell me."

"It feels so good," she said between pants of breath.

An unexpected sting of pleasure coursed through her body as he pinched the pearled peak through her shirt. "And that?"

"Yes," she moaned. "Do it again."

Damien crushed her to him in a searing kiss. Tabitha's body melted against his as he cupped her ass in his hands and lifted her up to meet his height. She kicked the boots from her feet as she shucked her jacket and wrapped her legs around his waist. He thrust up as he pushed down on her hips, forcing the thick length of his erection against her barely clothed and aching sex.

Holy shit, the man was sex personified.

He backed up until the bed stopped him and sat down on the mattress with Tabitha settled firmly in his lap. His kisses left her breathless, his tongue thrusting into her mouth in a slow, desperate rhythm that cranked her desire into overdrive. No one had ever kissed her this way before. Each deliberate movement carried with it a sense of possession: the way his mouth slanted across hers, each flick or swirl of his tongue, the slight scrape of his teeth on her bottom lip. In no uncertain terms, Damien laid claim to her and Tabitha was more than happy to give herself over to him.

At once demanding and careful, Damien cupped her face in his hands gently, as though she were something fragile. The kisses that had been frenzied and desperate only a moment ago were now soft and slow. A savoring of her mouth that made Tabitha's head spin. She was lost to him. Lost to his commanding, quiet presence, his body, the ink that decorated his skin. A slave to his scent, his callused fingers and smooth flesh, hulking form, the tousled locks of his light brown hair and the intensity of his golden gaze. This was an infatuation Tabitha would never find her way back from. And the realization of how far gone she was sent a trickle of icy fear through her bloodstream.

Chapter Thirteen

The sweetness of Tabitha's mouth, the soft texture of her skin and silken hair, her floral perfume and unabashed desire, latched on to every particle of Damien's body. The beginnings of an addiction he knew he would never have the strength to kick.

He couldn't hold her tight enough, kiss her deeply enough. His cock throbbed in his jeans, hot and hard and so damned ready to take her. It had been such a long damned time since he'd been with a woman that he wouldn't last a minute once he sunk himself into her slick heat. Entanglements of any kind while he was undercover were a huge no-go. But in the course of a week he realized that the longer he stayed away from Tabitha, the more he wanted her. And like the drugs he'd doled out so easily to eager addicts, he couldn't stay away from her, no matter how hard he tried.

He grasped Tabitha around the waist and lifted her. Her petite frame weighed almost nothing and he set her on her feet, between his legs. Sitting up straight, he was damned near as tall as she was standing. Her expression was curious yet heated as he wound his fists in the hem of her T-shirt and dragged it up and off of her, slowly, revealing her body to his hungry gaze inch by tantalizing inch.

The fabric met the resistance of her full breasts, and when he freed them from the restricting fabric, they gave a slight bounce that forced a groan from Damien's throat. Perfect and full, the dusky nipples stood proud and erect. He freed Tabitha's head from the neck of the shirt but left the garment at her wrists. Winding the fabric, he bound her hands together and stood, repositioning them so that she lay on the bed and he stood over her.

"Don't try to free yourself. Do you understand me?"

She answered with a nod and a low moan that caused his balls to tighten against his cock. As though in prayer, Damien went to his knees before her. The thin cotton fabric of the leggings hugging her legs like a second skin cooled his heated cheeks as he ran his nose up the inside of her thigh, inhaling her scent as he went. When he met the juncture at her thighs he said, "Spread your legs." And Tabitha trembled beneath him as she did as he asked. It was fucking torture not to simply strip the damned things from her body, but as he'd done earlier, touching her through her T-shirt, he grazed his teeth along her inner thigh.

Tabitha bucked at the contact, her back arching off the bed as she let out a quiet whimper. He repeated the action on the opposite side and she cried out, squirming as though fighting the urge to free her hands—which truly weren't bound in any sense of the word. But that was the point. It wasn't the binding that kept her arms high above her head, tangled in the T-shirt. Rather, his words and her trust in him garnered her compliance. That blind trust was as seductive as her body. No one had ever completely trusted him, and warm emotion swelled in his chest.

"Put your mouth on me."

The words were soft and pleading and Damien sealed his mouth over her sex, marveling at how damp the fabric was with her desire and how he could taste her arousal. Through the thin barrier, he knew her pussy was swollen, wet, and ready to receive him. *Goddamn.* This moment was heaven. The sweet torture of withholding himself from her almost more than he could bear.

"I want to touch you, Damien."

He grazed his teeth along the sensitive ridges of her sex, and she shuddered. "Not yet."

Like he'd taken off her shirt, Damien peeled the second skin of her leggings from her body slowly. He watched her reaction carefully, noting the quiver of her breasts with each pant of breath, the way her stomach muscles tightened when his fingers curled around the waistband of her pants. He eased them over her hips, kissing the juncture where her hip met her thigh, his attention divided between the newly exposed flesh and her arms, held high above her head and still tangled in her T-shirt. Holy Christ, she was a sight to behold.

He raked the pants down over her thighs and paused as he drank in the beauty of her glistening pussy. As he teased the short, damp curls, Tabitha let out a slow sigh. A release of breath that Damien felt over every inch of his body. With a quick tug, he freed the leggings from her ankles and dropped them somewhere behind him. He placed his palms on her thighs and urged them to part, sucking in a breath as he committed to memory how she looked, spread out naked on the bed, just as he'd imagined. Damn it, he should have gone down to the lobby and bought the condoms, gossip and reputations be damned.

"You are so fucking beautiful."

Tabitha's head came off the bed and their gazes locked. The emotion he saw in those crystal-blue depths shook Damien to his foundation. His fingers dug into her thighs and her lids became hooded as her head lolled back on the bed. Having her here, now, no matter the circumstances, was worth any risk both personal and professional. The world could fall down around him tomorrow, but tonight she belonged to him.

Most of the time, it was Damien who rattled others' nerves. Sort of came part and parcel with being a big, tattooed, scary-looking son of a bitch. But this petite woman spread out on the bed scared him more than any drug lord, arms dealer, or dangerous fugitive he'd ever kept company with. Because for the first time in his life, Damien finally needed someone. He needed *her*.

He backed away, standing for only as long as it took to strip his shirt from his chest. He wanted nothing between his skin and hers. Her lips quirked into a grin as she watched him, her hands still bound and immovable above her head. A reluctant smile tugged at his lips as he fumbled with the button of his jeans, unable to tear his eyes from her, focus on anything *but* her. He was starved to bury his face between those sweet thighs again. One taste wasn't even close to enough.

He finally managed to work his zipper down and when his cock sprang free of his underwear, Tabitha's eyes widened in appreciation as she rolled her bottom lip between her teeth. That one look was worth a thousand compliments, and it stroked his ego no small amount to know that his body pleased her.

As he moved to go back on his knees, Tabitha's voice stabbed through the quiet. "No." He stilled, brow furrowed with worry and she added, "If I can't touch you with my hands, at least let me appreciate you with my mouth."

"Holy shit, woman, are you trying to kill me?" The thought of her mouth on him while he lapped at her pussy was just too much.

"Not kill you." Her voice was a husky purr that slid down his spine in a pleasant shiver. "But I do want to enjoy you."

Damien scrubbed a hand through the tangles of his hair. "Not yet. Put your head on the pillows, keep your hands above your head, and open your legs for me." It wasn't a rejection of her attention. Good God, he wanted her mouth on his cock so badly he was trembling with need. But when he gauged her reaction to his gentle command—her quickened breath, liquid eyes, and the slight flush of her cheeks—Damien knew that he'd made the right decision. Whether she realized it or not, she craved the domination. And he was going to give her what she needed.

Tabitha did as he told her to, repositioning herself on the bed so that her head was on the pillows, arms resting near the headboard. Her back arched slightly off the mattress as she let her legs fall open and Damien admired her for a long moment before he came around to the foot of the bed and positioned his head between her thighs.

The woman was a fucking goddess, and he was about to worship her.

The first pass of his tongue on her soft flesh was bliss, and it sent him teetering over the edge of his control. As though he'd lived his life in a state of perpetual starvation, Tabitha became his sustenance and he finally knew what it was to be full. He took his time, learning the intricacies of her body, what made her moan, and what quickened her breath. A long drag with the flat of his tongue from her tight opening to her clit made her arch off the bed, and quick flicks of his tongue caused her to writhe in his grasp, her hips rolling and thrusting to meet his mouth.

When he sucked on the silky lips of her labia, she cried out, and when he took the swollen knot of nerves at her core between his teeth, she sobbed her pleasure. "Damien! Oh God, Damien."

He dug his fingers into the soft flesh of her ass, a pang of regret stabbing through his chest as she called out a name that was as much a part of his façade as the tattoos that graced his arms and chest. For the first time in as long as he'd been a member of the Marshals Service, he didn't want to be Damien anymore. He wanted to be Parker Evans, and that was the name he wanted on Tabitha's lips.

You should squash those fucking thoughts and thank God a woman like this is willing to give you the time of day, let alone the pleasure of her body.

Amen.

Tabitha laced her fingers and clasped her palms tightly together. She'd do whatever Damien asked as long as he kept making her feel this way, and that included resisting the urge to touch him. It was like he knew her body better than she did, every pass of his tongue a deliberate motion executed to achieve a specific reaction.

A gentle flick was followed up by a long, languid pass with the flat of his tongue and Tabitha cried out, not giving a damn who might hear her. He sucked, nibbled and licked, loving every inch of her throbbing sex with his talented mouth. Tabitha released her hands and gripped the pillow behind her, clutching the fabric like a lifeline. She floated on a cloud of bliss, pleasure like nothing she'd ever experienced, and if she didn't hold on to something—anything—to anchor her, there was a pretty good possibility she'd fly right into the stratosphere.

Damien slowed his pace and soon the pressure of his mouth was gone. Tabitha thrust her hips toward his mouth, eager for him to continue, but he pulled away and blew lightly over her heated, wet flesh, causing a delicious chill that made her bones go soft. *Oh . . . God . . .*

"Do you like that?" His voice was a sensual growl that vibrated up Tabitha's spine. He nipped at her inner thigh and a low moan escaped her lips.

"Yes." The word came as a desperate whisper, thick and rough.

"Should I do it again?"

"God, yes." She thrust her hips toward his mouth in frustration.

The pad of his finger teased her opening, the contact with her oversensitized flesh almost more than she could bear. He spread her wet arousal over her sex and blew again, the lightest breath that brought more of the intense chill that rippled over her skin like cool rain from a summer storm.

"Again?"

Words failed her. Mindless with need, all Tabitha could manage was a pleading whimper. The way he teased her was maddening. The most delicious torture she'd ever experienced. He caressed her, explored every inch of her with tender attention. Played with her. Tantalized her. A shock of heat as his mouth fastened over her sex. Blinding pleasure as he feathered the blunt tip of his thumb over her clit, just before his fingers rocked inside of her. Tabitha's body coiled, winding and turning over and around itself until she was nothing more than a constricted, quivering bundle of sensitized flesh, want, and need. Damien was going to break her apart and she welcomed the moment when he would shatter her completely.

His fingers bit into her flesh as he took her hip in his palm, his grip pulsing in time with every pass of his tongue. Tabitha cried out, her back arching off the bed and he reached up with his other hand to cup her breast, teasing her nipple with a slow roll and then a tight pinch that sent her toppling over the edge.

"Damien!" His name burst from her lips as she came, as reverent and solemn as a prayer. Wave after wave of the most intense pleasure she'd ever felt crested over her. Damien hadn't simply broken her apart. He'd obliterated her. She was nothing more than stardust, particles floating in a vast universe. This moment was unparalleled and it caused such intense emotion to roil in her chest that her heart felt as though it would burst. Even the men who'd claimed to love her had never *loved* her in the way that Damien just had. Dear God, she was ruined.

Tabitha lay still, panting through the aftershocks of what was hands down the most amazing orgasm of her entire life. Damien kissed the insides of her thighs, upward and over one hip. His mouth was a brand as it traveled across her lower abdomen, his tongue dipping briefly into her belly button. Up her torso, a light kiss to each one of her ribs and then over the swell of her breast before his mouth sealed over her nipple, sucking gently. She arched into his touch, desperate to comb her fingers through his hair and yet still unable to ignore his command that she keep her hands bound above her. Any other man would have been content to know that she'd gotten off, and would have been pounding away by now, or requesting that she return the favor with her own mouth. But she already knew that Damien was unlike any other man.

He attended her other breast with the same loving attention before kissing across her collarbone, up the column of her throat, beneath her ear—where he paused to take the lobe between his teeth before drawing it into his mouth. The deep inhale of Damien's breath caused chills to dance over Tabitha's skin as he buried his face in her hair and breathed her in. Her heart raced in her chest, on the verge of tears or laughter, she didn't know which. He was too good to be true.

"I could do that all night," he murmured, his breath hot in her ear. "Just lick and suck and taste you. Feel you come against my mouth. Again and again until the sun rose and we collapsed from exhaustion."

The words were so tender, a sharp contrast to the natural gruffness of his voice. Spread out beside her on the bed, his body felt even larger and more imposing. He braced himself up on an elbow and studied her with a quiet wonderment that made Tabitha's breath hitch.

"What?"

He smiled, showcasing the deep dimples in his cheeks that turned her bones to mush. "You're beautiful."

Heat rose to Tabitha's cheeks, though she doubted he'd notice with the flush of passion that was still no doubt on her skin. No man had ever called her beautiful before. And for the second time tonight, the compliment constricted her heart almost to the point of pain. Most of her life had been so hard and ugly, and at times it had made her feel ugly, too. Unworthy of praise. Her eyes searched his for any duplicity, but they were clear and honest. For the first time in her life, she truly felt beautiful. As though she was more than the low-class daughter of drug addicts. "Thank you," she said. It might have sounded silly, but it meant so much to her, she couldn't help herself.

"I want you. I need to be inside of you. I—" Deep grooves marred his brow as though he struggled with what he wanted to say. "I want you more than I've wanted anything. Ever."

"What's wrong with that?" He sounded so conflicted. Why?

"Because it scares the hell out of me."

Her stomach twirled into myriad tiny knots at his words. He'd been so honest with her and deserved an equally honest response. "I want you, too. And yeah, it's scary. But it's also *amazing*."

Damien positioned himself fully on top of her. Tabitha let her legs fall open, ready to accept him, but he held himself back, careful that only his torso made contact with her body. His arms trembled with the effort he exerted to keep himself suspended above her. "I'm a miserable son of a bitch, Tabitha. But I'm not a complete bastard. No matter how badly I need your body, it can't go any further than we already have tonight."

What? Why? Panic shot through her bloodstream. The night had barely begun as far as she was concerned. "What if I'm not okay with that?"

He brushed her hair from her face, lost for a moment as he rubbed the strands between his thumb and forefinger. He kept his gaze averted as he said, "You just want me to fuck you without any consideration of the fact that we have no protection? You don't really know me, Tabitha, yet you think I'm that trustworthy?"

Shit. She hadn't considered the fact that they had no condoms, or contraception of any kind. It had sort of become a non-issue in the heat of the moment. Did she find him trustworthy? She'd heard her share of excuses over the course of her adolescence, and even a few from Joey when they'd dated. *I'm sterile. If you loved me you would . . . I was just tested, babe. I'm totally clean.* And her all-time favorite, *I'm a virgin. You're my first.* Little did Eric Jones know that his last girlfriend flapped her lips about their sexual exploits to anyone who'd listen. She'd heard more than her fair share of excuses of why it was okay to have unprotected sex, but never had a man given her an argument for why they shouldn't.

It was true that she didn't know Damien well. But she did trust him.

"I'll take my chances. I want you. Please, just . . ." Her rational brain had taken a vacation the second he put his hands and mouth on her. She knew this wasn't a good idea, but somehow she didn't care. "Trust *me*. I'm not willing to let tonight end. Not yet."

He kissed her once. Softly. Just the slightest contact of his lips on hers.

"Baby, you're driving me crazy." He rolled his hips and the silky flesh of his erection brushed her thigh. "I can't get enough of you." Another thrust of his hips and he groaned, his teeth welded together as a look of near pain marred his strong features. "Sex is off the table. Tonight, at least. But you can do whatever else you want to me. Touch me, taste me. Fuck, I want your mouth on me. You're in control now, this is your show. I trust you, too."

Tabitha didn't know it was possible to experience this sort of intimacy without actual intercourse. At twenty-three, she wasn't exactly a seasoned pro, but in her past relationships, sex had always been the endgame. A frenzied mess of excitement and urgency that came and went like a passing storm. Tonight was more akin to an ocean tide. Ebbing and flowing, building to high breakers that lulled into gentle waves. Give and take. Urgent and easy. She'd never felt more comfortable in her own skin and yet so unaware of her own body. Damien had showed her all of this.

And now, he was giving her the reins. No sex, but other than that, he was hers. How could tonight get any more perfect? "Roll over," she said. "I want you on your back."

Chapter Fourteen

Damien propped himself up higher on his elbow and used his free hand to release the T-shirt that was now hanging limply from Tabitha's wrists. She'd trusted him completely, resisting the urge to use her hands despite the fact that they'd basically been free the entire time.

This was uncharted territory for him.

The majority of his past sexual relationships had been short-lived and sometimes anonymous encounters that scratched an itch for both parties and nothing more. Damien was usually very careful about choosing bedmates who weren't looking for more than a couple hours' worth of fun. His life was always in turmoil, traveling from one undercover assignment to the next. He didn't have the sort of stability in his life to support an honest-to-God relationship with a woman. And now that he'd finally met someone who made him want to stick around, he wasn't sure if a relationship with Tabitha would survive the laundry list of obstacles they'd have to overcome.

When her hands made contact with his bare skin, however, any obstacle seemed surmountable.

Warm and soft as satin, her fingers glided over him. She studied him with an intensity that made his heart race as she traced the outlines of the tattoos marking his pecs, ink that he'd recently become ashamed of because he'd begun to associate them with a lifestyle that he didn't subscribe to, yet had to pretend to live.

"I love this one," she said as she lovingly traced the artwork that crawled from his left pec up his shoulder. "The artwork is so intricate. What's the symbolism?"

Truth be told, he liked that one too. To the casual eye, the whorls and angles that made up the spines and scales of the dragon's head looked innocent enough. But to the discerning eye—the gangbangers and dealers who'd notice—the tattoo artist had hidden symbols that denoted his affiliation with the Russian mob. "The artwork is meant to represent Norse folk art. Dragons are considered evil in some of their mythology, but also creatures of immeasurable power."

"And this? Is it Norse too?"

She traced his opposite pec. This image depicted a snarling bear, and again, the artist had carefully hidden symbols meant to buy Damien street cred: stars that indicated stints in federal prison. Tabitha's fingertips traced each of Damien's knuckles and moved over the dots on the webbing between his thumb and forefinger, a false representation of the number of men he'd killed. These were the images—not the tattoos themselves—that Damien despised. Lies constructed to maintain his cover, permanently etched on his skin.

"The bear is associated with the berserker. Warriors

possessed with supernatural strength and fierceness in battle that made them more animals than men."

Her mouth spread in an enigmatic smile. "They're beautiful. I love them."

On and on she went, her palms roving the landscape of his body as though mapping every inch. She asked questions and he answered, more interested in observing her expressions than his own responses. He could watch her for hours.

"When I first noticed these, I thought they were gang symbols," she said with a laugh as she traced the ink tattooed between his knuckles. "But they're definitely not."

"Runes," he said.

"More Norse stuff?"

"Yeah," he said, trying to hide his embarrassment. He must seem like one of those idiots who'd succumbed to the tribal tattoo craze, inking his entire body in a theme. He dropped the façade of Damien's cover. She'd put her trust in him tonight. He could return the favor by sharing a little bit of Parker with her. "My mom's family are Norwegian. Most of them still live in Norway. I used to hear all of the myths and stories when I was little."

Tabitha brought his hand to her mouth and kissed each and every knuckle. Damien's stomach twisted into a knot so tight, he doubted it would ever unfurl. She kissed the inside of one wrist, and then the other, before venturing up his arm, across his shoulder, and down over the tattoos she'd traced just moments before. Her tongue flicked out at one nipple and he inhaled a sharp breath.

His stomach went rigid as she kissed a path down his abs, and he swallowed a groan as she went lower still, dragging the flat of her tongue across the juncture where his hip met his thigh. Hard as stone, his cock throbbed between his legs, and when she nipped at the flesh on his inner thigh, the sting of her teeth caused the bastard to twitch as though in anticipation of similar attention.

Tabitha took her time, acquainting herself with his body in the way he'd done with hers. Her will had to be stronger than his, because only seconds of her attention drove him crazy with desire. He wanted her so badly, every inch of him ached. She rose above him, settled her body between his thighs and bent, hovering over the one place he was dying to have her mouth.

"Tell me what you want," she said in a husky tone that tingled down his spine and settled in his balls. "And I'll do it. Anything."

Even after handing her total control, she gave it back to him. She trusted him. Wanted this give-and-take between them. He'd never known a woman like Tabitha. As though she sensed his need for control in the way he sensed her need to be controlled, they fit together like puzzle pieces. Perfect.

"I want you to suck the head of my cock."

Her gaze heated at his words and she dipped her full lips to his erection. A low moan vibrated in her throat as she wrapped her mouth around him and the sound tingled down his shaft. She curled her tongue around the engorged head, soft and slippery, before she sucked gently.

"Harder."

He didn't want anything tentative or light from her, and she increased the suction and pressure. Damien's hips rolled involuntarily, it felt so damned good. "Yeah, like that. Don't stop."

When the sensation was too intense for him to

take another second, he thrust, guiding his cock slightly farther into her mouth. He let out a moan that was as much in relief as it was pleasure. She pulled back to the tip, a clear sign that if he wanted her to take him deeper, he'd have to tell her so.

He reached down and threaded his fingers through the silken strands of her hair. "Deeper, baby. I need it deeper."

Tabitha's eyelids fluttered as she took him fully into her mouth, working her lips and tongue over his shaft in a steady rhythm that coaxed Damien's breath to come in deep, desperate pants. He pressed his head back into the pillow, one hand still wound in her hair, the other clenched in a fist at his side. The wet warmth of her mouth was heaven, but it only made him want to fuck her that much more. He'd sworn he wouldn't disrespect her. Wouldn't allow himself to be so irresponsible. But, goddamn, he wanted that joining of their bodies, he wanted to make that claim on her.

Like a fire tearing through dry grass, Damien's passion raged. He held nothing back, his voice an impassioned growl when he backed her off to where she'd started at the head of his cock. "Use your teeth." He was so far gone with want, the words barely made sense to him anymore. Her teeth scraped against the sensitive, engorged skin and he hissed in a breath.

"*Ungh*, God yeah," he said from between clenched teeth. "Again, harder."

Fuck, that felt *good*. Better than good. She nipped at him, alternating the intense sting with the silken heat of her tongue. Another sharp nip, a swirl of her tongue, followed up with the deep suction that hollowed her cheeks. He marveled at her soft beauty and fierce will.

On his first undercover assignment, Damien had had to sit by and watch a twentysomething kid shoot up with heroin for the first time. He'd hated how overcome the kid became, the look of utter bliss that stole over his features. Lost to the drug, he was instantly and irrevocably in its grip. He now knew what it felt like to lose himself in that way. Because he was hopelessly lost—addicted—to Tabitha Martin.

Tension built up in his body like water backed up by a dam. His thighs shook and muscles ached with the need for release. His balls drew up tighter with every deep pull of Tabitha's mouth and sweat beaded his skin. "Tabitha. Tabitha." Even the cadence of her name on his lips was euphoric. A shudder passed the length of his body. "Take it all."

She moaned around him as she worked her mouth over him in earnest, taking him as far into her mouth as she could before pulling back to the glossy head and back down. The deep suction constricted his shaft, squeezing it tightly in the heat of her mouth. Damien gripped the sheet in his fists, giving shallow rolls of his hips, denying his body's impulse to thrust hard and fast. "Don't stop." His breath sawed in and out of his chest, every muscle in his body going rigid. "You're going to make me come."

Chapter Fifteen

There was power in pleasure, and even though Tabitha had wanted him to dominate her, she'd still controlled the situation in her own way. She'd felt powerless for so long, had tried to control her out-of-control life until it felt like a wasted effort. Tonight, Damien gave her something back that she'd lost and she doubted he'd ever realize what that meant to her.

He showed so much restraint, his shallow thrusts not at all what she wanted. She needed more from him, she wanted him mindless. Frenzied. Taking her mouth until he shattered in the way that he'd shattered her. She wanted him to come with her lips wrapped around him. Wanted to taste him.

She worked her mouth over him, loving the satin glide of his erection, hard and smooth as polished steel against her tongue. Sucking, licking, using her teeth in the way that drove him crazy. His thighs held her tight as every muscle in his body went rigid. She took him as deeply as she could, sucked hard, and he shouted as the orgasm rocked him. Tabitha reveled in his salty sweet taste as jet after jet coated her tongue. With each jerk of his hips, his body relaxed and soon there was nothing but stillness and the sound of his labored breath.

They had both had their pleasure, explored one another's bodies. Tasted and indulged. But Tabitha wasn't even close to feeling sated, and she knew that Damien wasn't either.

His hands went to her arms and he urged her up, pulling her body along his as he guided her head to the crook of his shoulder. Fingers played idly with her hair, as though the act calmed him somehow. In the low light of the single lamp they'd left on, Tabitha looked up and studied the angle of his jaw, straight nose, the shadow of his cheekbones, committing each to memory. Quiet minutes passed and she drank him in.

"Why do you want to be a nurse?"

The question lacked the gruffness she'd grown accustomed to. Soft, curious, and a little sleepy. Tabitha smiled as she tucked her body closer to his. "People are at their weakest when they've experienced a trauma. Emotionally. Physically. Mentally. I want to do whatever I can to fix that. To help them."

"What about the excitement? The adrenaline that comes with an emergency situation?"

She found his curiosity endearing, and so honest. "Well, yeah. There's that, too. I'd be lying if I said I didn't like it. I chose trauma partially for that reason. But at the end of the day, I want to know that I made someone's life better. Or at least, know that I tried to."

Damien hugged her tight to him and kissed her forehead. "Is that why you're here now? Because you think that you can fix me?"

The question bit into her heart with sharp barbs. "Of course not." There was a duality to Damien that she didn't understand. She'd known dealers and petty criminals most of her life. Assholes who had about as much respect for a woman as they did the dirt on their boots. Damien wasn't one of those men. She couldn't reconcile the man he claimed to be with the man she knew he was. Did he fight the same battle of reconciliation? "I don't think you need fixing."

"You don't want to know why I'm living out of hotels, dealing on the weekends? You're not even a little curious as to what brought me here or how long I'm planning to stay?"

He could be a professional interrogator. Like those dudes who work for the CIA, getting you to spill your secrets before you even realized you'd done it. "If you want me to admit that I'm curious, I am. But your reasons are your own, and what I think or feel about it isn't going to change your mind about working for Joey."

He reached down to her chin and gently tilted her head up. His expression was gentle as his gaze delved straight into her soul. Tabitha's breath hitched as a silent moment passed while his fingers traced her jaw, over her cheekbone, the shell of her ear and her temple. "Can I change *your* mind?" The warm timbre of his voice cut through the silence. "Could I convince you not to work for him?"

"I don't work for him." Tabitha averted her gaze, ashamed.

"Then don't help him. Don't do a damned thing for him."

Tears stung at Tabitha's eyes, the need to trust Damien and confide in him overwhelming her. She'd been bearing the weight of this burden for so long there were days that she didn't think she could take another step. "I don't have a choice." Tabitha forced the words past the lump in her throat. "I have to help him."

"Look at me."

God, she didn't want to. Too afraid of what she'd see in the depth of his golden eyes. His arms came around her and he held her tight, the warmth of his body a soothing balm to Tabitha's now frayed nerves.

"I can protect you." Damien's words brooked no argument or doubt. "Whatever the reason you're mixed up in this, I'll help you out of it."

That was the problem, though, wasn't it? Tabitha didn't need protection. She'd spent most of her life getting Seth out of one scrape or another. It wouldn't be fair to transfer all of that onto Damien. "And who's going to protect you when Joey finds out you threw a monkey wrench into his operation?"

"You let me worry about that." So confident. It probably never occurred to Damien that he could ever lose.

Joey was scrawny, weak in comparison to Damien's sheer size and strength, but looks could be deceiving. What he lacked in physical power, he made up for in intelligence. "I practically raised my brother, even though we're only a couple of years apart." She couldn't bring herself to tell him outright that she'd made a deal with Joey to save Seth from prison time, but maybe she could steer the conversation in a direction that would keep him from pressing her on the issue.

"My dad was an alcoholic and a drug addict. My mom popped pills like they were going out of style. They were absentee parents for most of our lives. Partying, hustling, working the system, doing whatever they could for a couple of bucks and then spending it on booze or drugs rather than feeding their kids.

Seth and I fell through the cracks. Someone needed to be an adult, and so I stepped up. Every decision I make affects him because I've chosen to take care of him. Even my worst choices aren't made recklessly. Can you understand?"

Damien rolled them so that Tabitha was on her back; he was propped up on his side next to her. He stared down into her face, deep creases digging into his brow just above the bridge of his nose. Light as a gentle breeze, he stroked her bare skin, the rough pads of his fingers tracing a path down her throat, over her shoulder and down her arm. A shudder rippled over her skin as he skimmed her hip, worked his way up her ribs and around the outer swell of her breast.

"I understand that you're loyal." His fingers curled around the back of her neck, his grip possessive as his thumb brushed her jaw. "Fearless." His head dipped to her collarbone, where he kissed her. "Obviously stubborn." Tabitha's back came off the bed as his hand abandoned her throat and the flat of his palm passed down between her breasts, past her belly button. His fingers slid lower and she opened her legs to him, gasping as he teased her sex with featherlight strokes. "And that you love fiercely." One finger, and then another breached her opening and she moaned at the deep, delicious invasion. "But you're not alone. I need you to know that."

Her breath came in sharp pants as he pleasured her, as though he could buy her trust and loyalty with the ministrations of his skillful digits. For the record, it was sort of working. When he touched her this way, made her feel so good that it rivaled her best dreams, she wanted to tell him anything—everything—as long as he never stopped touching her.

"But I *don't* know that." Emotion choked the air from her lungs, the pain she felt a harsh contrast to the pleasure he gave her. "I don't know anything about you."

"Close your eyes." Tabitha's brow furrowed at his request. Damien didn't relent as his thumb circled her clit, slowly, gently, drawing a whimpering sigh from her chest. "Close them."

Under his spell and unable to deny him, she did as he asked. In the dark recesses of her mind, there was only this moment. The sensation of his fingers sliding across her slick flesh, the low rumble of his voice, and his breath hot in her ear.

Damien had become her entire universe.

He could lie here all night, and just watch her. With his mouth close to her ear, he held her close to him, one arm cradling her body, while the other slid through the soft, pink flesh of her gorgeous pussy. He'd never broken his cover before. Ever. He'd witnessed deplorable things, engaged in acts that tore at his conscience. Hell, he'd all but pistol-whipped those idiots who'd tried to hijack Joey's shipment the other night, an offense that would land any cop on administrative leave for a good, long while. And yet, Damien was given carte blanche. That sort of power and hubris would go to anyone's head.

And Damien wasn't above enjoying it.

No, he'd never broken character, never let that façade slip. But he wanted to break through the wall. Throw all of his hard work away. Now. For her.

"I enlisted right out of high school. Marines. Two tours in Afghanistan and two years in special forces."

He continued to pet her, slowly. He didn't want her to climax, only to feel enough physical pleasure to distract her mind from thinking too much about what he was saying to her. She let out a sigh that met his ears in a caress, and he continued, low. "I don't have any brothers. No sisters to look after. I never knew my dad, and my mom died when I was twenty-one. Stomach cancer. I didn't even get to say good-bye to her. She died while I was in that god-forsaken desert, and that's something I'll never be able to forgive myself for—not being there when she needed me."

Tabitha's eyes fluttered as though she fought to keep them closed. "Don't look at me. Keep your eyes shut."

He let a space of silence settle between them as he thrust his finger inside her tight channel, rocking his palm against her sex and coaxing tight, tiny whimpers from her throat. "I don't have a real home, I never stay anywhere for very long. I do what I have to do to get by and I won't apologize or make excuses for it." He was being as honest as he dared, giving her as much of a complete picture of who he was as he possibly could. She arched into his touch, her full lips parted, and he couldn't help but lean down to kiss her.

"Damien . . ."

His name left her lips on an exhale and he kissed her once again, reveling in the sweetness of her mouth. "I don't know if I'm a good man, but I do know that I'm not the sum of my mistakes and bad decisions." He caressed the outer edge of her labia, circled her clit with the pad of his finger before plunging back into her tight heat. "Let me be a better man for you. Let me in, Tabitha."

She cried out as her inner walls clenched around his fingers, gripping and releasing with each powerful wave of her orgasm. Her nails bit into his bicep as she rode it out, and Damien stared down at her, enraptured by the expression of bliss that crested over her features.

He put his mouth against her ear and murmured, "You're so beautiful." He couldn't say it enough to convey how truly lovely he found her. He'd done what he could to build some sort of trust between them, but now his words were nothing more than the flowery sentiments that guys whispered when they were hopelessly in love or some shit. "So soft and wet. I don't want you anywhere but in my bed. All day. Every day. Believe me when I say that I'll fucking *kill* any man who tries to hurt you or anyone you care about. I'm going to protect you whether you want me to or not."

He pulled away to gauge her reaction, and Tabitha's lids fluttered open to reveal the glistening blue of her eyes. A single tear trickled down her temple and Damien swiped it away with his thumb. Her hand found the back of his neck and she pulled him down for a kiss. Damien pulled her tight against him, crushing her soft, supple breasts into his chest as he slanted his mouth across hers. She returned his ardor with a fierceness that stalled his heart in his goddamned chest, stole his breath, and set him adrift in the haze of pleasure and need that he'd likened to the rush of heroin in his veins.

She kissed him until her body became limp in his arms. A precious, pliable thing that he cradled with care. Her breath left her and entered him on a sigh, as though his own lungs refused to function if she wasn't there to give him air.

"I don't want to go home tonight." Her voice was small, unsure, and it tore his composure to shreds.

"You don't have to," he said against her lips. "Stay. I told you, I don't want you anywhere but in my bed."

Tabitha nestled against him, and for the first time since he'd met her, Damien considered how fragile she truly was. And before this was all over, he vowed that Joey Cavello and anyone else who'd hurt her was going to pay for whatever it was they'd done to make her this way.

As light filtered in through a gap in the heavy blackout drapes, Damien woke to find his body cold and his arms empty. He shot up out of bed like the damned thing was on fire and checked the bathroom, and then the sitting area off the bedroom.

Tabitha was gone.

Panic gathered in Damien's chest, building in force like a tornado. He hadn't felt this sort of blind, senseless anxiety in a long damned time. Not since he'd trudged through the rocky desert mountains, his boots so heavy he didn't think he could walk another step. Shallow breaths were all he could manage as he reached for the door handle, only barely aware that he was naked and about to chase down the hall in pursuit of something that had already slipped through his grasp.

He'd scared her. What he'd considered to be a carefully orchestrated plan to earn her trust had done nothing more than send her running in the opposite direction. Damien rubbed hard at his sternum in an effort to banish the desperate ache that threatened to take him to his knees. Like the addicts who came to him for a fix, he felt himself slowly unraveling. Where was she? Who was she with? Was she okay? His limbs shook and his mouth went dry. His mindless need for her was almost more than he could bear.

The muffled sounds of Nirvana's "Heart-Shaped Box" played and Damien rushed back to the bedroom and rifled through his jeans, pulling the burner cell from one of the pockets. He checked the caller ID and damned near chucked the thing across the room when he realized that it wasn't Tabitha calling. *Motherfucker.* He swiped his finger across the screen and barked, "What?"

"Chill the fuck out, bro." Joey's voice in his ear was not going to *chill him the fuck out* anytime soon. The asshole was damned lucky he'd decided to call and not stop by for an impromptu visit. Otherwise, he'd be picking his sorry ass up off the floor.

"Late night. You caught me sleeping." Pretending to be even marginally pleasant was akin to eating glass. "'Sup?"

"You're off rotation tonight. I need you for something else. Tony will take over there. Meet me at Liquid at eight o'clock. You game?"

As if he could turn the son of a bitch down. "Sure. What about the suitcase?"

"The luggage stays. And leave a spare key card in the planter outside of the side exit so he doesn't have to hassle with the front desk."

Damien yanked his fingers through his hair, feeling the beginnings of one hell of a tension headache coming on. "I'll take care of it." He could at least be thankful that Tabitha had tonight off. "See ya at eight."

"Later."

Damien disconnected the call and tossed the

phone down on the bed just before his legs folded, sending his ass down to the mattress. He rested his elbows on his thighs, forehead in his palms and let out a forceful sigh. This investigation was going to be the death of him.

He grabbed the hotel phone from the nightstand and punched Ryan Gates's number into the keypad. The deputy answered on the third ring. "Gates."

"It's Damien."

There was a short pause before Ryan said, "Is everything okay?"

It was unusual for him to use his undercover name when checking in, let alone make contact on a weekend, especially since he should be deep in his cover as Joey Cavello's distributor for the next day and a half. Contact could be risky if someone caught him with a deputy marshal, but Damien needed to get some things straight with Gates and get him up to speed before he set out on whatever errand Cavello had laid out for him tonight.

"Can we meet around noon?"

"Sure." Ryan's tone showed his concern but he thankfully didn't press for information. "Where?"

"I want to avoid the downtown area." Just in case any of Cavello's buddies were out and about. "So anywhere else."

"I'll be at the Yard House in the Village at Meridian. Do you know where it is?"

Jesus, what was it with this Village? Did Idaho's population concentrate its attention on one trendy meeting place at a time? "No, but I can find it."

"See you there."

A shower would probably be a good idea. Make himself presentable and all that shit. But the prospect of washing Tabitha's scent from his body tied

Damien's stomach into knots. If he'd pushed her too far last night, the sweet floral perfume clinging to his skin might be all that was left of her.

The monster of mindless need raged at the back of his mind. He was worse than any addict, convincing himself that one fix was enough. It would never be enough. He'd go after her if he had to. Over and over again.

Dr. Meyers would have a field day with this one.

Chapter Sixteen

"I'm ruined. *Ruined!*"

"Oh, please. You're loving every minute of it. I'd pay good money for a man to ruin me right now."

Eh, Tabitha wasn't going to argue that point. Dave wished a man would ruin him at least once a week. He was such a tragically romantic soul. With a straw, she poked at the ice melting in her drink. It had definitely felt like a Bloody Mary type of day when she'd called Dave to meet her for brunch. But not even vodka could pull her mood out of the ditch it had curled up and died in.

"You know, when something's too good be true, it's usually because it *is*." Damien was everything she was attracted to in a man: big, rough around the edges, bulging with muscle, his skin decorated with glorious ink. He possessed a depth that she hadn't expected, a gentleness that blew her mind, and even though they'd yet to seal the deal, his skills in the bedroom far surpassed any other man she'd ever been with. He was too perfect for her. Too tailored for her every need. "It's like someone found my perfect-man wish list and crafted him in a lab. He's got a fatal flaw. I just don't know what it is yet." Well, that wasn't entirely true. He was a drug dealer. That was a pretty dark mark.

"Do you know what your problem is, Tabs?"

She rolled her eyes. "No, but I'm pretty sure you're going to tell me."

"You don't know how to be happy."

"What?" Please. She was totally happy. Smiley, cheery, rainbows and unicorns happy. "That's not true."

"Look." Dave took a long pull from the straw sticking out of his drink. "Life dealt you a shitty hand. You would have been better off an orphan." She cut him a look and he pursed his lips as though to say, *Well, it's true.* "And your brother, God love his fine, fine ass, is *trouble* and he's given you nothing but grief. You're so used to your life being shit that you don't expect anything better."

Tabitha took a deep breath and held it in her lungs. "Lila would tell me to suck it up and go find a guy who wears a tie to work."

"Sorry, but Lila's sort of a twat."

Tabitha laughed. "Seth's getting better. He's really turned his life around the past few months."

"And what happens the next time he gets in over his head?" Dave leveled his gaze on her, no longer playful. "What sort of deals are you going to make then?"

Her heart jumped up into her throat. "What do you mean?"

"Honey, I was born at night, but it wasn't last night. I know Joey's got you helping him with some lowdown shit."

"Dave." Tabitha leaned across the table, her heart

racing. "You can't say anything. If he found out that you—"

"Please, you know I'm not going to say anything. But *you* need to do something."

"I can't." The words lodged in her throat. "Joey said he'll go to the cops. If Seth gets another strike against him, he could go to federal prison this time."

"If Sandy finds out what's going on, it's you that's going to prison, not Seth. And would he step up to bail you out?"

She'd like to think that he would. Seth was misguided but he wasn't callous. "This guy that Seth hooked Joey up with, he only blows through town for a while. He uses people and then he drops them. It's his pattern. Joey won't have anything to sell for him after that. He won't have any use for either of us after that. If I can just wait it out, Joey won't have anything to sell and it'll be over."

"And the tattooed love god?"

Heat rose to Tabitha's cheeks. Even now the memory of the wicked things Damien had done to her the previous night heated her blood and caused her body to thrum with desire. "I don't know. He's not a bad guy, Dave. I know that sounds stupid, considering. It's like he's two different people or something. This guy that he expects everyone to believe he is and the guy that he really is under the act."

"But . . . ?"

Tabitha took a long drink of her Bloody Mary. "But what if I'm wrong? What if all there is is the bad guy, and I'm totally seeing what I want to see? Oh God," she moaned, throwing her head into the crook of her arm on the table. "Maybe I do need to find a guy who wears a tie to work."

"You just need to do what's right for you. And only you. Not Seth, not Joey, definitely not Lila, and not the tattooed love god, either."

"His name is Damien," she said.

"So. Sexy." Dave gave a sad shake of his head. "Don't feel bad about falling for him, Tabs. He's the total package."

She didn't feel guilty about it, and that was the problem. That non-guilt was enough to make her sneak out on him this morning. How could she possibly live with herself knowing what he did— selling drugs that did nothing but destroy lives and families—overlooking it all just because she needed him like she needed food and water. Like she needed air.

"He totally is." She shivered at the memory of his whispered words in her ear, so honest and heartfelt as his fingers did wonderful things to her body. It had been the most intimate encounter of her entire life. With his gentle touch and even gentler words, Damien had managed to shake her to her core.

"He could be married," she said with a wry smile. "So I guess it could be worse."

"I'll drink to that," Dave replied, bringing his glass up to hers.

Part of what made Damien good at his job was his ability to keep a level head under pressure. And this assignment was a low-stress gig in comparison to some of his past undercover assignments. But as he sat in the passenger seat of Joey's jacked-up truck, barreling down the freeway toward God knew where,

Damien had never been so damned on edge. The complete *opposite* of level.

Fuck.

"You sure Tony has his shit together enough to manage tonight's sales?" It wasn't that Damien gave a single shit if Tony was a competent employee or not. The asshole's run-in with Tabitha two weeks ago was what had him itching to bail out of the car and beat feet back to the hotel.

"Two weeks on the fucking job and you're acting like middle management or some shit." Joey's amused laughter grated on Damien's already raw nerves. "Tony's got it. I'm not half as worried about him as I am about putting these fuckers in their place tonight."

This wasn't the first time Damien had found himself in the middle of a turf war. What Joey didn't realize was that once Lightfoot pulled distribution out of Idaho, it wouldn't matter who sold on his turf. Joey would no longer have a product to push. Not to mention the fact his ass would be in jail.

After the ass-whupping Damien had delivered to Joey's rivals a couple of weeks ago, tension had been high between Joey and Milo Grankin, the distributor from the neighboring city. Damien didn't agree with Joey's tactics tonight, but neither did he have a say, and so he had no choice but to go along as the token muscle.

The drive to Nampa was just shy of a half hour. A tense, quiet half hour where Damien spent the time talking himself out of an act of violence against the guy sitting next to him. As soon as he got to the bottom of whatever it was Joey had on Tabitha's brother that he held over her head, there'd be hell to pay. And the bastard had better hope that Boise PD got their hands on him before Damien did.

"We're here."

Joey pulled up to a run-down building on the outskirts of the city. Several cars were parked outside: muscle cars, the souped-up Nissan from the other night, and a couple of pickups with lift kits like Joey's. Damien took a deep breath and tried to slow his pulse rate as his heart pumped blood through his system at about two hundred beats a minute. There was no way this was going to end any other way but badly. *Goddamn it.*

"I thought you said there would only be a couple of guys here." From the looks of the parking lot, they were outnumbered.

"Fucking Mike," Joey spat. "You can't trust anyone to get good intel anymore. Doesn't matter." His voice quavered with the words. "They don't know we're comin'. We've got the jump on them. We're going to show them that I'm not going to suffer their bullshit anymore."

He might have thought they had the element of surprise working for them, but Joey would change his tune pretty damned fast when he had ten semiautos pointed at his head. Damien checked the clip of the unregistered forty Joey handed him, and slid it home. He pulled back the slide and said a silent prayer that the power play about to go down would end peacefully without a single shot fired. *Yeah, right.* When the egos of drug dealers and gangbangers were involved, this sort of shit never ended well. Maybe what Damien should have been praying for was his own goddamned safety.

"Let's show these fuckers what's up."

Big words from Cavello. His ego and inability to plan further proved that he was the perfect middle-man for Lightfoot. Dude was fucking *dim*. Damien hung back and watched as the dipshit kicked open the door to the rival distributor's home base. He could dial 9-1-1 and end this now, but an arrest for either of them would slow down a timetable that they couldn't afford to disrupt. Kinks like these made Damien's teeth itch. *Damn it*. He didn't have time for this shit.

At the sound of angry voices, Damien charged in behind Joey, gun drawn and ready to defend himself if need be. The number of cars parked outside was misleading, thank God. Inside only three guys sat around a battered round table, cards and poker chips spread out on the surface, the smell of weed thick in the air.

"Cavello, you piece of shit!" Damien recognized one of the guys from a couple of weeks ago. The bruise around his eye was beginning to yellow, and when his gaze met Damien's the banger's dark eyes narrowed and a sneer stretched his lips. He stabbed a finger at Damien and said, "You're fucking dead, asshole."

The sound of the door swinging open behind them caught Damien's attention and he gave a quarter turn to discover that the rest of Grankin's crew had entered behind them. *Damn it*. He'd counted his blessings a little too soon. He raised his gun, aimed it at the son of a bitch's forehead. Adrenaline dumped into Damien's system and he locked his nerves down tight. He needed to keep his shit together if he was going to get out of this alive.

"You should have come with more people, Cavello." A tall, bulky, grimy-looking fucker stepped up to Joey, and Damien assumed this was Milo Grankin. He looked the part and carried the confidence of someone who'd cracked a few skulls to gain his position amongst his peers. "'Cuz the only way either one of you sons of bitches is going to leave this building is in a fucking body bag."

Joey's eyes met Damien's and he gnashed his teeth as he recognized the flash of panic. Joey was about to fuck up—big-time—and Damien was going to be the one caught in the crossfire. Without a word, Joey swung his arm around and pulled the trigger, winging one of the guys at the poker table. Chaos spread like wildfire, shots ringing out in a cacophony around them.

Damien hit the deck just in time to see Joey make a break for it, sprinting toward the door left open by Grankin and his buddies. Fucker. Damien fired off a couple of wild shots and rolled, propelling himself upward as he sprinted after Joey, convinced that if he didn't get his ass in gear, the little shit was bound to leave him there to die.

"Shoot that asshole!"

Damien stumbled as white hot pain ripped through his upper thigh. He fought through the pain, letting the adrenaline in his system take over. Turning back, he fired blindly once, twice, and again, squeezing off shots in quick succession in order to buy him enough time to get to Joey's truck.

The engine roared to life just as the passenger door flew open. Joey leaned across the seat and shouted, "Hurry the fuck up!"

Yeah, like that, and not the guys shooting at him, was going to get Damien's ass moving. In the distance, the sound of sirens grew louder and the panicked look in Joey's eyes was what really got Damien moving. He limped the last few feet, throwing the bulk of his torso up into the seat. Joey put his foot to the pedal, gravel spraying out from beneath the tires as he took off with Damien's legs still dangling out of the open door. He reached over and hauled Damien up by the neck of his T-shirt. Damien's leg throbbed, a bone-deep spasm shooting up the entire right side of his body. He managed to climb into the seat and shut the truck door moments before passing a Nampa PD cruiser going full-speed in the opposite direction, lights flashing and siren howling.

"Jesus fucking Christ."

"Are you hit?" Damien managed between pants of breath.

"Nah." Joey jerked the wheel to the right and Damien's head smacked on the window before he could right himself.

"Fuck, man!" The last thing he needed was a concussion on top of a gunshot wound. "Watch what you're doing!"

"I've gotta get us out of here."

Damien had a feeling that Joey had never been involved in a shooting before. The dude was straight up losing his cool. "Calm down." If he had to focus on managing Joey, at least he'd be too preoccupied to worry about his damned leg. "Slow down. If you look like you're running from something, the cops are going to stop us. Don't go too slow, but don't speed. Yield for the cruisers but don't stop. And for fuck's sake, turn on your headlights!"

"Oh, right. Shit." Joey flipped on his lights as he let up on the gas, traveling the darkening city streets at a respectable but not suspicious speed. He glanced down at Damien's leg, his eyes wide. "Fuck, man! Are you okay?"

They'd missed his femoral artery, so at least he didn't have to worry about bleeding out in the next two minutes. So he guessed he could rack that up in the plus column. "I'll live." That didn't mean he wouldn't bleed to death slowly if he didn't get the wound closed up soon. "Just get me back to my car."

Going to the hospital was pretty much out of the question. When someone came in with a gunshot wound, the police were automatically notified. But if he could shake Joey long enough to get ahold of Gates, they could get him to the hospital and have his leg taken care of discreetly. Damien let his head loll back on the headrest. The adrenaline rush was starting to wear off, and his thigh pulsed in an agonizing rhythm in time with the beat of his heart.

Joey Cavello had almost gotten his ass killed tonight and the only thought that had run through Damien's head was the fact that he might not ever see Tabitha again.

Chapter Seventeen

Tabitha checked her reflection in the rearview mirror one last time before getting out of her car. Sort of pointless in the low light of the parking lot's floodlights, but whatever. Her stomach was tied into so many knots, she doubted they would ever fully untangle, and her heart fluttered in her chest with the speed of a hummingbird's wings. She hadn't called to see if it was okay to come over. Maybe she should have. *Crap.*

It was only fifteen minutes later than when she'd come to the hotel last night. Surely, she'd given Damien enough time to have everything wrapped up for the night. As she pulled the master key card from her back pocket, Tabitha took stock of her outfit. Why did it matter at this point that she dressed to impress? Last night she'd shown up in her pj's. Ugh. She was *so* head over heels smitten with him it was pathetic.

She smoothed her palms over the denim of her skinny jeans, tucked into the Doc Martens combat boots—the most expensive pair of shoes she owned and her prized possession—with the black satin laces. The baggy black tank beneath her leather jacket with "hope" scrawled across the front in large white letters might not have been the best choice. Did the word broadcast some subliminal message? Make her look too desperate? God, what had she been *thinking*? Of course it made her look desperate! She might as well show up at his door, with *I'm begging you to fuck me* scrawled across her forehead in Sharpie.

Feet frozen in midstep, Tabitha turned on her heel and hoofed it back toward her car. She stopped again. Turned. Turned again. And once more back toward the hotel. *Oh, for fuck's sake!* She was making herself dizzy. He'd bent her over the bed and ordered her to bare her ass to him and they'd barely known each other. Called her last night and demanded that she present herself, front and center, within ten minutes' time. What did it matter what was printed on her shirt? If tonight went like any of their previous encounters, she doubted he'd take the time to even notice.

This time, the falter in her step had nothing to do with trepidation. Tabitha picked up her pace, jogging across the parking lot in her haste to get to Damien. The thought of his massive hands on her, cupping her breasts, his fingers kneading the globes of her ass . . . A delicious heat licked up her spine as she inserted her key card into the hotel's back entrance. Sneaky, sure. But she didn't want the night auditor—or anyone else—to see her there tonight. Dave knew about Damien and that was enough. None of her other coworkers needed to know what was going on between them.

Especially Sandy. If word got back that Tabitha was violating company policy by "fraternizing" with a guest, well, she doubted she'd get a high-five from her manager.

Her stomach floated in her abdomen as though suspended in space as the elevator took her to the fifth floor. Anticipation curved her lips in a secretive smile as she imagined what Damien's reaction to seeing her might be. Would he order her inside, like he had last night? Direct her in that commanding tone that made her shiver? She'd come prepared to play, the package of condoms tucked into her pocket. Presumptuous? You betcha. But she didn't care. Her want of Damien superseded good sense and caution.

Her knuckles made contact with the door, a tentative knock.

Breath stalled in her chest, she waited. When the door swung open she flashed an expectant smile, only to have it melt in an instant.

"Shit. Tonight must be my lucky night."

Tabitha's heart pounded for an entirely different reason as she took in the leer that stretched across Tony's face. What was he doing here? Where was Damien? Shit. Shit, shit, *shit*! She took a quick step backward, desperate to put as much distance between them as possible, when Tony pulled a handgun from the waistband of his jeans, letting his arm hang loosely at his side.

"Don't run off yet, girl," he said with a noticeable slur. "I think you oughta come in."

Nothing about Tony's words or demeanor suggested that Tabitha should turn him down. His pupils were pinpricks in his dull gray eyes, and not even close to tracking. She wondered what Joey would think if he knew that one of his guys was sampling the product he was supposed to be selling. One thing Tabitha had learned hanging out with dirtbags like

Tony: when someone was this high, it was best to proceed with a shitload of caution. The canister of pepper spray Damien had given her was tucked into her glove box—a lot of good it was doing her there!—and she didn't feel like testing Tony's mettle by turning him down.

He tapped the barrel of the 9mm on his thigh impatiently, agitation showing in his features.

"Okay, Tony." Tabitha felt as though the hallway was closing in on her, forcing her toward the open doorway. "I'll come in. But maybe you should put that away first," she said, indicating the gun.

Tony snorted and brought the gun up as though inspecting it. "Don't tell me what to do. You're not such a smart-mouthed bitch when I have this, are you?"

There wasn't enough oxygen in the world to fill Tabitha's lungs as she stepped into the suite. The door closed behind her with a finality that might as well have been the lid on her own coffin slamming down.

From the looks of the room, Tony had partied like a rock star tonight. The small dinette table in the far corner of the sitting area was strewn with pot, pills, and powder. Several discarded beer bottles lay strewn on the floor, and a half-empty fifth of tequila sat on the dresser in the bedroom area. It was a wonder he was still standing after what he'd put into his body. It certainly wouldn't do anything to make him less volatile. Tabitha made sure to stay close to the door, ready to bolt the first chance she got. Tony kept an eagle eye on her though, even as he staggered to the dresser where he snagged the bottle of tequila.

"Sit down and have a drink."

"I think I'll stand."

Tony brought the gun up and aimed it at Tabitha's face. "I said to sit your ass down."

Her pulse quickened, the adrenaline coursing so quickly through her veins that she became light-headed and her vision blurred. "Sure." Her voice quavered on the word as she swallowed down her nerves. "We're fine, right, Tony? No need to get upset."

He all but collapsed into a chair at the dinette, kicking out the one across from him in invitation. Tabitha balled her hands into fists, steeled herself against the tremor that rattled from her hair follicles to the tips of her toes. She never should have come here.

With a pop, Tony pulled the cork from the bottle of Patrón and slid it across the table. "Drink."

"No cup?" Nervous laughter fluttered from her throat as she lowered herself into the chair beside Tony. He slung one arm over the back of the chair, one leg jutting out in front of him. So gangster. *Please.*

"What, you don't wanna share a bottle that my mouth's been on?" Tony brandished the 9mm for emphasis, his finger too close to the trigger for Tabitha's comfort. "Too dirty for you, princess?"

"No." Yes. *God, yes.* She'd rather lick a Dumpster than put her mouth near anything Tony had touched. She indicated the wide, flat rim of the bottle. "It's just a little awkward to drink from, don't you think?"

"How 'bout I pour it down my body and you suck it off my cock. That any less awkward for you?"

Tabitha snatched up the bottle and brought it to her lips. On her list of preferred libations, tequila ranked just below toilet water. She gagged as the liquor hit the back of her throat, the pungent odor only adding to her disgust. Tony reached across the table and tipped the bottle, sending rivulets pouring down either side of Tabitha's mouth and dribbling from her chin. Her eyes watered as she began to choke and splutter, only adding to the mess that Tony was making. Hands wrapped firmly around the neck of the bottle, she jerked it down, slamming it onto the table with a splash.

"If I didn't know any better, I'd assume you think you're too good to sit and have a drink with me." Tony pushed himself out of his chair, leaned over the table with a rolled-up bill, and snorted a line of the white powder from the table. He sniffed, his eyes watering before he leaned over and inhaled a second line, his legs barely able to support his weight. Another loud sniff rent the silence and he wiped at his nose as he leaned in close. "But since you seemed to be okay fucking Joey, I know that's not the case. Right?"

"Tony—"

"You're giving it up to that new guy, too, aren't you? Damien." Tony's rueful tone sent a ripple of fear over Tabitha's skin. "Are you fucking him, Tabs?"

Armed or not, she wasn't going to stay here and play the victim. He was trying to rattle her. Intimidate her. She shot up from the chair and spun on a heel, put as much forward momentum as she could into running, when Tony reached out and snagged her wrist. With enough force to jar her neck, he whipped her around and pulled her tight against his chest. Before she could push away, he brought the barrel of the gun to her temple, the metal digging painfully into her skin.

"You're not going anywhere," he snarled in her ear. "It's time for Damien to share."

* * *

Damien paused next to the open door of his Shelby and pushed against it with enough force to take the damned thing right off the hinges. His leg was screaming at him, pain radiating from his thigh clear up into his hip. After Joey had dropped him off in the hotel parking lot like a sack of grain on the side of the road, his first instinct had been to call Gates or John Rader over at Boise PD and head for the hospital. But those plans fell by the wayside the second he noticed Tabitha's 4Runner parked a few spaces down. *Fuck.* Tony was here tonight and she'd already had one close call with the bastard. The bullet wound in his leg could wait until he knew that she was okay.

Seeing her car in the hotel parking lot was enough to throw him into a full-blown panic. But when she didn't answer her phone, his anxiety skyrocketed. She didn't work Saturday nights, which meant she must be there to see him. How fucking long had she been there? And more importantly, who was Damien going to have to kill if anything had happened to her?

His thigh muscle twitched, his entire leg growing stiffer by the second. "Mother*fucker.*" Damien ground his teeth to the point he was pretty sure there wasn't any enamel left, swallowing down the shout of pain that lodged in his throat. With a sound that echoed throughout the parking lot, he slammed the Shelby's door and headed for the side entrance of the hotel. Blood pooled in his shoe, making a sickening squishing sound with every step, and his jeans adhered to his leg and were stained crimson. Thank God it was past midnight and his chances of running into anyone would be slim. He jerked open the side entrance door and beelined it for the elevator. With each violent punch of his fist on the call button, Damien uttered a curse under his breath, his stomach knotting up tighter with each contact. The fucking stairs would have been faster, though at this point he was having a hard enough time just putting one foot in front of the other. Stairs would have hurt like a bitch.

By the time the elevator deposited him on the fifth floor, Damien was worked into a lather. The pain in his leg ebbed from the renewed burst of endorphins and he picked up his pace to a limping jog as he pulled the forty caliber Joey had given him from his waistband and chambered a round. If that slimy bastard laid even a finger on her, he was going to—

The sound of a scuffle sounded from behind the closed door, and Tabitha's muffled scream caused Damien's heart to jump up into his throat. He stabbed his extra key card into the lock and threw open the door, rushing into the room with a red haze of fury clouding his vision. Past the sitting area, Damien found Tabitha sprawled out on the bed, Tony on top of her as she struggled against him. The bastard had one hand over her mouth, the other between them, fumbling with the button on her pants.

A fierce growl erupted from Damien's throat as he grabbed Tony by the collar of his shirt at the scruff of his neck and hauled him off of Tabitha for the second time in two weeks. "I told you that if you so much as looked at her again, I would end you." He gave the other man a rough shake and Tony let out a pained yelp. The forty fell from Damien's grip and his fingers curled into a tight fist that shook from the anger built up in his system. With a shove, he put Tony at arm's length before pulling back his fist and letting it fly. It connected with the other man's face in a resounding *pop* that echoed off the walls and caused blood to pour from Tony's nose.

"I fucking warned you," Damien snarled as he hit Tony again, this time splitting his lip. His fist connected with Tony's face over and over, the force behind his blows increasing with each word. "You don't touch her." *Slam.* "You don't look at her." *Slam.* "You don't even think about her." *Slam.*

Tony whimpered, his hands held weakly in front of his face as though he could shield himself from the onslaught of Damien's fists. Something tugged at his elbow and he shook it off. Pulled back his arm to throw another punch, and met with resistance yet again. He twisted at the waist, ready to lay into whoever was trying to stop him, but froze as his eyes met Tabitha's, the blue depths glistening with unshed tears, panic, and worry.

"Damien, stop!"

The mindless violence that possessed him evaporated under her gentle words. He released his grip on Tony and let him collapse to the floor without a second thought. Damien's breath punched in and out of his chest, deep draughts that made him ache on the exhale. His body vibrated with unspent adrenaline, and he swayed on his feet. Probably the blood loss. Tabitha steadied him, propping her body under his arm to keep him upright. "Jesus Christ, Damien. You're covered in blood!" Her voice climbed to a panicked pitch as she ran a hand over his chest, his back, as though checking for wounds. "Where are you hurt?"

"Thigh." The word pushed past his lips in a pained bark. "Flesh wound. Take his gun and let's get out of here."

Her hands shook as she eased away from him and

Damien retrieved his own weapon while Tabitha grabbed Tony's 9mm from the bed. He held out his palm and she handed it over. Tucking it into his waistband along with the forty, he let her support him, the pain radiating from his leg with white-hot heat.

"Oh my God, Damien. Can you even walk?" Tony lay on the floor moaning and for all Damien cared, he could stay there and rot. Tabitha was worried if he was okay? Jesus, he was so shaken up, so fucking scared that asshole had hurt her, he could barely think straight.

"I'm okay."

"We've got to get you to a hospital."

"No." She paused at his emphatic tone, brow puckered with concern. Until a few minutes ago, he'd been prepared to call Gates and have him take him to the hospital so that the Marshals Service could keep his care off the books and under the radar. Drug dealers didn't go to the ER, especially when the local police were out looking for suspects in a reported shooting. *Fucking Joey.* What an idiot. His trigger-happy bullshit had almost gotten them both killed tonight.

"What do you mean, no?" Tabitha kept her voice down to a fierce whisper as they headed for the elevator. With every step, Damien's boot squished and from the corner of his eye he caught her cringe in time with the sound.

"No hospitals. Just get me somewhere that I can clean up and slap a bandage on it and I'll be good."

"What happened?"

The elevator doors slid open and they stepped inside. "Someone who likes Joey even less than you do shot me."

"Oh my God!" Her voice boomed in the enclosed space of the elevator. "What if the bullet is still in your leg? You might need surgery. Damien, you can't—"

"The bullet went through my leg. And I don't think there's any muscle damage, just the meaty part of my thigh." The elevator doors slid open and she helped him out and into the hallway.

Tabitha scoffed and he quirked a brow. She held open the door and Damien stepped out into the chill night air, taking a deep breath and allowing it to clear his head. "Sorry, but there isn't an inch of soft or meaty anything on your body."

His dick stirred in his jeans at the compliment. Apparently it would take more than a bullet wound to calm his libido. Shot and bleeding, all he could think about was Tabitha's warm skin and soft cries. Her lips. The curve of her ass. "How full is the hotel tonight? Would anyone have heard the commotion in the room?"

"We're pretty empty tonight," Tabitha said. "I made sure to book most of our rooms away from this floor. I'm sure no one heard."

"Good." The last thing he needed tonight was another fire to put out. "Ouch. *Fuck.*" A spasm of pain shot up his thigh, interrupting the course of his erotic thoughts.

"What? What is it?"

Tabitha's concern tugged at his chest. "Just hurts. No big deal."

Her derisive snort told him exactly what she thought of his explanation. "If you won't let me take you to the ER, you're at least going to let me look at your leg."

He cast her a sidelong glance and pointed to his car. He didn't want to give Tony a reason to vandalize it when the asshole came to. And if he touched Tabitha's car, he'd have more than a broken nose to worry about. "You have a secret exam room somewhere that I don't know about?"

"Keys." At her bossy tone, he dug in his pocket and handed over his car keys. "I'm taking you to my apartment, smart-ass. And you'd better be a good patient or I swear I will kick your ass."

She was taking him back to her place? His libido perked up at the thought of being alone with her away from prying eyes and ears. He groaned as Tabitha helped him into the passenger seat. Talk about pain. He needed to get good and drunk before he felt any better. "Honey, I'll be the best patient you've ever had."

"Ha. Ha." Tabitha climbed in and adjusted the driver's seat to get her closer to the pedals. "You'd better be."

Oh, he would be. He was as good as a slave to her will.

Chapter Eighteen

If there was ever any doubt that Tabitha had gotten in way over her head with Damien, there wasn't anymore. The only people who refused to go to the hospital after they'd been shot were gangsters, fugitives, and murderers. She already knew that Damien was something of a gangster. As for the other two, the more time she spent with him, the more she wondered if he was shielding her from even shadier parts of his past.

Had she reached the point of no return?

They took the stairs to her second-story apartment at a one-step-per-second pace. Damien was careful not to put too much of his weight on her shoulder. Every time he brought his right leg up to take another step, a growl that would have sent a wolf running scared vibrated in his chest.

"Just a few more steps." Tabitha wobbled as she steadied him. "Do you need to take a break?"

"No. Just get me up these stairs. I'll be fine once I can sit down."

The determination in his voice was admirable, all things considered. Sweat beaded his brow and his jaw squared from how tightly it clenched. The last five stairs were the toughest, and by the time they reached the landing, Damien was panting through the pain.

"Okay, we're here." Tabitha unlocked the door and poked her head into the apartment, a sigh of relief escaping her chest. Thank God Seth wasn't home. She wasn't interested in explaining any of this to him. Not yet, anyway.

Once inside the door, Damien paused beside her. While he caught his breath, Tabitha eyeballed the couch. No way was that going to work. Seth's bedroom was off-limits as well. That left only one option. "Come on, we're going to my bedroom."

Damien didn't argue, simply let her lead him past the living room down the short hallway to her room. Would it be rude to ask him to wait until she could lay a towel down? Tabitha eyed her light-blue comforter and then Damien's bloody leg. "Hang on. I'll be right back."

She grabbed a large bath towel from the bathroom and spread it out on top of the bed. Damien collapsed on the mattress, swinging his left leg up, and Tabitha grasped his right calf, easing him the rest of the way on the bed. "I'm probably going to have to cut your jeans away. I don't think I'll be able to get them off, otherwise."

Damien's eyes met hers and Tabitha had to have mistaken the heat that burned in the golden-brown depths. It was pain she saw there and not desire. Right? "It's not like I'll be wearing them again." The rough timbre of his voice sent a wave of chills dancing across Tabitha's skin. "Break out the scissors."

She was going to need a hell of a lot more than scissors to fix him up. And until she assessed the damage, she wouldn't even know if she could. "Don't move." He cocked a brow, as if to say *Where do you think I'll go?* Tabitha pursed her lips. "You know what I mean. Just try to relax. I'll be right back."

She left the room and shuffled down the hallway, the *snick, snick* of her boots gliding on the carpet the only sound. She wandered to her living room in a sort of trance, all of the emotions she'd put on hold in the crisis of Damien's arrival at the hotel finally rising to the surface. Her knees buckled and her ass bounced down on the couch cushion. The first tear spilled, searing a path down her cheek. Another one followed. And another, until she could do nothing to stem the steady flow.

Jesus. If he hadn't shown up, Tony would have raped her. He could have beaten her. Forced her to drink and snort whatever he wanted her to. Used her for God knew how long. He might have killed her. "*Fuck.*" The expletive left her lips in an emphatic burst. "*Fuck!*"

"Tabitha?" Damien called from the bedroom, his tone no less commanding despite his injured state. "Are you okay?"

She quickly swiped the tears from her cheeks and took several deep breaths. "I'm fine." Her voice was thick with emotion and she cleared her throat. "Just grabbing a few things. I'll be there in a minute."

On shaky legs, she abandoned the couch and centered her focus on taking care of Damien. There'd be plenty of time to break down later. Right now, she needed to get to work. She filled a bowl with warm water from the tap and grabbed several washcloths and snagged the kitchen shears from the butcher block on the counter. Not even a drop of rubbing alcohol in sight, she had no choice but to opt for the bottle of cheap vodka Seth had stored in the cupboard. When she found a box of gauze in the bathroom, Tabitha felt like pumping her fist in the air. No surgical tape, damn it. But she did have a roll of duct tape. It would have to do. She grabbed her razor from the shower and took her haul back into the bedroom, depositing everything on the bedside table.

"Damien?" Her heart skittered in her chest at his still form, eyes closed, chest barely rising with his breath. She laid tentative fingers on his throat, feeling for a pulse.

His hand came up and encircled her wrist. "Worried?"

Tabitha let out a gust of breath and tried to pull away, but Damien held fast to her wrist. His lids opened and his gaze burned through her, quickening her pulse for an entirely different reason. "If you weren't already hurt, I'd totally smack you right now." She tried for a playful tone but failed miserably. "How are you feeling?"

"I'm good." He patted the bed beside him. "Why don't you lie down and I'll show you just how good."

This time she did smack him. Just a gentle swat to his shoulder. Heat rose to her cheeks at the innuendo. "You've obviously lost too much blood and are delirious."

He flashed a wicked grin that showcased his dimples. "I'm right as rain. Just give me a chance to prove it to you."

Tabitha rolled her eyes. "Has anyone ever told you that you have a one-track mind?"

His gaze pinned her in place when he said, "Only when it comes to you."

As she tried to peel her eyes from his, Tabitha fumbled for the scissors. A deep breath filled her lungs and she let it out slowly. "Playtime's over. I don't have any painkillers. Nothing stronger than ibuprofen." She set the bottle of vodka beside him. "Feel free to drink away, but leave me some to sterilize the needle and your wounds, okay?"

"I don't need it."

"Oh, so you're a tough guy?"

"Depends." Damien's eyes raked her from head to toe. "Do you like tough guys?"

Oh hell. Tabitha's blood ignited like a flame to gasoline. Seriously, who flirted while bleeding out from a gunshot wound? He was absolutely a tough guy, and though she'd never admit it out loud, she really liked tough guys. Especially this one. "I'm, uh"—she cleared her throat—"going to cut your pants now. I'll try to be careful."

Tabitha grabbed the shears and set them on the bed. She removed both of Damien's shoes, careful not to jar his right leg, and peeled off his socks. "Just want to make sure you're comfortable," she said at his questioning gaze. "And we needed to get this bloody sock and shoe off."

A burst of nervous energy dumped into her bloodstream, but Tabitha was careful to keep her face impassive. If the soaked sock and his shoe were any indicator, Damien had lost a lot of blood. From the corner of her eye, she caught him staring at her, his expression pinched. "Did I hurt you?"

"Taking off my shoes?" he asked with a lazy laugh. "No."

Damien's lids drooped as she began to cut up his pant leg, careful to avoid the area on his upper thigh where the bullet had entered. She ran into resistance when the scissors met the additional fabric of his boxer briefs, and she separated them from the denim, cutting completely through the waist until the jeans parted away from his skin in two halves. "Sorry, but the underwear has to go, too."

"Mmmm." He blinked slowly. "Say that again."

The man was incorrigible. He'd flirt her into distraction if he had it his way, but his wounds needed to be closed before he lost any more blood. Tabitha made quick work of the briefs, spreading the halves apart, and inhaled a sharp breath.

A large hole oozed blood from his upper thigh, the wound raw and angry. She angled him onto his side to find the exit point and let out a relieved sigh. Damien was right. The bullet had gone through. "Is there anything I can do to convince you to go to the hospital?" He'd be so much better off if he'd just let a doctor clean and stitch him up.

"Nope. Just slap a bandage on me and we'll call it good."

"No can do. I'm going to have to stitch you up."

Yeah, he'd figured. Tonight wouldn't be the first—and probably not the last—time he'd been sewn up in a pinch, and if the wound had been worse, Damien probably would've taken Tabitha up on her offer to get him to the ER. As it was, he was damned lucky the shot had missed his femoral artery. Otherwise, he'd be kissing his ass good-bye.

"Do it naked." He was beginning to feel a little light-headed and his mouth formed words without his brain's permission.

"Damien." Her chiding tone only served to turn him on. "This is serious."

"I'm dead serious." His arm felt like it weighed a

metric ton as he reached out for her. "I want to see your body. Now. It'll distract me from the pain."

"You promised to be a good patient."

"Baby, I'll be the best you ever had."

Tabitha crossed the room and grabbed a rag to soak it in the bowl of water before wringing it out. "I was right. You're delirious." She came back to the side of the bed, her expression pinched and full of concern. Goddamn, he wanted to kiss her. "This is probably going to hurt, so prepare yourself."

Nothing hurt right now. He was too overwhelmed by Tabitha's presence to feel anything but awe. Despite everything that had happened tonight, she'd kept her cool. Cold steel under pressure.

"Did he hurt you?"

Tabitha paused, her gorgeous blue eyes glistening with emotion. She tucked a stray strand of short, blond hair behind her ear. Her voice was low in the quiet room. "No. You didn't give him a chance to. Now, hold still."

The muscles in his thigh tensed, a painful spasm traveling the entire right side of his body. His jaw locked down tight, aching from the effort it took not to shout. Especially when she concentrated her effort on the wound itself. "What's the razor for?" Damien asked as he panted through the pain. Anything to keep him focused and alert.

"I'm going to shave the hair away from the wound. I don't want anything in the way when I stitch you up, and it's more sanitary that way."

"I have to say, a woman's never shaved my legs before. Kinky. Ah, fuck!" He pressed his head back on the pillow and took a few deep breaths.

"I'm sorry. I just need to make sure the wound is clean. Believe me, this is going to be a cakewalk compared to what's next. You know, it's not too late to go to the hospital." Her gaze met his. Stern. "They've got all sorts of wonderful things there. Sterile instruments, trained professionals, painkillers . . . you won't feel a thing."

"Stop trying to sweet-talk me," Damien admonished. "Get back to work."

Tabitha gave him a half smile, half grimace that twisted his heart like a pretzel. "Just remember, you asked for it."

No one had ever treated Damien with such care. Tabitha's touch was gentle, satin gliding over his skin as she continued to clean the wound. He knew it was going to get a hell of a lot worse—hurt like a motherfucker worse—but he'd take it all and then some for her.

"Why did you go to the hotel tonight?" If he kept talking, focused on the sound of her voice, it would offer the distraction he needed. She kept her attention on the task at hand, the scrape of the razor against his skin the only sound in the room.

"Damien—"

He cut her off before she could chide him for not taking the situation seriously, or whatever she was about to lay into him for. "Just humor me. Talk to me, let me talk to you. Distract me. You're shaving my leg, for shit's sake. You *owe* me."

She sighed, but humor sparkled in her eyes. "I went there to see you."

Damien smiled wide as Tabitha cleaned off the razor on the wet rag and set it aside before she grabbed the bottle of vodka from beside him. "I'm less cranky about being shot than I am about missing that opportunity to be with you. I guess the night ended on a high note, though. I'm in your bed."

Tabitha's lips curved into a sweet smile. She pulled her bottom lip between her teeth and cast a sidelong glance his way before pouring the vodka on the wound. Damien's back bowed off the bed, his thigh on fucking fire as the alcohol seared through the hole in his leg. He gnashed his teeth but couldn't do a damned thing to silence the pained groan that tore from his throat.

"The bleeding has slowed, but we need to get this closed up. Can I keep going, or do you need a breather?"

"Keep going."

He watched as she poured a small amount of vodka into a cup. She dropped in the needle and a length of thread and swirled it all around, sterilizing it all. "A curved surgical needle would be ideal, but since I don't have a bag of them lying around, this is going to have to do. It's going to be tough to stitch you up with a straight sewing needle."

"Give it to me."

She fished the needle from the cup and handed it to him. It was long and thick enough that he could bend it without breaking it, and fashioned it into something crude but resembling a rounded curve. "Here."

She dropped the needle back into the cup of vodka and swirled it around for a couple of seconds before fishing it out again. "This is definitely going to hurt. Are you sure you don't want—"

"Do it."

Tabitha threaded the needle, her hands steady and sure. "What happened tonight?"

"Nothing you need to worry about." Tabitha was already in too deep. Damien didn't want to further complicate the situation by giving her any insight into tonight's cluster fuck. "When's your birthday?"

"That's totally off topic."

"I ask. You answer. When's your birthday?"

She pursed her lips before focusing her attention on the hole in his leg. The sting of the needle was momentary, and the pull of the thread only a minor annoyance in comparison to the vodka bath he'd just taken.

"May fourteenth."

"Favorite color?"

Her brow knitted as she continued to stitch, the tip of her tongue darting out with her concentration. "Black."

"Beer or hard liquor?"

"Depends." She paused to wipe her hands and dab at his leg with a dry cloth before continuing on. "I'm not a big beer drinker. Blue Moon is okay. And I like hard cider."

"Most heinous thing you were ever busted for?"

She paused, cut him a look that was neither guilty nor embarrassed. "Reckless driving when I was seventeen. Speeding." A sheepish grin spread across her face. "I like to drive fast."

His abs clenched and the pain in his thigh was nothing compared to the heat of desire that began to pool in Damien's gut. He'd love to see her behind the wheel of his Shelby, speeding down the freeway. So fucking hot.

"Pizza or burgers?"

"Burgers."

"Favorite body part?"

Tabitha ginned. "On the opposite sex?"

"Yeah."

A wistful sigh escaped her lips, the sound a full

body caress that heated Damien's blood. "The back. And for the record, you have an epically sexy back."

"Why don't you have any tattoos?" She'd been fascinated with his and it made his cock stir to remember the way her fingers felt as she'd traced the raised skin.

"I'm picky. I want to get a caduceus tattoo, but only after I graduate."

"Where?"

Tabitha shrugged. "I don't know. There are a lot of decent parlors around."

"No." Damien laughed. "Where on your body?"

"Oh." She flashed a brilliant smile. "Hold still. I need to tie this off and then I'll stitch the hole on the back of your thigh. I have no idea where I want it. Would you care to offer up a suggestion?"

"Between your shoulder blades. The small of your back right on your spine. Your hip. The back of your neck—that would be sexy as hell."

"You think?"

"Yeah." The blue of Tabitha's eyes darkened, deep ocean waters. "I'd kiss you there. Nip at your neck. Scrape my teeth across the ink."

Tabitha let out a slow breath. "If you keep talking like that, you're going to break my concentration."

"Oh, honey," Damien replied. "I'm just getting started."

Chapter Nineteen

Damien Evans was a criminal. A drug dealer. And God knew what else. But when he spoke to her that way, the words so full of heat and promise, Tabitha forgot all of those things. She wanted him more than any other man she'd ever met. How could she possibly lust after someone who would ask her to stitch up a gunshot wound, *Sons of Anarchy* style, in her bedroom? And what kind of woman did it make her that she was more than willing to do it?

"I need you to roll onto your stomach, and in the interest of logistics and comfort, I think we'd better get your pants all the way off."

"You don't have to ask me twice. But in the *interest of fairness*, I think you should do the same."

How could he be so playful at a time like this? "Slow your roll, buddy. You're in no shape for anything that would involve me taking my pants off."

"I'd have to be dead to not want to see you with your pants off. A little gunshot wound is nothing."

Tabitha grinned despite herself and circled the bed to his left side. She eased the intact half of his jeans and underwear down his leg, her eyes drawn to areas that a trained medical professional shouldn't be checking out. At. All. She caught him staring at her, mouth quirked with amusement, and heat rose to her cheeks. "Oookaaaay." Holy crap. She needed a cold shower. "Do you think you can turn over now? I need to sew up the exit wound."

"You just want to check out my sexy back."

The smile he flashed before easing over was just shy of wicked, and Tabitha's stomach shot up into her throat before floating down into her lower abdomen on fluffy white clouds. "You're not going to be quite so cocky when I clean this exit wound."

"If you give me a distraction . . . like your naked body to look at, I can guarantee you I won't feel a thing."

A lick of heat danced up Tabitha's spine. "Quiet, you." She reached over him to grab the bottle of vodka and a clean washcloth. When her chest brushed his back, he let out a low groan that caused a Pavlovian response in her body. Just the deep vibration of sound made her sex clench and her thighs tremble. *Jesus.*

As she gently cleaned the wound, Tabitha tried to focus on the task at hand and not the way the muscles in his ass flexed as she tended to him. God, she wanted to bite those round cheeks, knead them in her palms, run her thumbs up his spine as she let her palms explore the smooth skin of his muscled back. Damien sucked in a sharp breath and it brought Tabitha to attention. "Did I hurt you?"

"No." She heard the smile in his voice. "But your hand on my ass feels amazing."

Tabitha looked down as though just now noticing she'd cupped the very same cheek she'd been fantasizing about. She pulled away, mortified, and pegged her eyes to the still bleeding wound she was supposed to be sewing up. *Concentrate, you idiot.*

"Consider the pleasant groping an apology for what's next," she teased. "Get ready." Without any further notice, she drizzled the vodka over the hole in Damien's thigh. His grunt of pain was muffled by the pillows as his entire body went taut. It was totally pathetic that she found herself rapt to the play of muscles as her gaze caressed each ridge, hill, and valley. And not a little insensitive, either. *Good Lord, Tabitha.*

She laid a comforting hand on his shoulder as Damien panted through the pain. Without even realizing what she was doing, she leaned over him, laid her lips between his shoulder blades, and kissed. He relaxed beneath her, and let out a long, relieved sigh.

"Jesus Christ, Tabitha," he murmured against the pillow. His voice slurred, grew lazy and thick. "Who needs drugs when I've got you."

The quiet stillness that followed caused her heart rate to kick into high gear. "Damien?" Silence answered her and she gave him a little shake. "Damien?" She checked his pulse, slow but steady, and his breathing had become even as well. He was bound to pass out, though he'd lasted longer than she'd thought he would. The combination of pain, stress, and blood loss was too much for any body, even a strong, healthy one like his.

Tabitha worked quickly in the quiet, cleaning away the rest of the blood and shaving away the light dusting of hair that surrounded the wound before she re-sterilized the needle and fresh thread. The exit wound was messier than the entrance hole. More ragged and a little bigger. Unfortunately, it wasn't going to leave a pretty scar. Though on Damien, she doubted it would do anything other than make his body more attractive. Men like him wore scars well. And it showed just how ridiculous her infatuation was that she hoped he'd stick around long enough for her to see the healed marks in all their glory.

It took twice as long to stitch him up, but since she didn't have to worry about causing him undue pain, she tried to be more precise with each stitch. She took several breaks to clean fresh blood from the wound, and by the time she tied off the thread, Tabitha was confident that despite her hack job, he'd heal up nicely.

"Tabs? You home?"

Seth's voice called out from the living room, and Tabitha shot up from her hunched position over Damien's body. "Yeah! In my room. Give me a sec!"

There was no way she'd be able to explain the guy naked from the waist down, passed out on her bed and covered in blood, to her brother. Not that she hadn't walked in on much worse in his room a time or ten. From the foot of her bed, she grabbed a light throw blanket and slung it over Damien's waist. She adjusted the pillow under his head to make sure he wouldn't get a kink in his neck and cleaned up the mess she'd made, throwing the soiled washcloths in the hamper before closing her bedroom door quietly behind her.

"Hey, bro, what's up?"

Seth smirked. "*Bro?*"

He lounged on the couch, flipping through channels, a beer resting in his palm. His boots were caked with dirt and Tabitha fought the urge to freak out that he'd tracked it across the carpeting. "You know, bro, short for brother. You didn't just get home from work, did you? It's after midnight."

He slapped at his thigh and a plume of dust rose from his jeans. *Gah! He was getting dirt all over the couch!* "No. I went out with some of the guys, grabbed dinner, played some pool."

"Seth, you need to be careful. You can't afford to—"

"Fuck my life, Tabs, it was pool. I wasn't out knocking off a bank."

His tone, along with the added stress of the night, flipped a switch on Tabitha's composure. "Don't get an attitude with me, Seth. It's not like I don't have a reason to be wary of what you're doing and who you're doing it with. I'm the one who's been cleaning up your messes for the past seven years!"

"Hey, no one asked you to do that for me. You're not my mother." Seth leaned forward, his brows drawn sharply over his blue eyes. "So don't martyr yourself."

Wow. Her heart was overflowing with emotion from Seth's gratitude. "Someone had to take care of you! You think I should have just let you go to jail? Let Joey steamroll you?"

Seth gave an indifferent shrug before taking a long pull from the bottle. "Maybe."

"God, you are such a selfish jerk!"

"And you're a nosy, self-righteous, pain in my ass."

"So, what? You're actually butt-hurt that I'm trying to keep you out of trouble? Is that what you're saying?"

With a sigh, Seth settled back in the chair and turned his attention back to the TV. "Just drop it, okay, Tabs? I don't want to fight."

"No. You just want to insult me."

"Is everything okay out here?"

Tabitha and Seth turned in tandem toward the sound of Damien's voice. He stood in the hallway, the blanket slung around his waist. If his physical form hadn't been so damned imposing, his appearance might have been comical.

Her head whipped back toward Seth and he quirked a brow, a corner of his mouth hitched. "So, *sis*. What have you been up to tonight?"

The kid with the smart mouth had to be Tabitha's brother. He recognized him from the picture on her phone. If he'd been at even fifty percent, Damien would have shaken the little shit by the scruff of the neck and made him apologize and thank his sister a thousand times for everything she'd done for him.

"Everything's fine."

"Doesn't sound fine."

She didn't turn to face him, but instead kept her attention focused on her brother. Damien didn't have any siblings, but he sensed there was an unspoken argument going on that consisted of scowls and narrowed eyes. Seth looked away from his sister first and Damien felt a surge of pride that Tabitha had held her own and managed to put her brother in his place.

"No, it is." When she faced him, Damien could barely hide his amusement as she directed her stern, chiding glare his way. "But you shouldn't be out of bed. Come on, I'll go with you."

"You'd better tame that kinky streak, Tabs," Seth snarked from the couch.

How did Tabitha get through a day without clocking him?

"I'm young and impressionable and don't want to hear or see anything tonight that'll damage my delicate psyche."

Tabitha grabbed Damien by the arm and steered him back toward her bedroom, but not before she gave her brother the finger. "He's usually not such a pain in the ass," she said as though she'd read this thoughts. "I'm sorry if we woke you."

"No worries. I was already sort of awake."

Truth be told, her hot-tempered shouts had brought Damien to instant awareness from the dark void that had swallowed him whole. He'd come off the bed like a shot, regretting the quick movement when his leg buckled under his weight. Not even a bullet through the leg had kept him from making sure she was okay, though. He would have made his way out to the living room in an army crawl, his fists gripping the carpet, if he'd had to.

Once back in the bedroom, Damien steadied himself near the bed while Tabitha cleaned the bloody towel away and turned down the covers. "I'll get blood on your sheets." He wasn't used to someone taking care of him. But he'd be damned if he didn't like it.

"Now that you're awake, I can dress the wounds." Tabitha snagged a box of gauze and a roll of duct tape from the bedside table. "I don't have any surgical tape, so I'm apologizing in advance for the sticky goop that will probably stay on your legs for all eternity."

Damien laughed. "That's what makes duct tape so great. I've used it in place of a Band-Aid a couple of times. Obviously, I'm not used to fancy medical treatment."

Her brows pulled down. "Should you be bragging about that fact?"

He smiled. "Probably not."

"Can you stand? I'll dress the back first and then you can lie on your back in the bed."

Damien pulled the blanket from around his waist and let it drop to the floor. The sound of Tabitha's breath hitching gave him a smug sense of satisfaction.

"You're sort of my captive, you know." The seductive quality of her voice sent a tingle through his body that settled low in his sac. "Until I can get you some clothes, anyway. Where are you staying right now? I mean, when you're not working out of the IdaHaven. I could grab a few things for you."

The last thing he needed was for Tabitha to go to his hotel room across town. If she dug through the drawers she might find his badge and files on everyone involved with Joey Cavello—including her. "I don't want you going over there. The hotel is in a seedy part of town and there are more than a few tweakers hanging around." Though the story was fabricated, his concern for her wasn't. Okay, so she probably wouldn't see many tweakers at the Hilton the Marshals Service had put him up at, but he couldn't blow his cover. His stomach bottomed out at the deception. Lying to her fucking *sucked*. "I'll give you some cash. If you don't mind, you can pick me up something cheap at Walmart or wherever. I'm easy."

"Oh, all right." He didn't miss the twinge of disappointment in her voice. Why? Was she seriously bummed that he was concerned, or that he didn't want her in his hotel room? "I have tomorrow off so I can do that, no problem."

"What about school?"

The sound of tape being pulled from the roll sliced through the quiet. Tabitha's touch was gentle, her fingers cool as she placed the gauze on his leg and covered it with a piece of tape. "I wrapped up the semester a couple of weeks ago. I have a month off before I start my clinical rotation." Tabitha paused and another *ziiiip* of the tape followed. She secured the bandage at the bottom and a chill chased over Damien's skin from her touch. "Done. Can you get into bed yourself, or do you need help?"

Her body brushed against his as she stood, a whisper of contact that only made him want more. Damien turned on his left leg so he was facing her and peeled his T-shirt from his body. Tabitha's gaze heated, her eyes widening a fraction as she took in his bare chest. *Yep. Naked. And you're going to be joining me in a few seconds.* "I can manage on my own."

Damien stretched out on the bed and tucked his arms behind him, propping up his head so he could watch Tabitha work. The satin glide of her fingers soothed his aches and she used the same gentle care as she covered the wound with another square of gauze, securing it with a couple of strips of tape. "How does it feel?" She tested the skin around the edges of the tape, then looked over at him.

"Like I've been shot." She cringed at his words and he went on. "But not too bad. I could probably use a few ibuprofen if you have them."

She reached inside the drawer beside the bed and shook four of the little brown pills from a bottle. "These aren't super powerful, but it's the equivalent of the eight hundred milligram tabs you'd get at the hospital." Damien held out his hand and she placed the pills in his palm. "Let me go get you a glass of water."

"No need." He didn't want to give her any reason

to leave his side. He placed the pills on the back of his tongue and swallowed them down.

"You're not supposed to dry-swallow pills, Damien." God, that chiding tone made him hot. "It's bad for you."

"Worse than gunshot wounds?"

"Not funny."

"Get naked." If he didn't see her body in the next thirty seconds, he was going to put those scissors of hers to good use and cut her clothes off of her.

Her scandalized expression was a contradiction to the blush that colored her cheeks and the deep blue of her warm gaze. "Just like that, huh?"

"Yep. Get naked and get in bed with me. Now."

Her answering smile reminded him of moonlight, soft with a glow that illuminated her features. Damien sucked in a breath and held it in his chest as she toed off her boots and socks, her gaze locked on his. She unfastened her pants and shimmied out of them, discarding them beside her. "More?"

The way she teased him . . . The pain in his leg was nothing compared to the deep thrum of his cock as it began to grow harder with every inch of skin she exposed. "More." The word came out as a harsh bark, raw as it scratched his throat. "Your shirt."

It came off in a flash, drifting to the floor in a cloud of black fabric. Damien devoured her with his eyes, taking in the creamy flesh and soft curves barely concealed by a few triangles of lace. Her underwear was almost too tiny to be worthy of the word, and the bra—a pushup number that enhanced the natural swell of her breasts—was enough to make his mouth water. "Turn around."

She obliged him, turning to show off the thong back of her underwear, revealing the sweet bare

curves of her ass for him to admire. "Now the bra."
The thong was staying put for now, but he didn't
want anything to hamper the sight of her breasts.
She kept her back turned to him as she slowly un-
hooked the clasp and dragged the straps down and
off her arms. In a dramatic whisper, the garment fell
to the floor. "Let me see you."

There should have been a statue erected somewhere in honor of Tabitha Martin's breasts. It didn't
matter that he'd seen them before, held their weight
in his palms more than once. The sight of her tortured him, teased and tantalized. He could make a
meal of her body, licking, sucking, tasting every inch
of her. Sinking his teeth into the supple flesh of her
ass. He'd never actually wanted to bite a woman
before, but he wanted to bite her. Not hard, just
enough to make her moan.

One knee bent, curving inward as though she
wasn't quite sure what to do with her body. She fiddled with the lacy waistband of her thong and
Damien swallowed down a groan as he partook of
the visual feast she presented. "If you keep touching
yourself like that, I'm going to tear these stitches out
in my rush to get to you."

A lazy smile stretched across her face. Sweet and
seductive. "You promised me you'd be a good patient. Ripping my expert stitches would hardly be
classified as good behavior."

"I can be good. Let me show you." She'd demonstrated in the past that she liked for him to take control and dominate her. This was a game he'd enjoy.
He'd instruct her, watch from the bed as she touched
herself and teased him with the sight of her body.
And then, when they were both so mindless with
desire that neither one of them could give a shit

about his stitches, he'd take her. After the night he'd had, Damien wasn't sure he could keep his own desire in check for much longer. He needed a release. But he refused to push her if she was at all unsure.

Rather than answer, she climbed into bed next to him, nestling into the curve of his arm. "You are hereby grounded from anything that will cause you to tear those sutures. And if you think I'm kidding, I've got nine-one-one on speed dial."

"You'd rat me out to the paramedics?" he asked with a smile.

She answered with a wicked grin. "Absolutely."

Chapter Twenty

Was it possible to die from unspent sexual energy?

As Tabitha lay beside Damien, his body over-whelming hers with its sheer size, she wondered if she'd make it through the night. Her body pulsed with need, blood heated to the point that she felt the flush on every inch of her skin. He was hard and ready—a bullet to the thigh hadn't even slowed him down—and let her know in no uncertain terms that he wanted her.

Still, despite his cocky bravado, a gunshot wound was no laughing matter. And the truth of the situation was, the sutures she'd done were not the best. In fact, she'd never stitched anyone up before. That was a job best left to the MDs. She had no business tending to his wounds, and she'd meant what she said. If he stepped even a toe out of line, Damien was going to the ER.

"This is such a wasted opportunity." His lamented words were laced with humor, and Tabitha smiled against his chest.

"Will it help if I promise to bring you breakfast in bed?"

He traced an idle pattern on her arm with his fingertips. Up, down. Up, down. Tabitha shivered from the pleasant contact that relaxed her body from head to toe. "The only thing that can possibly make it up to me is bacon. A pile of bacon. A *mountain* of bacon. I will need to consume the Mount Everest of bacon if I can't make love to you tonight."

Tabitha's stomach twisted into a pretzel. Make love? Her bones went soft and liquid and she couldn't have moved a muscle if she'd tried. The words were so tender. So *honest*. Damien was an enigma. A contradiction to his very nature. Again, she thought of his duality, the face he showed to her in private moments like these and the fierce, violent criminal who'd nearly beaten Tony to death earlier tonight.

"I can probably manage some bacon. You might have to settle for a Boise foothills-sized plate, but I'll make it worth your while."

"Mmm." His chest rumbled with the sound. "Bacon."

He wrapped her in his embrace and pulled the covers up higher, tucking them around her. "I know I sound like a broken record, but are you sure you're okay? That fucker didn't do anything to you?"

Tabitha shuddered. "No. He was drunk and high. He roughed me up a little, shoved me. Forced me to drink some *nasty* tequila. But you showed up before anything happened. I owe you one. Really. Thank you."

"It's my goddamned fault," he all but growled. "I should have called you, told you I wasn't going to be there."

"You couldn't have known I'd show up."

"Still."

"Shush," Tabitha said with a playful swat to his abs.

Good Lord, the man was *marble*. "And I'm sorry that Seth was acting like a dick tonight. That was my fault, too. I egged him on."

"What's his story?"

Tabitha rolled fully on her side, enjoying the heat of Damien's naked skin on hers. She laid the flat of her palm against the hard planes of his stomach, marveling at the tight ridges of muscle. "Seth's had some problems, but he's really a good guy. He had a rough childhood, that's all. We both did. We weren't exactly taught good decision-making skills. Or responsibility."

"So, what? He's a troublemaker?" Damien tilted her face up to his. His gaze searched hers, his expression tense. "If you don't watch out, you're going to hit your quota for hard luck cases this month."

"Try this lifetime."

A comfortable silence settled. Damien's touch was reassuring, the gentle stroke of his fingers coaxing delicious chills to the surface of Tabitha's skin. She'd never talked much about her family with anyone other than Lila and Dave. And really, she'd barely broken the surface with the things she'd told them. In the quiet darkness of her bedroom, she wanted to lay herself bare to Damien. Wanted him to know everything about her. Trust was hard for her, but she wanted him to trust her, and in turn she wanted to put her trust in him.

"Seth and I . . ." God, the words were like broken glass in her mouth. "I told you that our dad was a user. And a dealer. He was an alcoholic and he was high more often than he wasn't. Our mom popped pills like they were Tic Tacs. Seth and I grew up in a really unhealthy environment."

Damien stiffened beside her and Tabitha's pulse

jumped. The reason why she rarely talked about her childhood was that she usually got two reactions from people: revulsion or pity.

"That must have been rough for you guys." His voice didn't carry any hint of pity or disdain. Instead, Damien held her closer, anchoring her to his strength.

"It was." Tabitha felt a fissure grow in the emotional dam she'd constructed. The tightness that was ever present in her chest began to loosen by small degrees. She'd always had a feeling that Damien didn't want to be a part of this world, either. Maybe what she'd needed all along was a kindred spirit to listen. "I mean, why is it so hard for some people to take care of their kids? If we wanted to eat, I had to cook. And honestly, there was rarely any food in the house. We wore dirty clothes a lot. We got teased when we were kids because we always looked ratty, we never had school supplies, and our mom couldn't even get her shit together to apply for supplemental lunch assistance. I lived every day of my life embarrassed. Couldn't wait to graduate so I could get the hell out of there."

"Social services didn't intervene?" In the dark, his voice was all-encompassing. Surrounding her, protecting her. "I mean, didn't the school district employees notice how bad off you were?"

She shrugged against him. "Health and Welfare came over once. A social worker did a home inspection and gave my parents a warning. Gave them a list of things that had to be fixed and improved in the house. My parents were good for about two weeks. Cleaned the house, filled the fridge with food, kept their nasty friends away. Then, when the smoke cleared, they just fell right back into their old patterns."

"Damn. That fucking sucks."

Tabitha gave a sad laugh. "Tell me about it. The thing is, I could've gotten over it. I could have forgiven them and just moved on with my life. But my dad had this friend. He was a total piece of shit. I feel like he had a lot to do with keeping my parents in the life and he was a really bad influence on Seth, too. He's the reason Seth was always getting into trouble. I thought things would get better when he moved out of town. But turns out Gerald was using Seth as a mule—transporting product from Seattle through Oregon and Idaho—and I didn't even know it."

Damien's fingers constricted, squeezing her arms. "This Gerald have a last name?"

Tabitha smiled into the darkness. "Why, you gonna go beat him up, too?"

"Maybe."

There was a tension in his voice that hadn't been there before. "Lightfoot. Gerald Lightfoot. I made it a point to stay as far away from my parents' bullshit as possible. But he was always around, treating Seth and I like we were his own kids. My parents even wanted us to call him Uncle Gerald. It was ridiculous. When I found out he was using Seth—probably because he was seventeen and still a minor—I went off. I left an anonymous tip with the Boise narcotics guys, and ratted my parents out. They didn't get Gerald, but both my mom and dad were arrested for possession with intent to distribute. I thought it would change things and Seth would get better, but it didn't. I found out about a year ago that he'd introduced Joey to Gerald. That's how Joey got me to hook him up with the hotel rooms for him to deal from. He said that if I didn't help him, he'd do the same thing I'd done to my parents and let the cops know that

Seth had been slinging. He promised to make sure there'd be plenty of evidence, too."

The silence that followed her confession choked the air from Tabitha's lungs. She'd just admitted to being a narc, and the one thing she'd learned growing up is that the lowest life form in the urban jungle was the rat. What did Damien think of her admission? Probably trying to figure out how quickly he could get the hell out of there before he wound up in police custody, as well.

"I've never told anyone the whole story before," she added. "Joey made a lucky guess and that's the only reason he knows. I couldn't tell Seth that I'm the one who turned in our parents. I'm too afraid to tell him. He'd hate me for it."

Damien's steady breath was the only sound in the room. Panic rushed hot in her veins. She shouldn't have said anything. Damn it, she should have kept her big mouth shut. Now it was too late to take the words back and she'd have to live with the consequences. For all she knew, Damien and Joey had gotten pretty tight over the past few weeks. And if he went to Joey with this story, Seth was as good as screwed. He'd set her brother up and hand him over to the narcotics task force on principle. Just to teach Tabitha a lesson. "Damien?" Oh God. *You really fucked up this time, Tabs.*

Damien's jaw was clenched to the point that his molars had begun to grind. Until he could get his anger under control, all he'd be able to manage was a few deep growls, and he didn't think that would do much to assuage Tabitha's fear. *Jesus fucking Christ.* If he wasn't laid up, he'd be halfway across town right now, beating the ever living shit out of Joey Cavello. All this time the Marshals Service had been trying to get their hands on Gerald Lightfoot. And Tabitha's clueless troublemaker brother—not Cavello—was the key to finding him.

"You did the right thing." The fear, the doubt in her voice made him feel as though he'd been shot again. That tremor of uncertainty ripped through his heart like a high velocity round. "Really, you should have turned them in a hell of a lot sooner."

"You don't think I'm a snitch?"

One of the things Damien hated about gang and drug culture was the cultlike nature of the "extended family" model. All disputes and issues were expected to be handled within the family. Bringing in outside authorities—especially social services or law enforcement—was a huge taboo. And those who did were treated like the lowest traitors.

"I think you're brave."

Tabitha let out a derisive snort. "I bet my folks would disagree with you on that one since they've still each got at least another year on their sentences."

Damien held her close. "They might share your gene pool, Tabitha, but those people weren't parents in any sense of the word."

"I felt guilty about it for a long time. I was only nineteen. But I'd had it. I couldn't deal with their drama or the fact that Seth was becoming too used to the lifestyle. I wanted him *out*."

"How does Seth feel about all of this? I know he's your brother and you feel obligated to take care of him. Does he want out as much as you want him out?"

"I think so." Her voice reached out in the darkness, sad and unsure. "He's been so good the past several months. He even got a legit job. His boss gave him an advance to buy some work boots and you should have seen him, Damien. He was beaming. Okay, so he did spend some of the money on a pizza, but for Seth this is a huge stride."

Damien wondered if Seth was truly as excited about his life on the straight and narrow as Tabitha thought. A lot of the time, family members of suspects lived in denial, emphatic to the very end in their belief that their loved one was innocent. Damien had been on the receiving end of a mother's wrath a time or ten in the course of making an arrest. But one of the things he loved about Tabitha was that she chose to see the good in everyone. There wasn't a soul who didn't first get the benefit of the doubt.

"Then for your sake, I hope he keeps his nose clean." Damien sought out her face in the dark, cupped her cheek as he brought her face toward his. "Because you deserve for someone *not* to let you down for a change."

He kissed her gently. For the first time since they'd met, Damien took his time to truly enjoy her. His raw need had been a physical thing, all-consuming, but now it was emotional as well. Under her tough façade, the combat boots, nose piercing, edgy haircut and sharp tongue, was a gentle, fragile soul with more love to give than Damien thought possible. She was a warm fire on a cold night. A tall, leafy tree in the storm. The levy that kept floodwater at bay.

Being with her made clear the lines that Damien had blurred over the years. Made him want to recall the man that he was beneath the fabricated covers, the conjured backstories. She washed the guilt of things he'd done and seen from his spirit, as though absolving him of sin. She deserved so much more than what life had given her. So much more.

"No one will ever use you again." The words were a vow spoken in the sanctity of darkness. He kissed her again and she sighed into his mouth, merging their breaths into one. "No one will exploit you. Abuse you. Disrespect you. I promise, Tabitha. I'll die before I let anyone hurt you ever again."

"Don't make promises you can't keep." Her whispered words carried with them the weight of sadness Damien knew far too well. "You never know, you might be the one to hurt me. I might hurt you. People aren't perfect, so it makes no sense to promise that we will be."

It would be a lie to deny it. Tabitha had put her trust in Damien, a man that she assumed knew firsthand the world she'd grown up in. Without her even realizing it, he'd hurt her. Betrayed her. Let her make confessions she'd never made to another soul but not to the man she thought he was. She may as well have turned her parents in all over again.

Because Damien had no choice but to go to the chief deputy and Boise PD with the information she'd shared. Arresting Gerald Lightfoot was the fugitive task force's number one priority. And Tabitha had given them a means to wrap this case up once and for all.

It would just take using her brother's freedom as leverage to pull it off.

"All right. No promises." He kissed her again, reveled in the petal-soft touch of her lips, the silky slide of her tongue against his. Tonight he'd let her believe the lie. But he'd have to come clean to her. Soon. Before Gates and Chief Deputy Callihan brought her brother in for questioning. When her lips left his,

Damien smoothed back her hair and said, "Can I at least thank you for sewing up my leg?"

She laughed, the sound rippling over him in warm waves. "Consider it payment for saving my life tonight."

As she settled into his embrace, Damien tried to stem the worry over what would happen after tonight. Would she forgive him for his deception? For using her brother with as much consideration as Joey and Lightfoot had? Or would she understand and appreciate that he truly wanted to help them both?

Moments passed and her breathing became deep and even, her palm relaxed on his chest. Her easy rest did nothing to calm Damien, however. No. His nightmare was only about to begin.

The scent of sizzling bacon could wake any man from a dead sleep. Damien let his head fall to the side and he stared at the empty pillow that Tabitha had slept on, her body tucked against his for long, blissful hours that felt more honest and real than anything he'd experienced in years. Jesus. Sappy much? He was a real tough son of a bitch, lying in bed all wistful and shit. Maybe that's why the SOG preferred unattached deputies for undercover work. Being in love seriously made a guy lose his edge.

But *was* he in love?

It had only been a few weeks since they'd met, yet it felt like years. His need to protect her, to shield her from all of the ugliness she'd lived through and continued to suffer was a physical thing that tied his stomach into knots. His body craved hers as surely as any drug, and the thought of being away from her for even a second sent him into a panic that clouded his mind and made him a useless sack of raw emotion. So if being completely ruined, physically, mentally, and emotionally meant that he was in love with Tabitha Martin, then yeah, maybe he did love her.

If that wasn't the craziest revelation ever.

"Hey." The door eased open and Tabitha walked in carrying a white plastic bag with Walmart scrawled across the front. Damien pushed himself up to a sitting position, surprised his leg didn't hurt as bad as he expected it to as he eased back against the headboard. "I hope you don't mind, but I borrowed your car this morning. I bought you jeans and underwear. Oh, and not quite a mountain, but a hill's worth of bacon. How's your leg?"

The sentences melded together in a rush that made Damien wonder why she was suddenly so nervous. "Pants are good. I don't think anyone needs to see me walking around in a blanket skirt."

She flashed him a quick smile that banished her previously tense expression. "I don't know, you could totally initiate a new fashion trend: man sarongs."

"The modern man's kilt."

"Exactly."

Damien welcomed the levity. Last night had been heavy-duty for both of them. How could anyone feel anything but awkward after so much drama?

"I was thinking that after breakfast I should check your stitches and change the bandages. We should probably get some antibiotic cream, too. Just in case. You're going to need to keep a close eye on the wounds to make sure they don't get infected. It wouldn't be good to get sepsis after we went through so much trouble to clean you up."

Aaaand, just like that, the awkwardness returned. Damien let out a slow sigh and stretched his neck from side to side. "Sounds good to me."

"Also, I have to go in to work for a few hours to do the food order and send out a few invoices. Would it be okay if I take your car since mine is at the hotel?"

"Sure. I'll go with you. I need to tie up some loose ends from last night, and I might as well get some of that cream while I'm out. How much do I owe you for the jeans?" Not even their first encounter had been as stilted as this. What the fuck had gone wrong during the night? *She opened up to you and is regretting the shit out of it. That's what went wrong.* Damien seriously needed a do-over.

"Okay. If you're sure your leg is all right to walk. And drive."

"It is."

"Don't worry about the pants," she said as she headed for the door. "They're on me. Breakfast is ready, by the way. Just come out whenever."

The door closed behind her and Damien swung his legs over the side of the bed—careful not to jog his injured thigh too much. He let his head hang between his shoulders and rolled them in an effort to banish some of the tension that had settled there. Goddamn it. While he'd been asleep, everything had changed. And all Damien wanted was to get back to that moment with Tabitha when it was only her and him and the quiet dark.

Chapter Twenty-One

Doing the walk of shame in front of her entire anatomy and physiology class would have been less awkward than the morning she'd spent with Damien. It was all her fault. Damien tried his best to salvage the day, chatting over breakfast and flashing those dimples that melted her insides. But she couldn't shake the sense of dread that since she'd decided to put her trust in him, everything between them would inevitably fall apart.

Which was pretty much on par for everything in her life.

You idiot. You never should have told him anything about your life. She should have kept things between them light and casual. A physical relationship with no strings attached. *He trusted you, though. Told you about his mom and the guilt he felt for not being there for her . . .* Which could totally be a lie, for all she knew. An emotionally charged sob story to manipulate her. *God, Tabitha, you are such a sap!*

"Hey, Tabitha?" Renee poked her head into the office. The Sunday front-desk clerk's expression was pinched, her brows drawn tight over her eyes.

"There's a guy here from HiTop Roofing who said he needs to talk to a manager. Something about his room."

Oh. *Fuck.* She'd been so busy worrying about Damien and what happened between them last night that she'd totally forgotten about Tony. Tabitha was getting pretty tired of visits from the drama llama. Why was it so impossible to break from the dysfunction of her life and start over?

"Go ahead and tell him he can come in." Tabitha rubbed at her temples and let out a slow breath. Twenty-three was too damned young for this level of stress.

Renee beat a hasty retreat, which did nothing to calm Tabitha's nerves. When Joey waltzed into her office, his expression dark, a burst of nervous energy skittered down her spine. She doubted Damien would come to her rescue this time. He closed the door behind him and the sound might as well have been an axe coming down on her neck.

"What in the *fuck* happened here last night, Tabs?"

Since becoming a "big-time" dealer, Joey's ego had grown about a thousand percent. She supposed being involved in a shooting last night probably elevated his opinion of himself as a high roller as well. Funny, he'd come away from the incident unscathed, while she'd had to sew Damien up last night. "Tony is out of his goddamned mind, that's what happened. He got out of line and thank God Damien showed up to put him in his place."

"Funny," Joey said, rounding Tabitha's desk to stand beside her. She inched away as he braced an arm on the desk and lowered himself to eye level. "That's not the story I got."

Tony and Joey had been friends for years. No doubt he'd believe his buddy over her. "I don't know what he told you, Joey, but you can believe me when I say he crossed a line. If you don't want to listen to me, ask Damien."

Joey snorted. "Like I'd ask him anything. That fucker is *done*. Tony told me what he did."

What an asshole. Tony was lower than the lowest pond scum. "And what exactly did he tell you?"

"Busted in after I dropped him off, beat the shit out of Tony and took off with the rest of my fucking product, that's what he did."

Tabitha couldn't help her disbelieving laughter. "Jesus Christ, Joey. That's so far from what actually happened, it's not even funny!"

"What's *funny* is that you'd say that, Tabs, because according to Tony, you helped Damien jack him."

Her jaw dropped. That asshole! That lying son of a bitch! "Considering the *arrangement* we have, why in God's name would I do that?" *How do you deal with someone who's blackmailing you? Simple. Rob him blind.* Tabitha snorted. Joey was such a fool.

"Since you've been chasing after Damien like a fucking bitch in heat, I doubt it was too hard for him to talk you into helping him."

Anger built inside of her like roiling storm clouds, so intense she tasted it on the back of her tongue. How did he even know she'd been seeing Damien? Tony obviously hadn't wasted any time in spreading the juicy gossip. "Get. Out." Tabitha stood from her chair and leveled her gaze on Joey. "Get out of my office right now."

Joey's hand struck out like a viper, catching her around the throat. "Don't get lippy with me, you little cunt. Because of your bullshit, Lightfoot is coming down and he'll be here *tonight*. Do you know how much of his shit went missing last night? Half of an entire goddamned delivery. And you can bet your uptight little ass it isn't going to be me that pays for the fuck-up."

He released his grip and Tabitha stumbled backward, gasping for air as she rubbed at her abused throat. "You're through," Joey spat as he headed for the door. "Your brother is fucking through. And so is that piece of shit boyfriend of yours."

The door slammed behind him with enough force to rattle Tabitha's teeth. Limbs shaking, she collapsed into her chair, her breaths coming in desperate gasps that made her see stars. She fumbled with her cell, dropping it three times before she could steady the stupid thing in her hands. She accessed the recent-calls screen and selected Damien's number from the list.

When his voice mail picked up, Tabitha cursed under her breath. Whether or not opening up to him had been a mistake, they were in this together now. She might not have been scared of Joey before, but he'd rattled her today. And if Gerald was on his way into town, they were all as good as dead.

"Damien, it's Tabitha." She tried to manage the panic in her voice, but that was easier said than done. "Tony told Joey that we beat him up and stole half a delivery's worth of drugs from him last night. Joey is pissed. He said Gerald Lightfoot is headed to town to sort it all out." A sob rose in her throat and she swallowed it down. "He said he's not going to take the fall for it and I know he's going to throw us all under the bus. Including Seth. I don't know what to do. Can you please call me?"

She disconnected the call and dialed Seth. He needed to get out of town. Now. Voice mail answered and Tabitha swore. Goddamn it, didn't anyone answer their phone anymore? "Seth, call me *as soon as you get this message*." She ended the call and stared at the far wall, tears springing to her eyes.

What she wouldn't give for a normal life. One that didn't involve being nearly choked to death twice in twenty-four hours.

"We need to get you to a hospital, Evans. Those stitches *cannot* be sanitary."

Despite the pain radiating from his thigh, Damien continued to pace the confines of his hotel room, his gut churning like the ocean at high tide. When he heard Tabitha's message, he'd been prepared to jump to action, but Chief Deputy Callihan insisted that they handle this by the book from here on out.

"I'm fine."

"The hell you are. What were you thinking, not reporting that shooting last night? John Rader is up my ass over this. He thinks we cut him out of the loop, and Nampa PD has had extra resources on this since last night. Would a phone call have killed you? 'Hey, Chief, just wanted to let you know I shot up a couple of gangbangers and took a bullet to the leg.' You know, just to give us a jumping-off point."

Neither his sarcasm nor his aggravation was lost on Damien. This case had been out of control since day one. *Way to instill confidence, dickhead.* "I didn't want to compromise my cover."

"No," Callihan snarked. "Of course not. Because fraternizing with a suspect didn't compromise you at all."

He had a point. "Tabitha Martin isn't a suspect. She's an asset. Her brother, too. They're the key to getting to Lightfoot."

The chief deputy snorted. "They'll be lucky if the U.S. attorneys' office doesn't file racketeering and conspiracy charges against both of them. You heard Martin's voice mail. She said Cavello thinks you stole from him. Lightfoot is on his way to put his business in order. We don't need Martin or his sister to get to Lightfoot now."

"We do," Damien asserted. There was no way in hell he was going to let Tabitha take the fall for *any* of this. "Lightfoot isn't an idiot; if he were, we would have made an arrest years ago. Since he's been on the run, he's been careful not to directly connect himself with any of his deals. He uses middlemen for everything. If we want an airtight case against him, we need both Tabitha and her brother's testimony. They have years of history with the man. Seth Martin was Lightfoot's mule for a long time. They might be the only two people who have personal knowledge of his involvement."

"Not true," Callihan argued. "We've got Cavello."

"Please." Damien needed to gain some ground and prove his case, now. "Do you really think Lightfoot is that stupid? If he's headed into town, like Cavello says, there is no way he's going to be stupid enough to initiate face-to-face contact."

"How else is he going to take care of business?"

"Simple," Damien replied. "He'll use the one

person he thinks he can trust. The only person in the area who's had face-to-face dealings with him."

"Seth Martin?"

"I'd be willing to bet my pension that if Lightfoot hasn't already contacted Seth, he will soon."

"Okay," Callihan said. "I'll bite. What do you want to do from here?"

"Bring Seth and Tabitha in. We'll make a deal— Seth helps us to make an arrest and we'll exonerate him of any wrongdoing."

Callihan gave Damien a pointed look. "How does Tabitha fit into the equation? As far as I can see, she brings nothing to the table."

"She flips on Cavello, Boise PD gets to make their arrests, and the state agrees not to press charges for her cooperation."

Callihan nodded. "This could mean WITSEC for both of them. Would they be willing to enter the program? You know it's a tough sell for people like them."

Damien gnashed his teeth and swallowed the sharp retort that sat on the tip of his tongue. *People like them*, meaning lower-class, white trash, dirty, uneducated . . . the list went on and on. He knew for a fact Tabitha had been trying to escape that stigma all of her life. The fact that people like Callihan insisted on making jackassed assumptions was why she found it so hard to find a life outside of her past.

"We'll deal with that issue when we come to it." Damien wasn't going to sit by and watch Tabitha disappear into the abyss of WITSEC anyway. Not if he could do anything about it. "But first we need to get them into custody before Lightfoot or Cavello gets their hands on them."

"All right. We'll play this your way. First I'm going to have to get the U.S. attorney to sign off on any deals we make. Then, I'll get Gates and a couple of Boise PD guys to bring them in. Get cleaned up. Because you're going to be brokering this little deal."

Damien swallowed down the anxiety that pooled in his gut. That nightmare he'd been worried about last night? It was just getting started.

Chapter Twenty-Two

"Where's Seth?" Tabitha's voice had reached supersonic proportions about fifteen minutes ago. She walked into the Boise police station flanked by the deputy U.S. marshal she'd met in the parking lot the other day and two cops. Wow. They must have thought she was dangerous. If she wasn't so scared out of her mind, she would have laughed. But if someone didn't tell her where Seth was soon, she'd show them dangerous and then some. "*Where is my brother?*"

Her entourage remained annoyingly stoic as they led her into a conference room. Seth was seated at the far end of a long table, a frown marring his face as he slouched in his chair. Sweet relief cascaded over her, and Tabitha let out a sob as she rushed into the room to give Seth a hug. "Oh my God," she sighed against his shoulder. "I've been worried *sick.*"

Seth gave her a look that said *Take it easy, Mom,* but she didn't care. When the marshal had showed up at the hotel and not-so-politely requested that she come with him, Tabitha lost her shit. Every worst-case scenario in the book had raced through her mind.

Number one on the list, that Joey had gotten his hands on Seth and her brother was dead. Arrested was way better than dead as far as she was concerned. Seth might not see it that way, but she didn't care.

"Have a seat, Miss Martin."

She stood up straight and squared her shoulders. "Not until you tell me what's going on."

Deputy Gates gave her a deadpan smile, one she suspected was reserved for smart-mouth detainees like herself. His tone was ice-cold, forceful. "Have a seat, Miss Martin."

Tabitha fell into the chair next to Seth's. The suspense was killing her and if something didn't give soon, she was going to throw up. Her stomach churned like an angry sea, her heart beating with so much force, she was afraid it was going to break right out of her chest like one of those creatures in the *Alien* movies. Should she have an attorney present? Could she even afford an attorney? How did one go about contacting a lawyer on a Sunday afternoon?

The door to the conference room swung open and Tabitha's brain froze as it tried to reconcile what her eyes were seeing. Behind an older man dressed in business casual was a towering mountain of a man, his height and bulk the most impressive form in the room. His light brown locks were still purposely mussed, but he looked out of place in a pair of form-fitting slacks and a white button-down. Around his neck, a gold badge hung on a lanyard, the five-pointed star glinting in the artificial light.

Tabitha opened her mouth to speak. Closed it. Opened it again, but words refused to come. What in the hell was going on?

"Miss Martin, I'm Chief Deputy U.S. Marshal

Dennis Callihan. This is Deputy Parker Evans. I think it's time we had a chat with you and your brother."

Parker Evans? Tabitha's brain cranked into high gear, along with an indignant fire that burned from the pit of her stomach all the way up her throat. What were the odds that Damien had an equally sexy twin brother who happened to work on the opposite side of the law? All signs pointed to *not a freaking chance*.

Seth began to run off at the mouth, a string of smart-ass remarks that Tabitha couldn't make a lick of sense of. The words were nothing more than gibberish, a cacophony of sound that amounted to white noise in the back of her mind. Her eyes met Damien's, and the look of regret that flashed across his handsome visage squeezed every ounce of blood from her heart and the last breath of oxygen from her lungs.

"You son of a bitch!"

Tabitha found her voice and it exploded from her in a shout that left her throat raw and aching. Angry tears stung her eyes, and she willed not a single one to pass over her lids. The thought that Damien—or was it Parker?—had used her, betrayed her trust, made her think that he felt *anything* for her, was like acid burning through her veins. *Oh God.* She'd thrown herself at him like some sort of sex-starved nympho. And he'd let her! Encouraged her! Played his little games of domination, making her think that she'd finally found a man who could give her what she needed. Had all of it been an act? Just a part he played to gain her trust so he could make an arrest?

The humiliation was almost more than she could bear.

"Come on, Seth. We're out of here." Her brother gave a superior snort, a secret fist-bump to encourage Tabitha's defiance. She pushed out her chair with so much force that it crashed against the opposite wall. Childish? Maybe. But it was either that or she was going to put her fist into Damien's not-too-soft gut. If she assaulted a United States marshal, she doubted anyone would think twice before slapping cuffs on her.

"Both of you need to sit back down." The older guy—Callihan—seemed to be running the show. Likewise, he didn't come off as the type of guy who took shit off of anyone. "Your brother might not know the kind of trouble you're both in, but you do, Tabitha. I don't think you want to take your chances out there."

Despair permeated every pore of her body, tightening Tabitha's skin to the point that she felt suffocated. Seth gave her the side-eye, and she knew that if she didn't play along, they were both screwed.

"Tabs, what's going on?" Seth's smart-ass tone evaporated into something altogether more concerned. It was the most adult he'd ever sounded, and if not for their abysmal circumstances, she would have been thrilled to see that for once, he was taking something seriously.

"Thanks to that lying son of a bitch over there"— she jerked her chin toward Damien—"Joey thinks I helped to steal a half shipment of whatever it is he's selling. Gerald is coming down to clean house."

Seth collapsed back down into his chair. "Holy shit, Tabs. This is bad."

"This has nothing to do with either of you." Damien approached the table and took up a place directly across from where Tabitha stood. She refused to demur and looked right into the bastard's eyes, hoping he could see the pain in hers. He deserved nothing less than to suffer for his deception.

"If it doesn't have anything to do with us, then why are we here?"

Damien gave Tabitha a look as though to say it was beneath her to play coy. Yeah, right. "We want Lightfoot. Period."

Jesus. She would have been less hurt to know it was Joey they'd been after. The admission speared her straight through the heart and twisted painfully. Had Damien known about her history all along? Weaseled into her life—her *heart*—in an effort to find a way to Gerald Lightfoot? God, she'd bared her soul to him, told him things she'd never told anyone else, and for all she knew, he'd already been up to speed on every sordid detail of her life!

"I can't get you any closer to Gerald than you already are," Tabitha replied. "You know that." Damien's gaze slid to Seth, and Tabitha's temper boiled. "It's not enough that you used me? Now you want to use him, too?"

Damien's shoulders slumped. It was a low blow, but Tabitha didn't care.

"The U.S. Marshals Fugitive Task Force has been after Gerald Lightfoot for years, Miss Martin," Chief Deputy Callihan chimed in. "Arresting him is our top priority. If you and your brother help us to make an arrest, we can guarantee your safety. We can take care of some of the dark marks on Seth's record and give you both a fresh start."

Tabitha snorted. "Sounds a lot like blackmail to me."

"Call it whatever you want. We can let you both

walk out of here right now, but what's that going to accomplish? You're facing racketeering and conspiracy charges, Tabitha. Your brother, too. Why take your chances out there when we can give you a sure thing right here?"

Yep, exactly like blackmail.

"Tabitha." Damien's voice was like a slow caress, lingering on her name with so much affection that it broke her heart all over again. "We're trying to help you. Both of you. We know that you were coerced into helping Joey by setting him up at the hotel. And as far as Seth's involvement goes, I know you don't want to see him pay the price for a few stupid mistakes. You said he's been straight and I believe you. Let me help you get a clean start. Let us protect you. Both of you."

Tabitha thought back to Damien's whispered words in the darkness of her bedroom. His emphatic proclamation that he'd protect her. That he'd never let anyone hurt her. She'd told him not to make promises he couldn't keep. He'd cut her more deeply than anyone in her entire screwed-up life. He'd gutted her. Hollowed her out and filled the empty space with his tender affection. And now, there was nothing left but a void.

"Let's say we do help you." Seth took Tabitha's hand and gave it a reassuring squeeze. "What do you want from us and what do we get if you arrest Lightfoot?"

An armor-piercing round to the chest wouldn't have hurt more than the pained look of betrayal marring Tabitha's delicate features. He'd wanted to explain things to her, come clean in private, away from the law enforcement setting. But this bullshit with Tony and the missing drugs had bumped up their time line. Damien had been too concerned for Tabitha's safety to risk not bringing her and Seth in immediately.

He'd never blurred the lines between his personal and professional lives before. Probably because he didn't have a personal life to speak of. This was a cluster fuck of epic proportions, and it was a wonder he was still allowed to wear his badge. Of course, once Crawford got wind of the situation, he might be turning it in after all.

"Right now, all Lightfoot knows is that half of his latest shipment is missing. That's almost a half-million-dollar loss for him and not something he's going to let slide. According to Joey Cavello, your sister and I stole those drugs and beat up one of his guys last night. I'd imagine that Joey is going to do whatever he can to avoid Lightfoot when he gets to town. It won't matter who stole what, only that it's gone. Joey is going to be held responsible. And if Lightfoot can't get his hands on Joey, he'll go to the guy who initially set him up with Joey in the first place. You."

"Damn, Tabs," Seth said to his sister. "You got into some *shit* last night."

Tabitha's face flushed with embarrassment and she sunk down into her previously discarded seat. As hard as she'd tried to separate herself from the life she'd grown up in, Damien knew that this situation had to be humiliating for her. He hated that she was involved at all. There was so much he wanted to say to her. But it didn't look like he'd get a second alone with her for a while.

"You're probably right," Seth said with a shrug.

"We're sort of like family to him. He'll call me if he can't find Joey. So, what do you want me to do? For the record, I'm not wearing a wire."

"We don't need you to." Callihan drummed his fingers on the tabletop as he spoke. "We're not trying to catch Lightfoot in the act of anything. He's a fugitive. We don't need any other reason to make an arrest. All we want is for you to arrange a meet."

"But you'll want Seth there to meet Gerald, right?" The accusation in Tabitha's voice stung, her blue eyes narrowed with anger.

"Yes. When we arrest Lightfoot, we'll arrest Seth as well. That way, Seth is protected from looking like a narc. After we've got Lightfoot in custody, we'll start the process of setting you both up in witness security."

Tabitha's eyes grew wide. She looked from Callihan, over at Gates, and back to Damien. "What's witness security?"

"You probably know it as the witness protection program, Tabitha," Callihan continued. "In exchange for your testimony—if needed—we'll set you and your brother up with new identities. In a new town. You'll both get a fresh start, and not Lightfoot, Cavello, or any of their associates will be able to find you. It's a chance at a real life and a little freedom."

"Freedom?" Tabitha's incredulous outburst echoed off the walls. "You call that freedom? You might as well throw us in jail!"

Tabitha's reaction wasn't out of the ordinary. Callihan's attempt to put a shiny spin on WITSEC crashed and burned like Damien knew it would. Witness security wasn't a cakewalk by any means.

"I know it sounds scary, but you should be focusing on the fact that you and Seth will be safe."

Tabitha looked at Damien with wide eyes, as though waiting for him to jump in and set the chief deputy straight. "I've got clinicals starting in less than a month! I'm so close to graduating. Seth's got a job and he's enrolled in college for the spring semester. You can't expect us to give all of that up. We've worked hard to get to this point, and you want us to throw all of it away?"

Callihan stretched his hands out imploringly. "You won't be throwing anything away, Tabitha. Seth can enroll in a school wherever we set you up, and as far as your education goes, we'll do whatever we can to make sure your credits transfer over so you don't lose any time."

Tabitha's eyes went wide. "I'm going to assume that you haven't been to college recently. Transferring credits between in-state schools is nearly impossible. Doing it with an out-of-state university? You may as well ask me to start over from square freaking one."

Damien leaned across the table, his hands itching to reach for her. "Tabitha—"

"You don't talk to me," she seethed, pointing an accusing finger his way. "You don't get to say another word to me. Ever."

She might as well have ripped his beating heart from his chest, thrown it on the ground, and stomped it into a bloody pulp. Damien welded his jaw together, the enamel grinding. The helplessness he felt grated on him, but not because he wasn't in control of the situation. Because he had this locked down. No, what pissed him off was the fact that he was in a room with three other colleagues and Tabitha's brother. And he wouldn't get a chance to plead his case with her.

She'd shut him down.

You don't get to say another word to me. Ever.

"How much time do we get to make a decision?" Seth asked.

"We need to know in the next thirty minutes," Damien replied. "I know it doesn't give you a lot of time to talk things through with your sister, but we need to get the ball rolling ASAP."

"I think we need a few minutes alone then." Seth had really stepped up to the plate. Tabitha was mixed up in all of this because of him, after all. And the fact that he was finally looking out for his sister elevated him in Damien's opinion.

"We can give you that." Damien and the chief deputy stood from their chairs and joined Ryan Gates and the Boise PD officer at the conference room door. "Talk it over and decide what you want to do. We'll check back soon."

They filed out of the room, Damien taking up the rear. As he went to close the door, he cast one final look at Tabitha. Their eyes met. The defiance, anger, and pain in her blue eyes cut Damien a little deeper, slicing through tissue and bone to add to the damage of his already mangled heart. "I'm sorry it had to go down like this." He looked at Seth, though his words were directed at Tabitha. "If I could go back and change it, I would."

He closed the door softly behind him.

"What do you think?" Callihan leaned against the opposite wall, his arms folded across his chest.

"They don't have a choice," Damien said on a sigh. "At this point, Joey is going to try to pin everything on Tabitha and me. Seth isn't going to let his sister take the fall." *Thank fuck.*

"I've gotta say, this is not how I envisioned this case

wrapping up. But if we get Lightfoot, it'll be worth it. I'll put in a call to John Rader. We'll want the Bandit task force in on this and maybe SWAT as well. Lightfoot is crafty, otherwise he wouldn't keep slipping through our fingers. Let's see him dodge an army when he decides to show up in town."

It was true. Lightfoot was notorious for dodging law enforcement officials and he possessed an uncanny ability to sniff out a trap. "What about Cavello?" Damien asked. Joey was still a threat to Tabitha and he wanted that SOB behind bars yesterday.

"We won't have any trouble getting an arrest warrant for Cavello," Callihan said. "We've got enough on him from your investigation that we shouldn't even need Martin's testimony to get a conviction."

With the amount of product Cavello was moving, he'd be facing a potential life sentence for drug trafficking. His associate—that piece of shit Tony—would go down, too. "The faster we can wrap it all up, the better." Damien wanted the least amount of stress on Tabitha as possible. "But, Chief, there's a possibility they won't agree to WITSEC." From the sound of it, Tabitha would have to be put in cuffs before she'd let them relocate her. "What then?"

Callihan shrugged his shoulders. "They can refuse, Evans. There's nothing we can do about that. We shouldn't need their testimony, you said so yourself, which means we can't force them into the program. If they refuse WITSEC, then their safety is in their own hands."

Damn it. Callihan was right. If he'd been thinking, Damien would have made sure that WITSEC was one of the conditions to wiping Seth's record and protecting Tabitha from possible charges. And as stubborn as she was, he knew she'd never willingly go into the program. If anything, to prove to him that he no longer had any influence over her. Rub his face in her disdain.

Awesome.

Twenty minutes and way too much small talk later, the conference room door squeaked open. Seth poked his head out into the hallway and said, "All right, here's the deal. I'll help you get Lightfoot. And Cavello, too, if you want, because he fucked with my sister and that shit don't fly. But in exchange for my help I want you"—his gaze slid to Damien—"to leave my sister alone. She's not doing witness protection or anything else for you guys. I'll go wherever you want, but she stays put. Understand?"

Callihan pushed himself off the wall and took Seth's outstretched hand. "Deal. I'll get some paperwork started and leave Deputies Evans and Gates to prep you."

Seth swung the door wide, and over his head Damien caught sight of Tabitha, her head in her hands, shoulders shaking with emotion. Goddamn it, he'd fucked up big-time. And there wasn't anything he could do shy of keeping what was left of her family intact, that would convince Tabitha to even consider forgiving him for what he'd done.

In doing his job, he'd ruined the only good thing in his life. If it was possible, Damien now had even more of a reason to hate Parker Evans.

Chapter Twenty-Three

Tabitha stared down from her apartment balcony at the traffic zooming by on Fairview Avenue, numb. Her heart was heavy with loss and she was still so pissed off at Seth she couldn't see straight. How could he just up and leave her? Disappear into witness protection for God knew how long, totally cut off from her.

"This is the best option for both of us, Tabs, and you know it."

The memory of Seth's words brought a fresh bout of tears to the surface and Tabitha swallowed them down. Seth was all she had. Her entire life had been about taking care of him. What was she going to do without him around?

"You're going to live your life, that's what."

Gah! Why did he have to pick today to be mature and responsible? U.S. Marshals and Boise PD had personnel staged outside of her building and parked around the block, all of them keeping an eye out for anything suspicious, in case Joey managed to track her down before they could wrap up their case. Because, you know, nothing about undercover cops camped out every five feet drew unwanted attention to her building.

Seth was holed up with the bigwigs from this morning—and probably Damien—back at the police station. His phone was being monitored and they were prepping him for what he could expect if Gerald did reach out to him. Despite the anger she felt, she was glad that someone was looking out for Seth and keeping him safe.

The suspense was freaking killing her, though.

She plopped back down on the cheap plastic lawn chair and snatched up the wine bottle sitting on the wooden crate that doubled as an end table. It was probably a sign of a potential problem that she was drinking in solitude, but Tabitha didn't care. She filled the glass three-quarters full with the last of the wine, wondering if she could sweet-talk one of the deputies into making a grocery store run for another bottle.

Tonight was definitely going to be a two-bottle night.

Tabitha craned her neck toward the sliding glass patio door, the knock at her front door barely audible from outside. Speak of the devils . . . If the marshals were checking up on her, she could totally use the opportunity to sweet-talk them into going grocery shopping. Maybe if she bought them a case of beer, they'd join in her misery. At least she wouldn't be drinking alone anymore.

She drained half of her glass in a long gulp before setting it down on the crate. Another round of obnoxious knocks followed on the heels of the first, and she blew out an aggravated breath. Pushy SOBs.

"I'm coming. Keep your panties on."

Tabitha threw open the door and froze, her fingers

curling around the knob in a death grip. "What in the hell are you doing here? You're supposed to be keeping an eye on Seth."

She moved to slam the door in Damien's face, but he stuck a booted toe against the jamb, blocking any attempt at a successful tantrum. "We need to talk."

"I don't have shit to say to you, *Deputy*." She tried to force the door closed again, but Damien was too damned strong. Instead, she turned her back on him and walked into the living room. Maybe if she ignored him, he'd have no choice but to get the hell out of there.

With her back turned, Tabitha stared out of the sliding glass doors as though entertained by the traffic whizzing by below. She refused to look at him, to let the emotion shining in his gaze affect her. Because she knew it was a lie. "If you're here, where's Seth?" She was pissed, but she wasn't going to let her anger stop her from checking up on her brother. "Someone had better have his back or so help me God—"

"Tabitha, look at me."

"Go to hell, Damien. Or I guess it's *Parker*, isn't it? I don't have to do a damned thing you say. Just tell me where Seth is and then get the hell out of my apartment."

Strong hands came around her shoulders and turned her with enough force to send her world reeling. The meager restraint she had over her temper snapped. God, she was tired of being used. It seemed that everyone in her life wanted a piece of her for some selfish reason. Didn't anyone just want her for herself? And why did it hurt more than any of the other hurts in her life that Damien had used her just as callously as everyone else in her crappy life.

Without thinking, she pulled back her hand and let it fly.

Her open palm cracked against his cheek, the sharp sting fueling her anger like dried kindling. Damien's brows drew tight over his eyes, and his nostrils flared. A spark lit in his golden gaze and for the second time since she'd met him, Tabitha experienced a cold tingle of fear. His fingertips dug into the skin at her shoulders, not enough to hurt, but enough to show her she'd better not try to pull away.

"That make you feel better?" His voice was a controlled burn, seething from between clenched teeth.

The fingers of her right hand curled into a fist, and as though Tabitha had no control over her own body, she struck out at him again, this time connecting with his broad shoulder. Her strength was a child's, uselessly lashing out at a wall of muscle that refused to yield under her pathetic blow.

"Come on, Tabitha. Don't stop there. Lay into me!"

His gaze drilled into her. The hard line of his mouth and squared jaw almost dared her to smack the stubborn expression from his face. His hands dropped from her shoulders and he took a step back, inviting whatever punishment she wanted to dole out. Blind rage and hurt sliced through her heart and Tabitha landed another weak punch to his shoulder.

He was immovable, a mountain that mocked her inconsequential existence. Tabitha let out a frustrated shriek. *None* of this made her feel any better. She could hit him again and again, until she couldn't lift her arms anymore, and it would do *nothing* to erase the pain slicing through her. Angry tears burned her cheeks and she balled her hands into tight fists, her nails biting into her palms.

"How could you use me like that?" Her breath hitched as she drew in a deep breath. "You lied to me!"

"Tabitha . . ." Every time he said her name it created another fissure in her heart. He raked his hand through his hair and blew out a breath. "I never wanted it to go down like this. And yeah, I fucking lied and I hated every goddamned minute of it. But I never used you."

Whatever. "Keep telling yourself that if it makes you feel better. Just don't stand there and pretend like you weren't working an angle with me. You saw a way to get what you wanted and exploited it. God! How could I have been so stupid?"

"Jesus Christ, you think I was working an *angle*?" Tabitha's stomach bottomed out at his angry shout, but she forced herself to stay planted to her spot on the floor. "I didn't tell you who I was or why I was really here. I'll own that. But the shit I told you was real. What happened between us was *real.* And I'm not going to let you cheapen that by accusing me of working a fucking angle with you."

A lump the size of a basketball lodged in her throat, but she shouted past it. "I trusted you! I told you things I've never even told my brother, and you took that trust and stomped all over it. I thought you cared about me, Damien, and you couldn't even be truthful with me! Jesus, that's not even your real name!" She laid her palms against his chest and shoved, but there was no force behind the action. He simply stood there. Took every ounce of it. Didn't even budge. "Do you know how many times I agonized over what was going on? Picked up the phone to call the FBI. Sat in the parking lot at the federal courthouse like some kind of freak!" Her strength began to flag, emotional exhaustion winning out over her rage. "Goddamn you!"

"You really think I have so little integrity that I'd play with your emotions like that?" His voice strained and Tabitha steeled herself against his tenderness. "It fucking *killed* me not to tell you the truth about what was going on. You're not the only one who put yourself out there, you know."

"Bullshit." Her gaze drilled into his. They stood not a foot apart, the air sizzling between them. Damien's nostrils flared with his heavy breaths and for once, Tabitha considered taking a cautious step back. "How can I possibly believe that *anything* that happened between us was real?"

Damien crushed her to him, his mouth claiming hers in a kiss that left her dizzy and breathless, though it did little to abate her anger. This time she turned it inward, berating herself as she thrust her tongue in his mouth, for wanting him. Craving him. Needing him like this despite everything he'd done to her.

Damien's large palm cupped the back of her neck before gathering the short strands of her hair in his fist. He tugged her head back and slanted his mouth across hers in a desperate, frenzied kiss that left Tabitha weak and shaking. And wanting more.

She tore at his shirt, popping buttons in her haste to get it off of him. He kicked off his shoes and she did the same, their mouths welded together as they worked the fastenings of each other's jeans, fingers fumbling and greedy for exposed flesh. He nipped at her bottom lip, the sting only goading her on as her sex clenched, a rush of delicious warmth spreading between her thighs. Their mouths parted only long enough for Damien to drag the T-shirt off of

Tabitha's body, and then he unfastened her bra, tearing it from her in a rush.

The cold air puckered her nipples to tight, aching peaks as Damien urged her backward, one hand clutching the back of her neck while the other kneaded her breast before he tugged on her nipple. Tabitha gasped, her head rolling back as he caught the other nipple in his mouth, sucking and licking, nibbling. Tiny bubbles of sensation burst over Tabitha's body, and she cried out, her hands diving into his hair as he continued to suck, the light sting of his teeth taking her dangerously close to the edge.

She soared on a cloud of bliss and her feet left the floor as though she'd floated away. Damien hoisted her up in his arms and cradled her against the heat of his chest, kissing her as though every beat of his heart depended on the contact. Down the hallway they bounced off the walls as he walked, fumbling his way to her bedroom, where he collapsed on top of her on the bed they'd shared the night before.

A primal growl worked its way up Damien's throat, rumbling in his chest as he grabbed her underwear and jerked it down her thighs. Tabitha's breath was ragged, her throat raw as she turned and pulled open the drawer of her bedside table to grab a condom from the box she'd bought. Funny, she'd been about to throw the damned things away when she got home. Thank God for small favors . . .

Damien grabbed the foil packet from her hand and wrapped his fingers around her waist, hoisting Tabitha up high on the bed. He spread her thighs and buried his face between them. She cried out with pleasure as his tongue swirled over her clit, already so swollen and throbbing that she ached with the need for release.

"Damien!" His name left her lips on a desperate gasp. She fisted the locks of his hair, holding him between her thighs, crying out with every flick, every thrust of his tongue.

He came up on his knees and Tabitha felt him shift as he ripped open the packet. "Oh God." Already she was close to the edge, her body humming with need, her pussy so wet that her thighs were slick with her arousal. Damien crawled up the length of her body like an animal about to consume its prey. He took her mouth again in a ravenous kiss, the taste of her on his lips driving him mad.

He entered her in a single purposeful thrust and the orgasm took her with an almost violent intensity.

Damien was mindless with desire. An animal with singular focus and goaded by pure instinctual need. Her pussy clenched around his cock, so fucking tight he welded his teeth together at the intensity of sensation, Tabitha's impassioned cries the sweetest sound in his ears as she came.

He couldn't get enough of her. The thought of losing her shook him to his very foundation, filling him with a sense of loss so deep and vast he knew he'd never recover from it. He buried himself to the root, taking her as hard and deep as he dared, and she opened her legs for him, urged him deeper, clawed at his back with the same ferocity. The same hopeless desperation.

"Harder." Tabitha's voice was a desperate whimper, her breath warm in his ear. "Oh God, Damien, harder!"

He cupped her ass in one palm, covered one full breast with the other. His muscles strained with every thrust, his jaw locked down and his breath heaved in his chest in time with every frantic beat of his heart. Her swollen bud brushed his shaft as he pulled out, teasing him as he buried himself deep. Each pleading sob from her lips was as sweet as honey, and he swallowed her cries in a kiss, as though he could taste those desperate whimpers as well.

Tabitha's second orgasm came on the heels of her first, so intense that she threw her head back as her cries grew hoarse from the effort. Damien's balls drew up tight, and he thrust hard once, and again, burying himself inside of her. "Tabitha." Her voice was a prayer, spoken in time with every thrust. "Tabitha." God, he needed her. Wanted her. "Tabitha." He *loved* her. "Tabitha!"

Damien's orgasm hit him in wave after violent wave of sensation, pulsing through his body with the explosiveness of an incendiary detonation. His blood was on fire, his lungs ached with the need for more oxygen. His body shook as his muscles tensed and spasmed. And yet he continued to pump his hips, milking himself on that sweet, tight heat that squeezed his cock.

He collapsed on top of her, no longer able to support his own weight. The only sounds in the room were their labored breaths that melded into one. On the heels of the most intense pleasure he'd ever experienced, a fear gripped at Damien's chest. Icy fingers that speared his heart and refused to melt. She'd been angry, and there was a fine line between rage and passion. Now that the spell was broken and she'd released all of that pent-up emotion, what now? Would she allow him to apologize, to explain himself? Or would she throw him out like she'd tried to do when he first showed up?

Like that night in the hotel room when he first tried to earn her trust, Damien spoke low against her ear in an effort to win her patience before the warm glow of her orgasm dissipated. "My name is Parker Damien Evans. I'm a deputy marshal with the U.S. Marshals' Special Operations Group. I've been working undercover on and off for the past four years and before I met you, I didn't think I could ever be anything but the part I'd taught myself to play."

Her breath hitched, too quietly for him to determine her reaction, so he pressed on. "Keep your eyes closed, baby, and please hear me out. I've never played a part with you, Tabitha. Ever. What I gave you was who I really am. And I wanted to tell you who I was, especially after last night. I was prepared to come clean, but then I got your message about Joey, and keeping you safe was more important than explaining myself to you. I meant everything I said to you. I kept the truth from you but I never lied. I know that doesn't make sense, but you can't just turn your back on me."

Damien wrapped his arms around her, held her close as though the simple act would guarantee she'd stay by his side forever. "I love you, Tabitha. I'm in love with you. And I swear, I will never lie, never keep anything from you, ever again."

Damien had never felt so emotionally or physically spent. Even in that godforsaken desert, surrounded by death and endless miles of cold and heat, sand and unyielding mountain terrain, hiding behind rocks, in caves, and convinced he'd never see home again, he hadn't been as totally wrecked as he was in this moment. Tabitha Martin had laid him low. Broken him down until he was nothing more than a blubbering pussy, begging her not to turn her back on him. Not to leave him. And damn it, he'd continue to beg, to plead, to do whatever the fuck she asked of him if that's what it took. He was so god-damned in love with this woman that he didn't think he'd be able to live through another day that didn't have her in it.

Damien rolled to his side so he wouldn't crush Tabitha beneath his weight. When he pulled out, separating their bodies, he fought the urge to go back to her. But if he expected her to give him a chance, he had to give her some space. And though their bodies seemed to crave each other, he needed to allow her to think with a clear head that wasn't influenced by lust.

Long moments passed. Damien kept his face buried against Tabitha's throat, breathing in her sweet floral scent. He let his fingers explore her body, memorize every soft curve. If this was the first and last time they made love, Damien wanted to be sure that he never forgot the way her hips flared from her narrow waist, or the freckles that dotted her shoulder. The supple curve of her breasts and the dusky nipples that stood out proud and erect, puckering as her body cooled. He brushed his thumb across her lips, petal soft and full. How he loved that mouth. Loved her taste, the methodical way her lips moved over his.

There wasn't any part of her that he didn't love.

His gut twisted into an unyielding knot as the silence stretched out between them. Her breathing was no longer heavy, but rhythmic and quiet as she feathered her fingers through his hair, her nails scraping lightly against his scalp with every pass. Tabitha's arms came around him and she cradled Damien against her body as though to offer him comfort.

"I think you should leave."

Her words were nothing more than a ragged whisper, thick with emotion. Panic welled in Damien's chest, burning like acid. He'd heard her wrong. She wasn't kicking him out. "Tabitha—"

"Please, Damien." She couldn't hide the tears in her voice as she continued to stroke his hair, her touch so gentle. "If you care about me at all, you'll do as I ask. If you stay I'll—" Her words ended on a sob. "I need you to go."

Damien's heart might as well have exploded in his chest. The ache was so deep, the damage so severe, it was a wound no man could survive. Her fingers left his hair, and her arms as well, taking with them any comfort he might have felt. Tabitha rolled away from him, the soft sound of her tears spearing every major organ in his body.

He rolled toward her and placed a light kiss to her temple before forcing his body off the bed. Each step felt like a thousand, his body rebelling the farther he took himself away from her. Damien eased her bedroom door closed behind him, determined to give her whatever solitude she needed.

Was it too soon to pray that she wouldn't keep him at arm's length forever?

Chapter Twenty-Four

Tabitha's body ached for him. *Ached.* A bone-deep pain that she feared would never go away. She curled into a ball on her mattress, her heart broken into so many pieces that she doubted it would ever be whole again. How could one man make her feel so complete and so absolutely wrecked, all at the same time?

The sound of Damien washing up in her bathroom had been comforting. The muted rustle of him moving around her living room as he got dressed, reassuring. But then he'd left, the front door of her apartment closing with a finality that stole the breath from Tabitha's lungs and hollowed her out until she was nothing more than a useless, empty shell.

He'd said that he loved her. And despite the things he'd kept from her, the lies he'd told, she knew in her heart that those words, spoken softly in her ear, had been the truth.

"I love you, too."

In the lonely quiet of her room, the words weighed heavily on her. As though once spoken aloud, they could never be taken back. Did she want to take them back? And seriously, how could she possibly fall in love with someone after a few sporadic weeks together? Still, there was something about being with Damien . . . Parker . . . whatever . . . that felt so *right* it was scary. Was fate making up for the crappy hand she'd been dealt by dropping the perfect man right in her lap?

Not so perfect, Tabs.

No. Not perfect. But really, who was? If she tried to see the situation from his perspective, she might be able to acknowledge that he'd done what he had to do. He was an undercover cop, in town to bring down a criminal. And for all he knew, Tabitha was as much a part of the entire operation as Joey was. She hadn't simply proved her involvement by setting Joey up at the hotel, she'd admitted to knowing the very fugitive Damien was searching for. Pretty damning evidence, to be sure. And though she'd given him glimpses into her life bit by bit, it wasn't until last night that she'd truly opened up to him. Trusted him. She supposed it had been a lot to process. Maybe she was being unfair in her anger. Wouldn't anyone need a little time after being hit with a bombshell like that? Especially when Damien realized that Tabitha had firsthand knowledge—not to mention a rocky history—with the man he was trying to arrest.

Afternoon faded into evening, and gray twilight swallowed the last of the light filtering into her bedroom. Worry settled on Tabitha's chest like a boulder, the weight unrelenting as she wondered if Seth was okay. Praying that Damien was with him. Protecting him.

Tabitha pushed herself off the bed, reluctant to part with the comforter that bore traces of Damien's clean, musky scent. It wouldn't do her a damn bit of good to lie there in the dark, second-guessing her decision to ask him to leave. She'd needed time to think, away from his magnetic presence and honest words that tugged at her heartstrings. Besides, Seth's safety was what was important, and Damien wasn't going to keep an eye on her brother while he was lounging in her bed. She'd made the right decision. There would be time later—when all of this business with Joey and Gerald was said and done—to work out the kinks of her personal life.

Thirty minutes later, someone knocked at her door. Tabitha muted the television, hoping that someone with the Marshals Service or Boise PD was there to give her an update. This time, she had the good sense to check the peephole before throwing the door wide but all she got was a close-up view of the logo of a Pizza Hut delivery shirt and the back of the guy's head. A tremor of anxiety rushed through her and Tabitha's heart began to race. She definitely hadn't ordered a pizza. It wasn't the first time something had been delivered to her unit by accident, though. All of the buildings looked the same and weren't clearly marked. It was easy to get lost. She let out a nervous chuff of breath. *Paranoid much, Tabs?* She eased the door open a crack only to have it shoved forcefully open. The nervous tremor transformed into panic as once again someone she didn't want to see barged through the threshold.

A sneer pulled at Joey's lip as he brought a gun up to Tabitha's face. "You make a sound, and I'll put a bullet in your head."

Tabitha took a step back. And another. How in the hell had he found her apartment? She'd been so careful, so sure that he didn't know where she lived. If he'd been watching the hotel, he would have seen the Boise PD guys escorting her to their cruiser this afternoon. *Shit.* How much did he already know? And what part of that knowledge was going to get her killed?

"Did you beat some poor guy up for that T-shirt, Joey?"

Joey snickered and Tabitha wanted to kick him. He advanced, stepping fully inside the apartment and letting the door close quietly behind him.

"I know you're upset, but you're obviously not thinking clearly. Don't do anything stupid, Joey."

Wrong choice of words. Joey lunged, pressing the cold metal of the barrel into Tabitha's forehead. "You think you can talk to me like that, you fucking bitch?" His pupils were blown and sweat beaded his brow. Wow. Joey was an idiot if he thought getting high would improve his situation. "Where is my shit? I want every last ounce of it right fucking now."

Where were the marshals who were supposed to be watching her apartment? The cops parked around the block and along the street? How had Joey managed to get past them? This was bad. He was obviously still operating under the assumption that Tabitha had stolen from him and was looking for someone to take the fall with Gerald so he'd be off the hook. If Gerald hadn't contacted him yet, he had to know that he was running out of time. Tabitha tried to swallow the lump that rose in her throat, willed enough saliva into her mouth to speak. "Joey, I don't have your stuff. Neither does Damien. I tried to tell you earlier today. Tony stole those drugs. Not me. He attacked me, and Damien beat the shit out of him. But your drugs were long gone before any of that went down."

Joey pressed the barrel tighter into Tabitha's

forehead and she winced. If he kept it up he was going to draw blood.

"That's bullshit. You're fucking lying. And you're going to give every single motherfucking ounce back to me before Lightfoot shows up. Do you understand me?"

A tentative wave of relief rippled over Tabitha's flushed skin. Okay, so all she had to do was convince him to go to the meet. They didn't need him there to bust Gerald, but if he did show up, Damien could kill two birds with one stone. At least, that's what she was hoping for. "You need to talk to Tony." Tabitha's mind raced as she tried to think of anything that might shift Joey's focus from putting a bullet in her head. It would have helped to know if Gerald had gotten in touch with Seth yet. *Shit.* "Joey, if Gerald is coming to town to straighten things out, you know he's going to call Seth if he can't get ahold of you. That's not going to look good. You can't dodge him and expect it to make this situation better."

Joey grabbed her just above her left elbow, his fingertips biting painfully into her skin. "I'm not planning to dodge him." He sneered. "But since I can't find that piece of shit you're currently fucking, I'm going to bring Lightfoot the next best thing. There's no way in hell I'm going down for this, Tabitha."

Well, hell. If she hadn't been nervous before, this new development was sure getting it done. "Joey, let's talk about this."

He wrenched her arm behind her back with enough force that Tabitha thought it might snap. She cried out from the pain, doubled over and helpless. "Joey, the police are watching me." It might have been a stupid move to show her hand so quickly, but unless Tabitha wanted to be stuck in the middle of a potential shoot-out, she needed to do something to defuse the situation. "They're parked outside and around the block. If you try to take me out of here, we're both screwed."

"For someone so concerned about walking the straight and narrow, you sure stepped in it, didn't you, Tabs?"

Boy, wasn't that the understatement of the year. She wondered what Joey would think if she told him that the guy she was "currently fucking" happened to be a deputy U.S. marshal. "Yeah, well, I think I have you to thank for that."

Joey wrenched her arm again and Tabitha swallowed down a scream. If he kept it up, he'd dislocate her shoulder. "I think you have your fuck-up of a brother to thank for it." Joey's text alert went off and he released Tabitha's arm, keeping the gun trained on her forehead. "Time to go, sweetheart. Lightfoot's plane touched down twenty minutes ago and we're going to get this shit settled once and for all."

"Did you not hear me?" Tabitha rubbed her injured arm. She was going to have some class-A bruises. "The cops are watching my apartment. Really, it's a wonder you even got to the front door, Joey."

"Not really. The cops are fucking stupid. They don't think twice about whose name they say over the radio. Anyone with a scanner can keep an eye on where they are and what they're doing." He gave an arrogant snort. "Or who they've got in custody. We're going to sneak out of here the way I snuck in. Do you think I'm a fucking idiot, Tabitha?" Did he really want her to answer that? "Those assholes think they're all stealthy and shit hanging out in their cars. Like that isn't as lame as fuck. Let's go. We're outta here."

A surge of fear-driven adrenaline coursed through Tabitha's veins. Her only consolation to being dragged out of her apartment at gunpoint was the thought that wherever Joey was taking her, Damien would likely be. Would he protect her like he'd promised to, despite the fact that she'd kicked him out of her apartment only minutes after the most intense sexual experience of her life? Who knew. There wouldn't be time for her to explain herself, to tell him that she'd been scared and confused and hurt. That her feelings for him ran far deeper than any crush or simple attraction, and she worried that he'd burrowed so deeply into her soul that she couldn't live without him. All of that would have to wait. She just prayed that her faith in him wasn't misplaced. Because he was going to have more than just Seth to protect at this point.

Joey bent down and snatched Tabitha's tennis shoes up from the floor. He chucked them at her feet. "Get your shoes on and let's go."

She obeyed without another squeak of protest. It didn't do much good to argue with someone who was not only high as a kite, but armed. Joey dragged Tabitha through the door and directly into her neighbor's apartment which was situated at the far corner of her building. The jamb was splintered and the lock broken. She said a small prayer of thanks that no one was home. She didn't know her neighbor well, but Tabitha did know she was a single mom with two young kids. Joey pulled her through the apartment to the balcony, where he'd slung a knotted rope made from a bedsheet. Looked like they were fleeing the scene like a couple of ten-year-olds running away from home. Good God.

"You first." Joey poked her in the ribs with the

barrel of the gun. *Ouch!* "When you get to the ground, don't even think about running or I'll put a bullet in you. Got it?"

Tabitha nodded. She slung one leg over the balcony, gripped the first knot in the sheet, and then slung her other leg over. In choosing to escape from the balcony that was shielded from the view of the parking lot and the street, Joey had demonstrated that he wasn't as clueless as she'd given him credit for. God, she hoped Damien was good at his job. Because right now, he was the only thing standing between her and death.

"I've gotten into some shit in my life, but this takes the fuckin' cake."

Damien gave Seth a sidelong glance. The kid was bouncing around like he was about to take the court in the NBA playoffs or some shit. It was sad to think that he was so young and already had such illustrious criminal connections. Damien could only imagine what Seth and Tabitha's childhood must have been like. And he admired Tabitha all the more for the way she fought to distance herself from that life. "Just calm down, Seth. You don't want to give Lightfoot any reason to be nervous. This is just business as usual, got it?"

"Sorry." Seth stuffed his hands in his pockets and his shoulders slumped. He even sounded like a dejected kid. "So, how's the whole witness protection thing, anyway? Am I going to have to get plastic surgery or wear dark glasses everywhere I go?"

Damien laughed. "Hardly." He hadn't worked a rotation with WITSEC in a long time, but he knew that the Marshals Service would make sure Seth was well taken care of. "It'll be nice and chill. You'll get to be a normal twenty-one-year-old kid and live your life. And it won't be permanent. I'm sure once the dust settles, you'll be able to come back here if you want."

"Cool." Seth craned his head out of the window of Damien's car like a squirrel poking its head from a hole. "But Tabs will probably be better off if I stayed away. For a while anyway. At least until I get my shit together."

Damien opted not to respond. Seth's relationship with Tabitha was none of his business. Hell, at this point he doubted that Tabitha was his business. He'd gone to her apartment this afternoon, prepared to explain himself and at least reach some sort of understanding. Instead of a simple understanding, he'd gotten everything he'd ever wanted and more.

Tabitha was heaven.

There would never be another woman for him. Every encounter he'd had with Tabitha before today had been nothing more than play. A tantalizing peek at what being with her would truly be like. Damien could never have prepared himself for the intensity— the intimacy—of making love to her. It had never been that good with any other woman and would never be better. She was *it*.

"My sister likes you, you know."

Damien glanced at Seth and swallowed down a disbelieving grunt. *Yeah, sure she does.* Which was why she'd all but thrown him out of her apartment this afternoon.

"Your sister throws a mean right hook." Damien figured Seth didn't need to know everything about their afternoon together.

"She *so* does. But—and this is going to sound totally

fucked up—she wouldn't have decked you if she didn't care. The last time I got in trouble, she smacked me upside the head so hard I swear I saw stars." Seth chuckled. "You ever see a bear with her cubs? They get out of line and that big paw comes out to swat them around and bring them into line. That's Tabs. She's a mama bear. Always has been."

Damien could totally picture her laying into her brother that way. Maybe Seth was right. If he gave Tabitha some space, let her vent her frustrations with him and put him in line, she'd come around. Even if she didn't, Damien would be at her front door every day, more than willing to act as her punching bag until she forgave him. He wasn't going *anywhere.*

A pair of headlights turned onto Federal Way, toward the fenced-in yard of Lightfoot's shipping company where Damien and Seth waited. The kid resumed his nervous bouncing, shaking the Shelby until Damien felt like they were cruising down a bumpy road and no longer parked. "Relax, Seth. There are marshals, DEA, Boise PD, and SWAT staged at the perimeters of the property and we're all going to walk out of here in one piece. Got it?"

Seth turned and gave him a sheepish smile. "Got it. But, man, I am so going straight after tonight. This shit ain't worth the stress."

Wasn't that the fucking truth?

"Shit." A jacked-up Ford pickup pulled up beside them and Damien's hands wrapped around the steering wheel in a white-knuckled grip.

"What?"

"Joey beat Lightfoot here." Damn it. As far as Joey was concerned, Seth and Damien would have no business to be here together. He didn't want anything throwing up red flags at this point. If Joey decided to call them out on it and give Lightfoot any reason for suspicion, it would be a disaster. "Here." He shoved a Glock into Seth's hand. "You found me at the hotel and forced me to come here. Got it?"

"Shit!" If Seth wasn't panicked before, he sure as hell was now. "What if something happens? How are you going to arrest anyone—or save any of our asses—unarmed?"

"Don't worry. I've got an extra holstered at my waistband. This is just for show. Make Joey think that you've got the situation under control. Damien locked his gaze with Seth's. "You can do this. For your sister."

Seth visibly swallowed and nodded his head. "No worries. I've got this."

"Okay, then. Put on a good show."

Damien got out of the car with a scowl fixed into place. He put his hands behind his neck and interlaced his fingers as though Seth had already given him the order to do so. Seth trained the gun on him and Damien had to admit he was sweating a little with a nervous kid pointing a loaded weapon at his head. It might have been a good idea to remove the damned clip. *Jesus.* Just another day at the office . . .

He came around to the front of the Shelby, the headlights of Joey's truck shining too bright for Damien to see anything but shadows. Joey got out and the passenger door swung open. Damien's gut clenched at this new variable that had been thrown into the mix. Could Joey have come with Lightfoot? Then his stomach took a nosedive and landed with a splat somewhere near the soles of his feet when he realized the shadowed form was much too curvy and feminine to belong to Gerald Lightfoot.

Motherfucker.

"Damn, Seth!" Joey followed up with a slow whistle. "You're a certifiable badass. Brought in the big game tonight. Nice fucking job, dude."

Damien's teeth gnashed. He was going to kill that little son of a bitch. *Kill* him, if he touched one hair on Tabitha's head.

"Lightfoot said he wanted everyone involved rounded up. I do what I'm told."

Seth's tone was cool and level. Perfect. In the glare of Joey's headlights, Damien couldn't see Tabitha's face. Was she okay? The loose perimeter of officers watching her apartment had been an obvious fail. Damn it, he should have had her taken into protective custody. She would have been pissed but at least she'd be safe. Damien pushed the myriad worries to the back of his mind and focused on the situation at hand. Whether or not Tabitha's protective detail had fallen through, he had backup here. And he was going to get all of them out of this alive.

"Seth, are you out of your *mind*?" Damien would have laughed at Tabitha's enraged tone if the situation had been less dire. "What are you doing?"

"What I have to."

If Damien didn't know any better, he would have been nervous at Seth's Oscar-worthy performance. He wished there was some way to convey to Tabitha that everything was okay, but unfortunately, she'd have to remain in the dark for the duration.

"You oughta take a page from your brother's book, Tabs," Joey said. Damien's gaze slid to where Joey's hand bit into Tabitha's arm and it was all he could do not to tackle the fucker. "He knows what's what. Seth, why don't you talk some sense into this bitch? The quicker I get my shit back, the better."

"She's still my sister, asshole." Seth's voice burned with barely veiled rage. "So watch your fucking mouth."

Joey snorted. "Whatever. It's not going to matter to Lightfoot that she's your sister, so you better get her to cough up the goods before he gets here."

What a cluster fuck. Though if Damien had known a simple theft would get Lightfoot to show his face, he would have played this assignment differently from the start. With Lightfoot as hard to lay eyes on as Santa Claus or the Easter Bunny, the marshals were keeping their distance. Damien was prepared to take a beating in order to get the arrest, but he wasn't interested in getting shot. With Tabitha here, it added a more dangerous layer to an already volatile situation. Despite her family connection to Lightfoot, there was no guarantee that he wouldn't kill her just to prove a point.

"You know, it's my own fucking fault for trusting a guy who just blows into town, free as a bird, when the rest of his crew is sitting in a federal prison." Joey pointed his revolver at Damien and the tension in Damien's shoulders relaxed a couple fractions of an inch. Anything was better than having that barrel trained on Tabitha. "I mean, what the fuck? You get pinched with a bunch of fucking arms dealers. The feds lock everyone up and you skate? Did you narc on your buddies, Damien? Cut a deal to save your own ass? Because you're a punk-ass bitch if you did." He moved his arm just to the left of Damien's head and pulled the trigger.

The report of the shot cracked as the headlight of Damien's Shelby exploded, sending sparks and shards of glass flying. Tabitha lurched, as though ready to tackle both him and Seth to the ground in order to protect them, but Joey reached out and wound his fist in her hair, pulling her back with a cruel yank.

Joey Cavello had abused both of Damien's girls tonight—Tabitha and his Shelby—and the bastard wasn't going to walk away from this with his nuts intact. "I told your buddy Tony that if he so much as shot a mean mug Tabitha's way, that I would end him. He didn't listen and I beat the ever-living *fuck* out of him. He'd be a dead man right now if it wasn't for the woman standing beside you. So, unless you want to die right here, right now, you'd better take your goddamned hands off of her."

Joey brought up the gun and fired again, shattering the windshield of Damien's car. A riot of chatter went off in his earpiece, Ryan Gates shouting orders to his team and the DEA agents on scene, to be ready to move in at Damien's word. They'd agreed on *bandit* as the code word to signal the marshals and SWAT to move in, and the highly trained tactical team wouldn't move a muscle until given the green light. Joey was blowing off steam—and pissing Damien right the fuck off in the process—but he wouldn't kill Damien. No, he'd wait until Lightfoot showed up before he did anything too rash.

"You gonna end me, Damien?" Another shot rang out and the side mirror exploded. Tabitha grunted in pain as Joey twisted his fist in her hair, wrenching her head back. He put his face against hers and bit Tabitha's earlobe hard enough to cause her to cry out in pain. "Come on. If you're such a tough motherfucker, do something."

Damien's entire body went rigid. Anger burned in his gut like molten metal, slogging through his veins and searing every nerve ending in the process. He took two rapid steps, closing the distance between them, and Tabitha's eyes went wide. "Damien, don't." The urgency in her tone froze him in his tracks, but it did nothing to slow the frantic beat of his heart or heavy breaths puffing in his chest.

"You took something that belonged to me, asshole." Joey brought the barrel of his revolver to Tabitha's temple and she cringed. "I think it's only fair I take something of yours in return."

Chapter Twenty-Five

Joey egged Damien on in an attempt to goad him into doing something that would justify killing him before Gerald showed up. If everything went south before the star of the show made an appearance, all of this would be for nothing, and Tabitha refused to let that happen.

You're okay, you're okay, you're okay.

The self-coaching was helping to slow her racing heart, but it wasn't doing shit for the fear that threatened to choke the air from her lungs. She was pretty sure her ear was bleeding and she wanted to return the favor so badly, she shook with unrestrained rage.

"Seth, don't!"

Her brother's shadowed form cut a swath through the beam of headlights as he rushed at Joey. The situation went from bad to worse in about half a second as Seth's shoulder made contact with Joey's chest. Joey fired off a wild shot and Tabitha went down with them in a tangle of limbs and a cloud of dust. Someone's elbow caught her in the chin, jarring her head back with enough force that it rattled her teeth. Pain radiated through her face, so intense she saw stars.

Or were they headlights? She choked as a second cloud of dust swirled over her, the crunch of gravel barely audible over the sound of the scuffle.

"Jesus fucking *Christ*!"

The sound of that voice rocketed Tabitha into the past and chilled the blood in her veins. Jagged like the rocks and dirt beneath her, dry as the dust coating her lungs, and as deathly cold as a grave. She kicked and rolled away from the mass of struggling bodies, desperate to free herself from the melee.

"Seth, stop." Her tone was low but frantic as she straightened and tugged at her brother's shoulder. "Seth." Memories of Gerald beating a poor kid who'd stiffed him for fifty bucks flashed in her mind. If he'd broken someone's arm over a few bucks, what would he do to them for losing an entire half of his shipment? "Seth!" She kicked at Joey, desperate to get him away from Seth. "Please. Stop now!" Strong arms pulled her upright and Damien hauled her backward, away from the chaos. Seth was next, hauled up by his collar like a helpless kitten being relocated by its mother.

Joey scrambled to retrieve the gun he'd dropped during the fight and brought it up as he came to his feet, practically foaming at the mouth. "You're fucking dead, Seth."

"No one here dies unless I say so." Gerald pulled back the hammer on a monster revolver, the swirling dust lending a dreamlike, gossamer backdrop to the scene. He poked the barrel into the back of Joey's head and for the first time tonight, the jackass had the good sense to look scared.

Joey lowered his own gun and let it hang limply at his side. "Hey, man." His voice cracked like a prepubescent teen as he faced Gerald. "I was just trying to get this situation under control before you showed up."

"Yeah, looks like it." Gerald did nothing to hide his disdain, and Tabitha's mouth went dry. Damien's back was a wall of muscle, shielding her and Seth. There was no way in hell any of this was going to end well.

"Come here, little man." Gerald's endearment to Seth did little to settle Tabitha's nerves. Instead, a sense of foreboding crept over her like an early morning frost. She grabbed Seth's hand, reluctant to let him go. He gave her fingers a reassuring squeeze before walking past the protection Damien offered and over to the man who'd ruined all of their lives.

Gerald Lightfoot was a walking cliché. He looked older than his fifty years, the product of hard living and even harder fighting. Salt-and-pepper hair was drawn back into a long, bedraggled ponytail, deep wrinkles fanned from the corner of his eyes and mouth, and when he smiled at Seth, he revealed a row of crooked teeth with more than one gap. Tabitha's dad had knocked out one of those teeth one night when they'd both been too drunk to stand. It had pissed Gerald off to the point that he'd given her dad a concussion in retaliation.

He was a throwback to the heyday of motorcycle gangs. Hell, Tabitha knew Gerald still had connections with the Demons of Speed, an infamous local biker gang that was well-known for being violent, racist, criminal scumbags. He could easily be their leader, the king asshole. And the funny thing was . . . Damien's rough-around-the-edges appearance fit right in with Gerald's. Joey—all six skinny, grungy feet of him—looked like a clueless newb in comparison.

"How've you been, little man?" Gerald embraced

Seth and gave him a few robust pats on the back. Tabitha's stomach churned with nervous energy and she swallowed down the bile that rose in her throat. Gerald's gesture of fatherly affection was nothing more than show. He'd kill Seth in a heartbeat and not even think twice about it.

Gerald's eyes locked with Tabitha's over her brother's shoulder and he gave her a slow smile that made her skin crawl. "It's been a while, sis. You don't got any love for me?"

She *hated* when he called her that. Even as a kid, the endearment had carried with it an undertone that made her sick. It'd been almost seven years since she'd seen the son of a bitch and he was treating it like some kind of dysfunctional family reunion. Her body sought out Damien's, her steps mechanical as she pressed herself against his broad back. Every inch of her vibrated with fear. Why hadn't anyone called in the cavalry? That was the plan, right? Get Gerald to show his face and then the marshals would move in and arrest him. Where in the hell was everyone?

"Get on over here, Tabby Cat, and give me a hug."

God, the pet names. Sis . . . now Tabby Cat. And there were many more. They seemed to be never ending. With each usage, she was reminded of a life she'd fought so hard to put behind her. A life she didn't want anything to do with ever again. Gerald shifted so that Seth stood beside him, though Gerald kept the hand holding his gun slung casually over her brother's shoulder. Tabitha wasn't an idiot. She knew what he was trying to do: separate them from Damien.

"Come on now, Tabitha. Don't be shy." Gerald's tone was no longer playful or even moderately pleasant. The order was firm and promised retribution if she didn't obey. In front of her, Damien stiffened. What was he waiting for? Where were the troops? Did he need some sort of visual confirmation? Surely Damien knew what Gerald Lightfoot looked like. Her gaze slid to Seth and his furrowed brow urged her forward.

Joey's lips puckered into a superior sneer as she left the protection that Damien offered and approached the man who'd been her parents' friend, business partner, dealer, enabler, and undoing. Gerald kept one hand on Seth as he wrapped Tabitha in his embrace, the smell of stale cigarette smoke causing her to gag. He disgusted her. Gerald kissed Tabitha on the temple and she recoiled from his touch. A hoarse, almost wet chuckle rumbled in his chest. *Ew.* The man was the poster child for why years of smoking, drinking, and drug use was a *bad* idea.

"I gotta say, you two kids are more trouble than you're worth." Gerald's fingers dug into Tabitha's shoulder and she bit her lip to keep from crying out. Dark shadows hid Damien's face, but Tabitha knew by the way his hands were balled into fists that he was barely hanging on to his temper. Seeing the situation from this new angle, Tabitha knew why Damien hadn't called in the cavalry. Gerald now had in his possession two human shields. Insurance in case shit went south. *Oh God.*

"I don't like handlin' business myself," Gerald remarked. "Which is why I trusted Seth to set me up with someone I could depend on." His fingers worked on Tabitha's shoulder, kneading the flesh with too much force. "People who cross me usually die before any questions get to be asked. But since you kids are like family to me, I'm willing to hear you out. So, sis. What sort of trouble did you and your old man over there make for me?"

Joey obviously hadn't wasted any time ratting her out when he was caught empty-handed. What an asshole.

"Whatever Cavello told you is a lie." Damien took a step forward and Gerald leveled the massive revolver at his head.

"I don't remember asking you to say a goddamned thing. But since you're so interested in jumping right in, let's get down to brass tacks. Who the fuck do you think you are, son? And where the fuck is my product?"

"Gerald—"

He squeezed the nerve between Tabitha's neck and shoulder and a jolt of pain shot down her right side. "Quiet, sis. Your old man wants to tell me something."

"Yeah, I do." Damien's voice was a controlled burn, every syllable forced through his teeth. "I'll be more than happy to talk to you about your missing product. But not until you let Seth and Tabitha go."

Dry laughter answered Damien's request. "These are *my* kids. And they're right where they belong."

"Evans, say the word and we'll move in."

Gates's voice in his earpiece was a distraction Damien didn't need. Lightfoot hadn't slipped through their fingers time and again because he was an idiot. Though he doubted his cover had been blown, Damien knew that Lightfoot was wary of him. Anyone who'd been on the run for almost a decade would be. Gates was as antsy as a kid in line at an amusement park, ready to fire the cannons and storm the castle. But Damien wasn't willing to risk Tabitha's or Seth's safety. Lightfoot was using them as a human shield. The son of a bitch wouldn't think twice before shoving either one of them in the path of an oncoming bullet.

"It doesn't matter who I am," Damien all but growled. "All that matters is who I'm with. You think Tabitha would steal from you?"

"That's a good question."

Beside Gerald, Joey squared his shoulders. Yeah, the bastard was only tough when he was bullying a woman or standing next to someone who could back his play. He leaned toward Lightfoot's ear and said, "If he's so trustworthy, why did Seth show up with a gun on this asshole?"

Gerald turned to Seth. "That true, son?"

Tabitha's expression soured at the endearment. Her discomfort with that man did nothing but further rile Damien's temper. Prison was too good for Lightfoot. The bastard would be better off dead.

"It's true." Seth's words carried the slightest quaver. "I didn't know who to trust so I thought I'd better cover all of my bases."

"I'll tell you who to trust, son. *Me.*"

Gerald's arm left Seth's shoulder and swung around until the revolver crossed right in front of Tabitha's face. He pulled the trigger and the shot rang out like thunder. Joey Cavello crumpled to the ground like tissue paper, the point-blank shot to the chest killing him in an instant.

Tabitha clasped her hands over her ears. Damien lunged forward to grab her as her knees buckled, but Gerald refused to let her fall, hugging her body tight against his. "Oh my God!" The words burst from her in a breathless, frantic gasp. "Ohmygodohmygodohmygod."

"Quiet, sis." Gerald gave Tabitha a rough shake and her frantic sobs ceased, muffled as she brought her hands to her mouth. She looked at Damien with wide, disbelieving eyes, every inch of her trembling violently. "See what happens when you trifle with men's hearts? They don't think straight. Your ex couldn't manage his shit like a man's s'posed to. Couldn't keep your sassy ass in line. Now he's dead." Gerald leveled the revolver on Damien and added, "One down, one to go."

"No!"

Tabitha shot upright and grabbed Gerald by the shirt. "Don't. Don't kill him, Gerald. Damien didn't do anything. He didn't steal *anything* from you. I didn't steal anything from you. You're right, Joey didn't manage his people but Damien isn't the problem. I promise."

Damien hated to see her beg that piece of shit for anything. Fear widened her eyes, thinned her lips, and hollowed her cheeks. Her chest heaved with quickened breath.

"Evans, we're moving in."

"Wait."

He let the word hang. It could have been spoken to Lightfoot, though Gates would know the command was meant for him. Seth took a slow sliding step away from Lightfoot and then another. It only put inches between them, but any ground gained was good. Damien couldn't save them both, and if he chose Tabitha's safety over her brother's, he knew she'd never forgive him.

"Let's get somethin' straight right now." Lightfoot pulled back the hammer. "I don't wait for *anyone.*"

As though Tabitha and Seth were communicating via telepathy, they both acted at once. Seth knocked Lightfoot's arm high in the air as Tabitha used the distraction to spin away. The second shot exploded from the gun just as Damien reached to his back for the 9mm tucked into his waistband. He whipped it around at Lightfoot's face just as the older man aimed his revolver once again.

Lightfoot smirked. "This is what you call a good old-fashioned standoff."

Damien shrugged. "Guess so."

In her haste to get away, Tabitha tripped and landed beside Joey Cavello's body. Without missing a beat, Lightfoot stomped a booted foot down onto Tabitha's ankle with enough force to snap it in two. She stifled a scream that ended on a pained sob. "Seth, you do somethin' stupid like that again, and I'll make you watch while I skin your sister alive. You understand me, son?"

Seth looked to Damien as though for guidance, but he had to stay focused on Lightfoot.

"No one's doing shit. Back away from Tabitha and I won't put a bullet in your chest."

Lightfoot laughed, the sound like the crackle of dry autumn leaves. "You think you can shoot me before I shoot you? I'll give it to you, you've got a pair on you. So, if you don't have my product, who the fuck does?"

Damien kept his gun leveled on the other man, his attention divided between Lightfoot and Tabitha. "One of Cavello's buddies. But since you killed him, I doubt we'll be able to find your thief now."

"I don't need that pissant to find anyone." His gaze narrowed and he studied Damien as though deconstructing every particle of his being. "You're a fed, aren't you?" he asked with a leering smile. "What are you? FBI? CIA? DEA?" Lightfoot laughed. "Department of Homeland?" He spat to his left. "Seth, you really fucked up this time, hooking me up with a bunch of goddamned pigs."

It was time to end this shit. Damien took a deep breath and spoke loud and clear. "Bandit."

Dark forms moved out of the shadows, the U.S. Marshals, Boise PD SWAT, and DEA in full tactical gear, an armory's worth of weapons leveled on Lightfoot. He lowered his revolver and pointed the weapon at Tabitha this time. "You really wanna take me down so bad you're willing to risk her pretty neck?"

"Go ahead and pull that trigger." Damien could barely get the bluff to leave his mouth, he was so fucking scared. "If you do, you're dead."

Lightfoot cocked a brow. "So is she."

"Check your men, Gates," Damien said. "You copy?"

"I copy," Gates responded in Damien's earpiece from wherever he was stationed. "No one's going to do a goddamned thing. But you need to secure this situation, ASAP. You know we can't risk him getting away."

No matter the cost. Damien filled in the blank without Gates having to say a goddamned word.

Lightfoot was caught and he knew it. Killing Tabitha out of spite would be right up the bastard's alley. If he was going down, he was taking anyone he could with him.

"I hate bullshit, don't you?" Despite the army of law enforcement surrounding him, Lightfoot kept his eyes glued to Damien. "A man oughta know what he's up against when he comes face-to-face with his enemies. So, who are you really? It's all out in the open now. No use bullshitting."

Damien reached for his badge, tucked into his shirt.

"Careful, son. My trigger finger's twitchy."

Slowly, Damien curled his finger around the chain draped from his neck. He pulled the badge from his shirt and let it dangle for Lightfoot's inspection. "Parker Evans, U.S. Marshals Service. Fugitive Recovery Task Force."

Lightfoot's raspy laugher echoed in the quiet. "Tabby Cat, you shacked up with a U.S. fucking marshal?" He kicked at Tabitha's ankle and she cried out.

If he touched her again, Damien was going to kill the motherfucker with his bare hands.

"Well, Deputy. Here's where things are going to get interesting. See, I'm not so keen on being arrested today. And since I know better than to show up anywhere in the States without having my exit plan ready to roll, you're going to call off your fucking pig friends and I'm going to get in my car—with my goddaughter—and you're not going to do a fuckin' thing about it. Understand?"

Damien snorted. "It's not going to happen. You're outgunned and surrounded. Surrender now and let's end this peacefully. I'd think you'd rather live another day than die here in the dirt, Lightfoot."

The man wasn't even fazed by Damien's threat, and his lack of fear caused the hairs to prickle on the back of Damien's neck. Lightfoot was an escape artist. A ruthless one. He dug into the pocket of his tattered jeans and Damien tensed, ready to pull the trigger if need be. He could do it. He could take Lightfoot out before anything happened to Tabitha . . . He *had* to.

"See this?" Lightfoot held up the palm-sized detonator switch for the inspection of all. No doubt every night-vision scope in the vicinity was zeroed in on the piece of plastic. Damien's stomach bottomed out and adrenaline coursed hot and thick through his veins. Lightfoot smirked at Damien's realization. "There's enough C-4 in the trunk of my car to incinerate everything in at least a mile radius. So unless you want to blow us all to hell, you'll let me get in my car with Tabby Cat and leave."

"Bullshit." No way could Lightfoot have had the time to rig the car up like that.

"Believe it, son. Seth," Lightfoot barked. "Go on over and pop the trunk for the marshal, here."

The chatter in his earpiece was so distracting that Damien had to pull it from his ear. Gates and his team were on high alert, not taking anything for granted. "Slowly, Seth." If there were explosives in the trunk of Lightfoot's car, any minor disturbance could set them off. What kind of crazy son of a bitch drove around with a carful of fucking C-4? *Jesus.*

Lightfoot tossed Seth his keys, and even in the shadows cast on him by the headlights, Damien could see the worry and fear etched into the kid's face. Seth approached the beat-up Toyota Corolla like he was walking up to a grizzly bear. He slid the key into the lock slowly and popped the trunk, easing it open inch by inch.

"What do you see, Seth?"

"A shitload of weird-looking bricks. Like clay wrapped in plastic." Seth's voice quavered. "A red blinking light, lots of wires and cords. It's all housed in a big black box."

Fuck. It sure as hell sounded legit. He popped his

earpiece back in and said, "Did you get all of that, Gates?"

"Yeah." Gates didn't sound any happier about the situation than Damien was. "We've got a DOD bomb squad from Gowen Field on alert. They'll deploy in fifteen minutes."

"I'll blow us all to kingdom come before I let you fuckers take me!" Lightfoot shouted so everyone within earshot would hear him loud and clear. "So you're gonna let me walk out of here with what's mine, or I'll see you all in hell!"

The Boise Airport was only five minutes away. The task force had suspected for a while that Lightfoot— an accomplished pilot—had been flying in and out of the country in a private plane under an assumed name. But how he'd managed to get his hands on this much C-4 was a mystery. Had the crazy son of a bitch flown it in on his plane?

Every second that Lightfoot had his gun pointed on Tabitha felt like a lifetime, and Damien prayed that he'd have the strength to protect her. To keep her safe, get her out of this alive. He needed more time with her. More kisses, another word from her honeyed voice, just one touch more.

The bastard flashed Damien a superior smile that made him want to rip his lips right off his face. "Come on, sis. It's time to go."

Chapter Twenty-Six

Tabitha's eyes were glued to Damien. What had started out as a cut-and-dried plan had taken such a nosedive that she doubted he'd be able to pull them out of it. Beside her, Joey's body lay lifeless, his sightless eyes staring up at the night sky. A sob hitched in Tabitha's throat. She'd hated Joey for everything he'd done to her, but she never would have wished him dead.

"Come on, sis. It's time to go."

She stared at Gerald, eyes wide. "My ankle is broken," she said through the thickness in her throat. "How in the hell do you expect me to go anywhere?"

"Don't get lippy with me." His tone promised a second broken ankle if she didn't watch out. "It's your own damned fault. You always were the weak one. Your brother knows how to play the game. You went against your family, sis. That's why you're in the mess you're in."

Of course Gerald would see it that way. His self-appointed title as their godfather let Gerald think that he had some sort of claim on her and Seth. And likewise, he expected her to play by the rules of the life they'd grown up in. Number one: you never go against your family. Number two: you never involve the authorities. Ever. Number three: you are always, *always* loyal to the family, no matter what they do.

"You're not my family," Tabitha said through clenched teeth. "Go to hell."

With his gun still aimed at Damien, Gerald reached down and shoved the detonator in her hand. He forced her thumb down on a red button and she felt something click. Oh God, no! Had he just engaged the detonator? He hauled Tabitha up by her hair, the sounds of strands releasing from her scalp sickening her as she screamed from the pain of trying to stand on both feet. She took the weight off her broken ankle, supporting herself solely on her right foot. Tears streamed down her face and there was nothing she could do to stop the flow. Whether or not Gerald managed to escape this situation, Tabitha knew that she was going to die.

"If she takes her finger off that button," Gerald said to Damien, "we're all fucked."

Tabitha's chest fluttered with her racing heart. She couldn't do anything to slow the rush of air that hiccuped on each intake, the hyperventilation coaxing stars in her vision. "Damien," she said through each desperate pant, "I . . . think . . . I'm going . . . to pass out."

In which case, they were all *definitely* fucked.

Damien put his gun down and raised his hands in supplication to Gerald. He took one slow step forward, and then another.

"That's close enough, Marshal," Gerald drawled.

"Tabitha, look at me."

He fiddled with something in his ear and leaned down, forcing her to meet his eyes. He blurred in and out of focus and Tabitha swayed as she tried to steady herself on her good foot. Pain radiated from her ankle, so intense that it made her nauseous. She couldn't do this. She wasn't strong enough. At least if they all died in a fiery explosion it would be quick and painless. Right?

"Tabitha. Look at me."

She choked back a sob as she took in every detail of Damien's face. If she had known tonight was going to end this way, she never would have asked him to leave her apartment. She would have begged him to stay. Pleaded with him to let Gerald go. She would have told him how she felt about him. That she'd fallen so hard there was no climbing back from it. That he had invaded every pore of her skin, every particle that made up her being. In just a few short weeks, she'd fallen in love with him. And it didn't matter if he was Damien or Parker, or anyone else. She wanted him. Needed him. There would never, ever be another man for her.

Damien was it.

And now, it was too late to tell him any of it.

"I don't think I can do this, Damien." Understatement of the century. Her thumb was beginning to cramp from the force she exerted to keep the button on the detonator pressed down. She was so tired. Exhausted. She just wanted to let it go and fall to the ground.

"Yes, you can." His tone was firm but so reassuring. "You're strong, Tabitha. Just hang on. I'm going to get you out of this, I promise."

"I told you, you shouldn't make promises that you

can't keep." She gave him a sad smile. From the moment she met him, she'd known that he wasn't like anyone she'd ever met. Even when he knew they were all screwed, he was trying to save the day.

"I'm sure as *hell* going to keep this one," he assured her. "Don't you dare give up. Do you understand me?"

She nodded, unable to respond through the lump swelling in her throat. He'd never give up on her, would he? Tabitha knew that Damien would fight for her. Would do anything in his power to keep her safe. Emotion swelled in her chest, and the frantic rush of air slowed in her lungs until she no longer felt light-headed. So many people had disappointed her, taken advantage of her, neglected and abused her. But Damien never would. He loved her. She felt that love in every determined word he spoke. He'd never let her down.

And she wasn't going to let him down, either.

"Get your ass in the car, Tabitha." Gerald tugged at her elbow, his gun still pointed at Damien's face. "Now."

A calm settled over Tabitha with Gerald's words. She wrapped her free hand around her fist, adding additional pressure to the detonator and swung out with her joined fists, catching Gerald in the gut. He doubled over with a *whoof!* and his free hand swung out in a backhand that caught Tabitha high on her cheek. She spun away, her good leg unable to retain her balance. Everything seemed to happen in slow motion as she clutched her fists tight to her chest, protecting the detonator button at all costs. Damien dropped to the ground and rolled, avoiding a wild shot from Gerald's gun that stirred up a cloud of dust. He grabbed his discarded weapon and fired three successive shots. She didn't know if any of them had hit, but Gerald flew backward just the same. Time sped up as an army of law enforcement wearing head-to-toe black converged on the scene. Tabitha squeezed her eyes tightly shut and waited for the inevitable explosion. She peeked through one lid at her fists, still clutching the detonator. The switch still pressed firmly down.

Thank God.

"Tabitha!" Seth scrambled through the chaos, going to his knees at her side. "Are you okay?" She'd never heard Seth sound so scared. It broke her heart, but she couldn't help but hope that if they made it out of this alive, tonight would put Seth on the right path once and for all.

Because even though Gerald was down, they were still far from safe.

"Give her some room, Seth." Damien tugged at Seth's arm, pulling him upright. "The bomb squad is on their way, but I need to get you out of here, do you understand?"

"Bullshit." Seth disengaged from Damien's grasp. "I'm staying with her."

"Seth, no." Tabitha wanted to sit up, but every inch of her body ached and she worried that any shift might loosen her grip on the detonator. "You need to get out of here. If you think I went through all of this tonight just so you could get your ass blown up, you've got another think coming."

"And if you think I'm just going to abandon you, you're out of your fucking mind!"

"She needs a clear head," Damien chimed in. "She's not going to be able to focus if you're in danger, Seth. Let Deputy Gates get you out of here. I promise, I'll keep you posted. I'm not going anywhere. I'm not going to let anything happen to her."

"Come on, Seth." Deputy Gates came up behind Damien. "Let us take care of this. Do your sister a favor and give her one less thing to worry about, all right?"

Seth turned to face Damien and stepped up until they were almost nose to nose. "I'm holding you to every single promise you've made to her. Don't you dare let her down."

"I won't. I swear."

Tabitha waited until Deputy Gates led Seth away. She watched the darkness swallow them as they left the perimeter of light offered by the headlights of the cars. Damien squatted down beside her and brushed his fingers through her hair, pulling the strands back from her forehead. "I'm going to help you sit up, okay?"

"Damien." She took a deep breath and released it slowly. "I don't want to die."

He should have killed Lightfoot. Put a bullet straight into the bastard's brain instead of his shoulder. Death would have been an easy out, though. No matter how badly he wanted Lightfoot to pay for what he'd done to Tabitha, Damien was going to have to settle for letting him rot in prison. Living out the rest of his days in a super max wasn't exactly a cakewalk but still, Damien wanted him to *suffer*. To feel every injury he'd inflicted on Tabitha, experience every ounce of fear a thousandfold.

"You're not going to die, honey. I'm not going to let that happen."

Tabitha's humorless laughter did little to lighten the mood. "You might be used to getting your way, but there's a first time for everything. I want you to leave, too, Damien. Get out of here before something bad happens."

"I already told you, I'm not going *anywhere*. Now hang on to that detonator. I'm going to lift you up."

As though she were made of bits of glass held together by cobwebs, Damien eased his arms around her and lifted Tabitha into his embrace. Her hands shook as she held the detonator button down with both thumbs, and he pulled her close to his chest, steadying the tremor that passed through her, into him.

"Where are we going?" She tucked her head into his shoulder, and it was one of the best feelings in the world. "I was thinking Cabo might be nice right about now."

Damien chuckled. "That might be a little too far at the moment, but once this is over, I'll take you wherever you want to go."

In the distance, flashing lights sped down the freeway toward the Federal Way exit, a procession of ambulances, additional law enforcement, and several fire trucks. Boise PD was in the process of evacuating everyone within a five-mile radius, and additional support was in place to create roadblocks and divert traffic.

"Honestly, if we make it out of this alive, I'd be pretty damned happy with a trip to the ER."

Damien's gut burned with churning acid. The Marshals Service had better pray he never wound up in a room with Lightfoot. "Where do you hurt?"

Tabitha snorted. "I think the more appropriate

question would be, where don't I hurt? We've gone through the wringer this week, haven't we?"

In the harsh glare of the multiple sets of headlights arriving on scene, Damien could see Tabitha's bruised and swollen face more clearly. Her jaw was bluing and her lip was split and caked with dried blood. Her left cheek didn't look much better, swollen and purple and darkening under her eye. And that was just the injuries he could readily see. "How's your ankle holding up?"

"Oh, it's broken," Tabitha replied matter-of-factly. "I just hope it's not shattered. A clean break will be easy to fix. I don't really want surgery."

"Deputy Evans," a voice said in his earpiece. "The bomb squad is here and they've requested that you take Miss Martin to the command center they've set up at the north quadrant of the scene."

"Copy."

"What?" Tabitha searched his face, her brow furrowed.

"The bomb squad is here." He changed course and headed toward the north side of the property. "They want you at their command center."

"How do you know?"

"Earpiece."

"Oh."

Silence settled over them and it made Damien twitchy. He needed the sound of her voice to reassure him, to keep the fear he'd stuffed to the soles of his feet from surging up to overtake him.

"Damien, stop for a second."

He looked down at her and slowed his pace. "It's going to be okay, Tabitha. These guys know what they're doing."

"It's not that. I need to say something and I don't want to say it in front of an audience."

Damien stopped dead in his tracks. He braced her against him with one arm and with the other he disconnected the wireless mic connecting him to the rest of the personnel on scene. His breath stalled and he swore his heart froze mid-beat. "I'm listening."

"I . . ." Tabitha's tongue flicked out at her swollen lip and she cringed. "Earlier today . . . I didn't want you to leave. I thought that—"

Damien put his lips to hers, careful to make the contact featherlight. He kissed her jaw, her bruised cheek. "That's not important right now," he said against her ear. "Let's get you out of this mess first. We'll talk about everything else later. Okay?"

Her eyes drifted shut and she let out a slow breath. "Okay."

As they approached the incident command post, a flurry of activity swarmed around them. Damien was reluctant to let Tabitha go, but they transferred her to a gurney with paramedics on scene ready to take care of her as soon as the bomb in Lightfoot's car was disabled. Everyone was outfitted in thick protective gear: Kevlar, thick padded vests lined with space-age shit meant to protect their bodies from damage in the event of an impact. Damien was given a vest that he slipped into, and another was draped over Tabitha's shoulders.

"Parker, I need a minute."

He all but ignored the chief deputy's request as he lost sight of Tabitha in a sea of explosives experts. She was scared, exhausted, stressed . . . "Later, Chief." She needed him.

"Evans, now."

Callihan's tone brooked no argument, and unless Damien wanted to be brought up on review for insubordination or some shit, blowing a superior off wasn't a good idea. "Yeah. Sorry. What's up?"

"Lightfoot's plane is in a private hangar at the airport. We need to get a team over there ASAP to clear the contents and seize it. This is your operation. You need to run point so we can wrap this up."

"Tabitha—"

"Is not your responsibility. The guys from Gowen have this under control. Let them handle it."

Damien pushed past the chief deputy, bound and determined to talk to Tabitha before he set out on this fool's errand that any guy with a badge could do. "Evans!" Callihan barked. "You need to take a step back."

As though just realizing there were more people than the two of them standing there, Damien noticed many sets of curious eyes watching his every move. His jaw clenched, his hands balled into tight fists. At any other scene, he would have passed off any witnesses, victims, innocent bystanders to EMS personnel or the first available officer of lower rank while he focused on tying up each and every loose end. But as soon as Lightfoot had been nullified, Damien's whole world became attending to Tabitha. It obviously hadn't gone unnoticed.

"I told her I'd stay with her, sir. I promised."

"We can let her know that you had to leave. She's well taken care of."

They could launch an IA investigation if they wanted to. He wasn't going anywhere. "With all due respect, I'm staying. At least until that explosive is defused. After I know Tabitha is safe, I'll wrap up at the airport."

Callihan let out an exasperated sigh. "You're a stubborn son of a bitch. You know that?"

Damien brushed past the chief. "I do, sir."

He pushed through the throng of Gowen Field's best as he heard the frantic, pleading tone of Tabitha's voice. "Can't I just let it go? My fingers are going numb. I'm tired. My ankle is killing me. Please, I just want to let it go."

Damien found her surrounded by a group of explosives experts trying to talk her out of taking her hand off the detonator until they could disarm Lightfoot's bomb. Damien slid in behind her, not giving a single shit about the looks he got from the people around him, and eased her back against his chest. "I'm here, Tabitha."

"I don't know how much longer I can hold this damned button down, Damien."

He closed his fists over hers to still the violent tremor of her hands. "Close your eyes."

When her body relaxed against his, he knew she'd done as he asked. He let his own eyes drift shut, blocking out everything until there was just the two of them. "When I first laid eyes on you, I couldn't breathe. Couldn't even form a coherent thought. No woman ever stopped me in my tracks before, but you did."

Tabitha's breath hitched and the tremor in her hands calmed by a small degree.

"Working undercover is hard. It's fucking torture on my mind. I spend a month after every case in goddamned therapy, trying to talk out the anxiety that has become so normal that I didn't think I could function without it. But in three weeks, you've done more for me than years of bullshitting with some shrink ever accomplished. You leveled me out, calmed that part of me that could never settle down. You're like the best muscle relaxer on the market, honey. I'm addicted to you, Tabitha. I can't live without you. So you've got to be strong and just hold down that button for a while longer. Can you do that for me?"

Something warm and wet dripped on his hand. *Tap.* And then again. *Tap.* Tabitha sniffed and Damien peeked through one lid and caught sight of a woman in full tactical gear. She held up the splayed fingers of one hand and mouthed, "*Five minutes.*"

Damien put his lips to Tabitha's temple. "You're doing great. Don't cry, honey. Just a few more minutes."

"Is Seth okay?" she whispered.

"Seth's fine. Deputy Gates got him out of here and he's okay."

Her grip loosened but not enough to release the button. Good. The tension in her fingers led to the cramping. He needed her relaxed. Just five more minutes . . .

Damien continued to murmur in her ear, words of encouragement, mundane things, a story about the time he camped out on a cold snow-covered mountain in Afghanistan for three days without sleep. Minutes passed and Tabitha sat still, her thumbs holding down the button.

"Damien," she said quietly, turning her face toward his. "I'm in love with you."

His eyes flew open at the admission, his chest swelling to the point he thought it might burst. He'd been so scared that he might lose her tonight, too many close calls to count. He met the gaze of the woman marking the explosive ordnance team's progress, and she smiled. Gave him a thumbs-up and said, "We're good. The bomb's disarmed."

He leaned over Tabitha and squeezed her tight. "I am *so* in love with you, Tabitha. Open your eyes, baby. You can let go now."

She couldn't release her grip, but Damien helped to loosen her fingers from around the detonator. He handed it over to the woman standing beside them and shushed Tabitha as she cried quietly in his arms.

"It's over, Tabitha. You're going to be okay."

Chapter Twenty-Seven

Tabitha stared at the carts, machinery, and myriad medical tools in the too-bright hospital room. It sucked to be the patient, but she wasn't about to give any of the nurses even a tiny bit of flak. She'd been examined, X-rayed, and her ankle was now sporting a bright pink cast—they didn't have any black casting—and she'd just said good-bye to her brother for God knew how long.

The U.S. Marshals Service sure didn't waste any time. Seth had been hauled from the scene of Gerald's arrest and his belongings promptly packed. She'd hoped for more time with him. A few hours at least, but according to Deputy Gates, part of what made the witness protection program effective was the Marshals Service's ability to relocate a witness quickly and quietly. She hadn't been given enough time to say everything she'd wanted to say to her brother. Just a hug and a quick good-bye. And all she was left with was worry and guilt.

"All righty, I've got your discharge papers here, Tabitha. We just need you to sign them and you're good to go."

"Thanks." She gave the nurse a wan smile as she mechanically signed each of the papers and took the little business card with the information for her follow-up appointments. The nurse handed her a baggie with a bottle of pain meds and a prescription for more if she needed them.

"Do you have someone to help you out at home, Tabitha? You're going to be sore for a while and you won't be running any races anytime soon."

Did she? Uncertainty and doubt clawed away at her. After riding in the ambulance with her and getting her settled in the ER, Damien had had to leave to wrap up with the other marshals on the scene. Of course she understood and refused to let him feel bad for leaving her. He had a job to do, after all. But in the quiet aftermath of the worst ordeal of her life—and that was saying a lot considering her life— she couldn't help but worry. What would happen now? Would Damien leave Boise? He'd said he loved her, but in the grand scheme of things, what did love matter when compared to his other obligations? He had a job. A life somewhere else. Would she be a part of Damien's future or just a memory in his past?

"Tabitha? Are you sure this is what you want?" Deputy Gates stood just outside the exam room, his brow furrowed. He'd been designated Tabitha's baby-sitter for the night, responsible for making sure she made it home safely.

"I'm sure. I don't want to start over. Or hide. I'm tired of being scared and worried and I'm going to take my life back on my own terms." It might have been the Norco talking, but she hadn't felt so brave in a long time. "I'm just glad that Seth is going to be taken care of."

The nurse interrupted any further conversation

when she came up beside the exam table with a set of crutches and a wheelchair. "You're good to go." She handed Tabitha the crutches, while Deputy Gates took her paperwork. "Just take it easy for the next few weeks and don't push yourself too hard."

Tabitha settled into the wheelchair and put the crutches across her lap. She had a month until fall semester and her clinicals started, and since she doubted she'd have a job after tonight, there was a pretty good chance she'd have plenty of downtime. Not to mention weeks of ramen noodles ahead of her, since she wouldn't have a paycheck for a while.

She waited with the nurse while Deputy Gates brought the car around. He parked under the ER's portico and held open the passenger-side door. "Ready, Tabitha?"

Seth was safe, Joey was gone, and it wouldn't be long before the rest of Joey's partners, Tony included, would be rounded up by Boise PD. She had a fresh start ahead of her in a life that was one hundred percent in her control. So why did she feel as though she was about to lose everything?

Damien watched as Lightfoot's Cessna was loaded up onto a trailer, ready to be hauled off to impound. His plane was loaded down with automatic weapons, a stash of emergency cash, and several fake IDs and passports, as well as more C-4 and the additional bomb-making accoutrements Lightfoot would have needed to blow the hangar to shreds. The guy wasn't just dangerous, he was certifiably insane.

"This is a huge win, Parker. Huge."

Bill Crawford had flown in to personally oversee

Lightfoot's arrest and processing. He'd missed the big show, but he was fine with basking in the aftermath of the arrest and seizure of Lightfoot's property. Crawford was right: It was a huge win. One that would define his career. So why was Damien's stomach churning like an angry sea?

"Thank you, sir. I'm just glad the son of a bitch is in custody."

Crawford gave him a robust pat on the back. "We'll want you in charge of Lightfoot's transfer. His shoulder is patched up and we're moving him out ASAP. Can you be ready to roll in fifteen?"

Leaving Boise was the last thing Damien wanted. But getting Lightfoot as far away from Tabitha as possible was more important right now, and Damien didn't trust anyone else to see it done. "I'm ready. I'll fly back after he's processed and tie up my loose ends here. It won't be a problem."

Crawford continued to talk, about what Damien had no fucking idea. His thoughts were elsewhere, the worry over Tabitha eating him alive. Was she okay? Had they been able to set her ankle without any trouble? And what about her face? Was anything else broken? Her physical injuries were nothing compared to his concern over her emotional state, though. She'd been reluctant to let him go, her anxiety apparent in the visible tremor that shook her slight form.

Tabitha thought she was weak. But in truth, her strength, her fortitude, astounded him. His own fear ran far deeper than hers, shaking him deep in the pit of his soul. What would happen after tonight? He'd been one hundred percent honest with her when he'd spoken low in her ear. He needed her. Craved her. Loved her. But sometimes emotional attachments were forged in brutally intense situations like the one Tabitha had just endured. What if her reciprocating words were just empty promises made during stressful moments? Had she perhaps projected an imitation of honest emotion, professing her love for him because he was offering her the support she needed in a life-or-death situation?

Maybe Tabitha didn't want him the way he wanted her. If so, where did that leave him?

"So, what do you think, Evans?"

Damien turned to the SOG director. "Sorry, sir. I didn't get that last part." Yeah, right. He didn't get any of it, he was so caught up in his own damned head.

"I said that after tonight you'll be able to write your own ticket. You can go anywhere, work any detail. Hell, I wouldn't be surprised if the FBI, CIA, or even Department of Homeland tries to court you. But I've gotta say, I'm going to do what I can to keep you on my team, Parker. Just tell me what it's going to take to keep you around."

Damien knew what he wanted. It was a huge risk, one that might result in his undoing. But the truth of it was, if this didn't work out he'd be undone anyway. Might as well pull the trigger and see what happened. "I'm not interested in working for another agency," Damien replied. "But as long as we're talking about what I want, I'd like to talk to you about a transfer."

"We can do whatever you want," Crawford replied. "Just say the word."

Chapter Twenty-Eight

"I wish you could have been there to see it. Sandy looked that guy from corporate straight in the eye and told him where he could stick it. If I'd been thinking, I would have recorded it on my phone so you could watch the awesomeness for yourself. It was probably the best thing I've ever seen."

No doubt Dave's drama meter had topped out when Sandy went to bat with the corporate executive who'd demanded that Tabitha not only be fired, but suggested that charges be filed for her role in Joey's operation. What Mister Big Executive didn't realize was that for her role in all of it, Tabitha had immunity from prosecution in exchange for her testimony. Likewise, it was sweet that Sandy had stood up for her. But Tabitha wasn't so sure she was going to go back to her job at the IdaHaven. She only had six months of clinicals left in the fall before she could get a nursing job. Maybe she could find something in a restaurant or grocery store to float her until graduation.

"Tell her thanks for me," Tabitha replied with a smile. "I bet it was a killer scene."

Dave finished putting away the few groceries he'd picked up for her, and leaned against the bar. "Looks like I didn't need to buy you much. You're pretty well stocked."

"Lila," Tabitha said. "She's been bringing me food, magazines, movies . . . Even hanging out when she's not at work or with Charlie." Things were heating up with the investment banker and Lila had been pretty scarce. Still proving she could be a good friend, though, she'd checked in on Tabitha regularly over the past couple of weeks.

"I'm going to have to step up my game," Dave remarked. "No way am I going to let Lila be a better friend than me."

When she'd left the hospital after her ordeal, Tabitha had thought she was alone. Dave and Lila, even Sandy, were proving her wrong, though. She wasn't alone. There were people besides Seth who cared about her. They were a family of sorts, and she felt blessed to have them in her life.

"You're still my favorite person to gossip with, Dave. You've got Lila beat in that department."

He smiled. "Damn straight. So . . . in the vein of being a good friend, have you heard from the tattooed love god lately?"

Tabitha hobbled over to the couch, careful not to catch her crutches on the coffee table. "He's called." Damien—damn it, she should probably get used to thinking of him as Parker—called at least once a day. He had to wrap up his case against Lightfoot and until then, he was going to have to stay wherever it was that undercover marshals took their top level prisoners. Dam—*Parker* said that the less she knew about it, the better. Tabitha had to agree with him. She didn't want to know anything about where

Gerald Lightfoot was. She didn't want to think about him at all.

"And . . . ?" Dave looked as though the suspense was killing him.

"We talk." Tabitha was usually more than ready to discuss her love life with Dave, but things had changed. She'd changed. Her feelings weren't girlish, or fleeting. This wasn't some crush that she'd get over later. She was in love with a man she wasn't sure she even knew. Maybe Parker was a completely different man than Damien. She'd always sensed a duality in him. What if she was in love with the undercover persona and nothing more? What if she didn't love Parker Evans?

Dave leaned forward, eyes wide. "Dirty talk?"

"Like I'd tell you," she teased. "Mostly it's just boring, everyday sort of talk."

Tabitha didn't miss the way Dave deflated at her lack of juicy details. "Is he coming back?"

That was the big question, wasn't it? "I don't know," she said with a shrug. "I hope so."

A knock came at the door and Tabitha stifled a groan. It was such a pain to move around her tiny apartment on her crutches.

"Stay put," Dave said. "I'll get it."

Thank. God. Maybe she could talk Dave into moving into Seth's old room until she was given a walking cast. She'd already tripped several times in the past couple of weeks, and she wasn't really interested in breaking anything else. All she needed was to trip and crack her wrist or something. "Thanks, Dave. You're awesome."

"Oh, don't I know it." He flashed her a grin as he crossed the living room to the front door. "Well, speak of the devil." Dave opened the door wide, and standing on the other side, head and shoulders above her friend, was the very object of Tabitha's obsession.

Holy crap. In the weeks they'd been apart it seemed as though he'd grown more commanding, a specimen of masculine perfection without equal. Dave didn't even bother to hide his own look of admiration as he took in all six-plus feet of sculpted muscle and gorgeous ink. He was everything Tabitha could have possibly wanted. A bad boy on the outside with a heart of gold on the inside.

Perfect.

"Hi." The word lodged in her throat, nothing more than a pathetic squeak.

"Well, I'm thinking this is my cue to GTFO," Dave said with a laugh. "Call me if you need anything, Tabs, though it looks like you've got everything you want."

Heat rose to her cheeks and her eyes grew wide. It's like he went out of his way to embarrass her. "Thanks, Dave," she said through a tight smile. "I'll call you later."

Dam—uh, Parker—stepped through the doorway as Dave exited. The door closed behind him with an echoing finality that caused Tabitha's pulse to jump in her veins. After two weeks apart, she was as giddy and nervous as she'd been the first time she'd laid eyes on him.

He tied her into knots. Who cared if he was Parker, or Damien, or whoever? He was here now. That's all that mattered.

A couple of weeks might as well have been decades spent away from her. For a long moment, Damien stood and just took in the sight of her. Goddamn, she was beautiful. His gaze lit on the cast encasing her leg and he felt a stab of regret that he hadn't been there for her at the hospital, and afterward to help her.

"How's your leg?" He'd practiced what he was going to say to her on the four-hour flight. Each word planned and precise. But now that he was standing here, so close he could touch, every single thought-out word was sucked from his brain like water down the drain. *How's your leg? It's broken, dumbass.*

"It's starting to itch." Tabitha gave a nervous laugh. "I made Dave bring me a wire hanger the other day so I could scratch it. By the time they put the walking cast on, I'm going to scratch all of my skin off."

"I broke my ankle when I was thirteen. It sucked."

"Yeah. I won't be running any marathons for a while, I guess." She gave a nervous laugh. "Is it weird that I have no idea what to call you? I've been trying not to think of you as Damien, but it's tough, you know? I can only imagine what the duality is like for you."

An awkward quiet swallowed up all of the breathable air and he cupped the back of his neck to try and massage away some of the tension pinching the muscle there. Why was he ruining this moment? All he'd been able to think about for the past two weeks was getting back to Tabitha. And now that he was right here in front of her, he was letting his own damned insecurities get the better of him. Damn it, not anymore. He wasn't going to let the best thing in his life slip through his fingers because of his own stupid doubts.

He rushed to the couch and hauled Tabitha up into his arms. "You can call me any goddamned thing you want as long as you love me." Damien navigated the coffee table and carried Tabitha down the hallway to her bedroom, careful not to bump her leg in the process. "I always thought that I had to be one or the other. Damien or Parker. There was no in-between. But with you, I can be both. I can be more." He set her gently on the bed and stretched out beside her, brushing the hair from her face. "I'm here for good, Tabitha, but only if you want me."

"What do you mean, for good?" She searched his face as though for the truth in his words.

"I mean, I asked for a transfer. No more undercover. I want to put down roots. Here. With you."

Tabitha's eyes glistened with unshed tears and a quick smile lit her features. She was the brightest star in a night sky, shining just for him. A beacon calling him home. "Are you sure you want this?" The soft timbre of her voice caressed every nerve ending, filled his chest with so much emotion he thought it would burst. "My life is so messed up. I mean, God . . . Parker, I've got so much baggage it would fill a school bus."

Parker. His name used to grate on his own ears, didn't sound right after so many years of living undercover. But the way she said it, with so much gentle affection . . . It was the sweetest sound he'd ever heard.

"Say my name again."

Her bemused expression melted into a brilliant smile. "Parker."

He kissed her, slow. "Again."

A bout of sensual laughter rippled over him like warm water on a cool evening. "Parker."

He let out a low growl before he kissed her again, this time sliding his tongue against hers. She met him with equal fervor, winding her arms around his neck and threading her fingers through his hair. Chills cascaded down his spine as he held her close, loving the way her body fit against his. "I wouldn't care if you had enough baggage to fill six school buses. I love you, Tabitha Martin. I love everything about you, including your baggage. There is nothing you could throw at me that I can't take. And I'm more than ready to trust you with my baggage, too. Believe me, mine would fill up a few buses, too."

She smiled against his lips. "Well, you did let me sew you up. If that doesn't prove that you trust me, I don't know what does."

"I trust you," he assured her. "With my life, my heart, everything."

"I trust you, too." She kissed him once, her lips lingering on his. "With my life, my heart, everything. You keep your promises, Parker. No one has ever done that for me. I love you."

And he'd keep on keeping those promises to her. "I love you. So much." His mouth found hers and he lost himself to her taste, the silky glide of her tongue and petal softness of her lips. Tabitha was his drug; there was no doubt about it. "I'm addicted to you, honey. I hope you know, you won't ever be getting rid of me."

She pulled away and gave him a brilliant smile. "Everyone's got a vice, right?"

He traced the line of her jaw, brushed his thumb over her full bottom lip. "I think so. What's yours?"

"My addiction?" Her voice dropped an octave and her voice sparked with mischief. "Well, I can't seem to get enough of this certain deputy marshal. He's a good guy wrapped up in a bad boy package. Pretty perfect if you ask me."

"I'm far from perfect."

"You're perfect for me, Parker. Isn't that all that matters?"

"It is. You're perfect for me, too." Lying here with Tabitha in his arms, he knew he was finally home. "Say my name again."

Her throaty laughter stirred his blood. "Parker."

Perfect.

Keep reading for a sneak peek
at the latest in the
U.S. Marshals series,

AT ANY COST,

available in Summer, 2016.

Nick stared out the window, through the steady fall of snow outside, at the woman he'd spent weeks tracking down. She might be going by Olivia Gallagher now, but that didn't matter. He was on the money. The kitchen of the rented cabin provided the perfect vantage point with a direct view of her driveway, and he watched as she talked to her shovel as she moved scoop after scoop of snow. Her grumbles, spoken between bouts of profanity could be heard even through his kitchen window, would have made a sailor proud.

She'd done a damned good job of flying below the radar, but not good enough. No one can simply vanish. People talked, there were paper trails. Sporting a new name and Social Security number wasn't enough. Living in an obscure town in the middle of BFE wasn't enough. Nick had only set up shop in the cabin yesterday afternoon. Not even twelve hours in McCall, Idaho, and he had eyes on his target.

She wasn't quite what he'd expected.

"Frank, you piece of shit! How could you do this to me?"

Nick's lips quirked as Olivia continued on with her tirade, loud enough to wake up everyone on the lane. Well, it would have if anyone else was living on the lane. He grabbed a notebook from the kitchen counter and scribbled the name Frank with a question mark beside it. According to his research, she lived alone. Maybe Frank was her snowplow guy. Or an ex-boyfriend. That wouldn't make Joel Meecum very happy, would it?

A tingle of excitement raced from the base of Nick's neck down his spine, sending a killer rush of adrenaline through his system. Who needed coffee when he could live off of the excitement he felt every time a lead panned out. He'd hit the jackpot with Olivia. Pure solid gold. He watched as she continued to struggle in the fresh snow, wading through a drift that had to have been pushing three feet as she made her way to the back of the car. In the dull red glow of the taillights of the still running car, he could barely make out her profile. Two long braids on either side of her head trailed down from a large, slouchy beanie that she pushed back up on her forehead. She was decked out in snow gear: ski pants, coat, gloves. Nick watched as she plopped down on the ground to check something out under the car. Hell, she looked like a little kid whose mom had gotten her dressed for the trek to the bus stop.

Where was she going this early in the morning, anyway? Nick hadn't been there long enough to determine any patterns in her comings and goings yet. This could be part of her daily routine for all he knew. He noted the time in his notebook as he flipped on the light in the kitchen. She straightened, her head turning in his direction. Now was as good a time as any to introduce himself. From the rage fest going on outside, he already knew that Olivia Gallagher had a bit of a temper. What would a conversation with her reveal?

She continued to wrestle with the snow and Nick left her to it as he headed for the bedroom to get dressed. Her car was buried to the hood in the deep drift; she wasn't leaving anytime soon. And for that matter, neither was he.

The sleepy town in the heart of Idaho had to have taken her some time to get used to. He wondered how she'd come to the decision to move here. Had she closed her eyes and stabbed her finger down on a map? Motorcycle-club life was a far cry from the picturesque tourist town she'd settled in. He'd have to ask around, shake the bushes and see what fell out. People loved to gossip in tiny communities like this. Someone had to be willing to talk. Was Olivia an upstanding member of the community? Did she pass bad checks? Hang out at the local bars? When you knew the right questions to ask and how to ask them, people could be pretty damned informative without even knowing they were being questioned.

Nick had yet to unpack his shit. He tossed his duffel onto the bed and dug out a pair of jeans, T-shirt, and a sweater. He searched around in the bottom of the bag and found a pair of wool socks that he added to the pile. His boots were in the mudroom along with his coat, gloves, and hat. Probably should have brought long underwear or some shit. Another angry shout came from outside and spurred Nick into action as he threw on his clothes.

He didn't have a snow shovel, damn it.

Hell, he didn't have much of anything. No groceries

and a little over a week's worth of clothes. Was it wishful thinking that he'd get the job done and be out of there in a little less than a week? Probably. Which meant if he was planning on sticking around Ski Town, USA, then he should probably get his ass in gear and load up on some shit. It might not be a bad idea to get his hands on a snowblower if he had any intention of making it up the lane to the city street. He had four-wheel drive and good tires, but still. This was some serious fucking snow on the ground.

Jesus, it took less time to get outfitted in his vest and tactical gear to go out in the field. Once he got his boots laced, Nick headed out onto the porch. Olivia stood beside her car, digging snow out from underneath it as best she could with the snow shovel's scoop, which was way too big and awkward for the job she was trying to use it for. But since Nick didn't have even a piece-of-shit broken shovel to help her out with, he supposed they'd have to make do.

She kept her back turned to him, completely oblivious to his presence. It was a vulnerable position, one that left her exposed to all sorts of danger. He found himself wanting to chide her, but why? No doubt Joel Meecum's old lady could take care of herself. Meek and weak didn't cut it when you rolled with bikers. He waded through the knee-deep snow, closer. Olivia straightened to lean on the shovel and pushed her slouchy hat up on her forehead. A frustrated shriek sent a cloud of steam billowing up into the air above her. "Son of a bitch!"

This snowstorm was absolute, fucking *bullshit*.

Fingers of trepidation speared Livy's chest as she tried to focus on the task at hand and not the lights that had sprung to life at the neighboring house. This time of year, most of the cabins along the lake went uninhabited or rented to vacationers, like the cabin that faced hers from across the narrow lane. She hadn't met her new neighbors yet and she didn't plan on it. Livy kept to herself and she couldn't help but be a little annoyed that her peaceful, deserted haven had gained another resident. No matter how temporary.

That light flicking on—a simple, everyday act that probably had nothing to do with her—was a sore reminder that not a fake identity nor a life a million miles from anywhere in all directions was enough to make her feel safe.

She continued to dig, but with every scoop of snow she moved, it seemed that twice as much sloughed from the drift to take its place. "Stupid, fucking, powdery pain in my ass!" Snow might be pure and white, but it was surely a device of the devil. Five months and counting till spring . . .

After what felt like a year's worth of shoveling, Livy got in the car and put it in gear. The Caliber's wheels continued to spin and the engine growled as she punched down the accelerator. "Come *on*, you Dodge piece of shit! Move!"

From the corner of her eye, she glanced at the cabin next door. No doubt she'd given her neighbor a lovely six a.m. wake-up call with her revving engine and swear-fest. The Toyota pickup parked in the driveway looked like it had the clearance to maneuver through the accumulated snow with little effort.

Maybe they had a tow strap . . . *No.* Livy banished the thought from her mind. She had no idea who had rented the cabin. It could be anyone. And she'd managed to stay hidden the past four years by *not* taking chances.

A frustrated growl grated in Livy's throat as she threw the car into park and got out. She scooped several more shovelfuls of snow out from under the car, her breath coming in quick pants. Was twenty-five too young for a heart attack? Because she was pretty sure she felt one coming on. Her back ached as she straightened and leaned on the shovel handle. Damn it, she needed to take a breather. The wood splintered under her weight and broke in two. "Are you fucking kidding me?" she shouted as she held the splintered remains of her snow shovel. The damned thing was beyond ancient, and she'd needed a new one about two winters ago. But when forty dollars could be better spent on groceries, she'd decided to live dangerously and work the poor thing to death.

"Well, Frank, I wish I could say it was fun while it lasted."

Frank totally sounded like the sort of name a snow shovel would have. Utilitarian. All business. Frank didn't take any shit. He plowed through the accumulated feet of powdered evil and made that snow his bitch. Sort of.

The scoop was bent and the sharp metal dug grooves into the wood of her deck every time she tried to clear the snow away. Like her life, Frank was useless and pathetic, hiding out in the shed when he wasn't being put to use. For the hundredth time she wondered how she hadn't died from the excitement.

Commercials always made you think that a four-wheel drive vehicle could go anywhere and do anything. But after a winter storm dumps two feet of snow overnight, even the most stalwart of cars is going to have some trouble. High-centered in a snowdrift, and now no shovel to dig out with. She wasn't going anywhere.

"Goddamn it!"

She pulled her gloves up tighter on her hands and went to her knees with the scoop end of the broken shovel. If she could clear some of the snow out from under the car, she might have a chance of getting unstuck. She was already late for work, and since her paycheck was dependent on the number of students she had, she couldn't afford to miss a half day getting her car out of the driveway.

Nope, she wasn't going to ask for help. She'd gotten by this long on her own.

She kicked at the back bumper and her boot slipped against the slick plastic. Her legs went out from under her and she landed in the snow squarely on her ass. "Fuck!" Her voice echoed in the quiet of snowfall. "Fuck, fuck, *fuck*!"

She took the broken handle and wedged it underneath one of the back wheels of her car for traction and went to her knees. The cold soaked through her heavy ski pants. Ass up in the air, toes anchoring her to the snow, she continued to shovel the packed snow out from under her car. Who needed to go to the gym for a workout? With every scoop of snow, the calories were melting away . . .

"You stuck?"

The rumble of a deep voice behind her sent Livy's heart up into her throat. She could practically feel the icy barrel of a gun pressing into the exposed skin at the back of her neck. A shiver of trepidation traveled down her spine and Livy's brain went absolutely blank. Her mouth went dry. She froze; one-half of Frank's severed body clutched in her fists.

Slowly, Livy rose up to her knees. The fact that she wasn't dead yet was a good sign. Either that, or she'd grown so paranoid that she couldn't even carry on a simple conversation with another human being in fear that he might be one of Joel's thugs sent to get her. With the shovel clutched close to her chest, Livy stood. Took a deep breath, and turned to face the source of that deep voice.

She brought her gaze up, up, *up* to the face of the man standing just to the left of her headlights. His features were indistinguishable in the dark, making him look sinister and strangely alluring all at once. Livy's heart raced and she swallowed the lump of fear that rose in her throat.

"H-high-centered," she rasped just before clearing her throat. "The road's drifted shut. The snowplow hasn't been by yet."

He tilted his head to one side as though studying her. She could make out the outline of a strong jaw, and his lips curved as though in amusement as he turned his attention to her car. His profile displayed strong, sharp features and a shock of hair poked out from beneath his beanie, brushing his brows. "You're trying to go forward when you should be backing up." He jerked his head toward the driver's-side door. "Get in. I'll push."

Livy regarded him for a moment. *Bossy neighbor is bossy.* But his voice wasn't at all as threatening as her first impression had led her to believe. Instead, it was decadent and warm, like a bubble bath on a cold night. It eased the tension that caused her muscles to ache and filled her with a sense of calm. Holy shit. If he could bottle his voice, he'd make a fortune. It had been a long damned time since she'd felt comfortable in the presence of a stranger. Anyone, really. "Okay. Thanks."

Her tongue stuck to the roof of her mouth and she was suddenly painfully aware that she was decked out in five layers of clothes and a slouchy hat that she had to keep pushing up on her forehead. If he was there to kill her, he'd have no problem catching her. She looked like that kid from *A Christmas Story*, and if she fell down, Livy was pretty sure she wasn't getting back up.

She knocked the snow from her boots on the front tire before getting in the car. With her teeth, she pulled her gloves from her hands as her neighbor rounded the car. Livy shifted into reverse and braced both hands against the wheel. He stepped into the glare of her headlights and brought his head up to look at her through the windshield.

Dear God.

Livy's breath left her lungs in a rush. There might as well have been a cape waving in the breeze behind him. Those chiseled features weren't simply a play of shadow. And the warmth of his voice was nothing compared to his deep brown eyes. The dark hair that brushed his brow curled just a bit at the ends. He smiled, showcasing a row of straight white teeth, and Livy thought her ovaries might explode right then and there. *Ka-boom!* It would totally be just her luck that her assassin would show up with killer good looks to match his profession.

"Straighten out the wheel. Then give it a little gas and let off. We'll see if we can rock you out." Oh, he could rock her out all right. His good looks had to be an illusion. Like a reverse mirage brought on by the cold and snow. Livy's jaw went slack as she continued to stare. One brow arched curiously over his eye. "Ready?"

Huh? Ready for what? If it wouldn't have made her look insane, she'd have given herself a solid slap across the face. "Oh yeah. Right." She hit the button on her armrest and lowered her window a crack. "I'm ready. Just say when."

"Okay." He braced his arms on the hood of the car. "Now."

It took a moment for her brain to kick into gear. He was Atlas, and Livy knew that under the layers of clothes, there was a body that could easily shoulder the weight of the world. Why did it have to be the dead of winter when a hot guy rented the cabin next door? Mid-August would have been *soooo* much better. He paused and looked up, quirking a brow. Shit! Her boot slipped in her haste to hit the gas and the engine revved. "Sorry! I'm ready now."

"Okay." His eyes locked with hers and Livy's insides went molten. She hit the gas and the car rocked backward. "Again."

He gave the car a solid shove and she eased her foot down on the accelerator. The snow gave way under the car and moved several feet back before rocking forward.

"One more and I think we've got it!"

He put all of his weight into the action and Livy stomped her foot down on the pedal. The car gained traction and backed out of the drift with little effort. Free of the deepest snow, she put the car in park and opened the door. "Thank you so much. I would have been screwed if you hadn't come out to help. I owe you. Big-time."

"Big-time, huh?" Good Lord, that smile should've been illegal. "What do you have in mind?"

GREAT BOOKS,
GREAT SAVINGS!

When You Visit Our Website:
www.kensingtonbooks.com
You Can Save Money Off The Retail Price
Of Any Book You Purchase!

- **All Your Favorite Kensington Authors**
- **New Releases & Timeless Classics**
- **Overnight Shipping Available**
- **eBooks Available For Many Titles**
- **All Major Credit Cards Accepted**

Visit Us Today To Start Saving!
www.kensingtonbooks.com

All Orders Are Subject To Availability.
Shipping and Handling Charges Apply.
Offers and Prices Subject To Change Without Notice.

Thrilling Suspense from
Beverly Barton

__Every Move She Makes	0-8217-6838-7	$6.50US/$8.99CAN
__What She Doesn't Know	0-8217-7214-7	$6.50US/$8.99CAN
__After Dark	0-8217-7666-5	$6.50US/$8.99CAN
__The Fifth Victim	0-8217-7215-5	$6.50US/$8.99CAN
__The Last to Die	0-8217-7216-3	$6.50US/$8.99CAN
__As Good As Dead	0-8217-7219-8	$6.99US/$9.99CAN
__Killing Her Softly	0-8217-7687-8	$6.99US/$9.99CAN
__Close Enough to Kill	0-8217-7688-6	$6.99US/$9.99CAN
__The Dying Game	0-8217-7689-4	$6.99US/$9.99CAN

Available Wherever Books Are Sold!

Visit our website at **www.kensingtonbooks.com**